CREATURE COMFORT

Rob Rosen

FIERCE
PUBLISHING

Published in the United States by Fierce Publishing

Edited by Christine Van Zandt

ISBN-10: 0983767823
ISBN-13: 978-0-9837678-2-4

For Kenny,
my snap, my crackle and all of my pop, forever and always.

PRAISE FOR ROB ROSEN'S PREVIOUS NOVELS

Queens of the Apocalypse
"One part tongue-in-cheek humor, one part sweet romance, and one part paranormal free for all. The action in the novel is stunningly fast paced, the dialogue clever, and the characters simply hysterical! ... Rob Rosen is one of the most cleverly gifted m/m writers on the scene today." – Joyfully Jay

Vamp
"This is a highly original twist on the whole vampire/werewolf genre. Snarky, saucy, witty. It will keep you howling."
– The San Francisco Examiner

Queerwolf
"You have to read this book. It is by far the funniest, best crafted novel I've read in a long time! It marches on without a pause, and sweeps you along in its action packed wake, leaving you gasping for breath and wiping the tears from your eyes from laughter!" – Reviews by Jessewave

Southern Fried
"Hands down, this is one of the funniest and oddest books I've ever read, and I mean that in a really good way!" – Rainbow Book Reviews

Hot Lava
"Hot Lava by Rob Rosen is, for this reader, another vastly entertaining and winning book. Actually, I'd go so far as to say that it is a winner for anyone who loves humor, mystery, adventure and, oh yes, men… lots of sexy men and some very steamy lovin'" – Dark Divas

Divas Las Vegas
"A rollicking, roller coaster of a read, sure to keep you smiling. Five stars out of five on your fun reading slot machine!" – Echo Magazine

Sparkle: The Queerest Book You'll Ever Love
"A gloriously, uproariously funny and immensely touching novel that's impossible to pigeonhole into a single genre. Part who-dunnit, part satire, part memoir, with a perfectly portioned serving of poignancy on the side, this story will surely touch your heart and tickle your funny bone." – Top 2 Bottom Reviews

CHAPTER 1
FEEL THE BURN

I can feel it, you know—the radiation, I mean—feel it snap, crackle and pop inside of me. All these years later, decades now, centuries even, it's like a constant hum, as if I'm a forever percolating pot of coffee.

As to real coffee, sad to say but nuh-uh—water and zombies, you see, simply do not mix. Sizzle City, girlfriend. *Ouch*. Not that I feel pain, mind you, but I'd imagine it wouldn't be all that delightful to suddenly go out all Wicked Witch of the West like. Nope, all I ingested back when this whole sordid tale began, once every week or so, like clockwork, was a heaping helping of iodized salt, poured down my gullet by one of my various human minions.

Sorry, not bragging here, not that being the Queen of All Humanity isn't brag-worthy, I know, it's just that that's what they were and still are: my minions. Besides, humanity, really, was nothing more than a couple of hundred surviving men and women and children, as far as I was aware.

And the other zombies? Fine, there were a few billion of them, and though they did indeed heed my every command, I tended not to interact with them all that much. Kind of like talking to a toaster, if you know what I mean. And without electricity, beyond the solar power we utilized, a toaster isn't all that much fun to chat with. Plus, it always ended up being a rather one-sided conversation: I talked, they groaned. Suffice it to say, it wore kind of thin on an undead person, like real fast.

As for that salt I regularly swallowed and continue to swallow to this very day, the one of the iodized variety, it's the next best thing when you don't have potassium iodide radiation pills. See, it's the salt that keeps the radiation in check and allows for my humanity, what's left of it, to rise to the grayish-purple surface. Which is why, for the past few centuries plus some change, I ruled the roost from a salt factory in Utah. Funny how in life I wouldn't have been caught dead in Utah, and then I found myself trapped there, both alive *and* dead. Still, without my regular iodized intake, I too would've been just like one of those groaning toaster-like zombies, aimlessly milling about for all eternity—or at least until those infernal internal nuclear power plants of ours goes poop instead of pop. And Lord only knows how long that will take.

So that, in a rather stiff nutshell, is me, Creature Comfort, undead zombie queen.

Wait, wait, undead zombie *drag* queen. *Mhm*, such a nicer ring to it that way, don't you think? The silver lining to my rather tarnished existence. Or maybe let's make that lining lamé. Goes nicely with my brown hair (sans blonde wig) and brown eyes (sans the ever-present bloodshot) and cheekbones for days (too many to count), all topping my average height and fabulously slender body. Though of course nothing else is even remotely average about me. *Nothing.* It bears repeating.

Yep, ages-old Creature Comfort, fabulous to the bitter end. Emphasis on the bitter. As to the end, well, I think we've already covered that. And based on my exceedingly limited knowledge of radiation, which is slim to say the least, plus that snapping and crackling and forever popping going on, the end ain't coming any time soon.

As to the beginning, what made me *me*, well here goes: one massive solar flare equaled one dead planet, minus anyone that was lucky enough (if you saw your glass as half full) to be walled up inside anything thickly metal at the time of the blast. Me, I wasn't so lucky (glass empty, as it were), but a few of my drag sisters were. They figured out the iodized salt routine, which in and of itself was a miracle, considering that they could barely make it through a Madonna number without miserably tripping over themselves. In any case, "Creature Comfort: Drag Queen" promptly became "Creature Comfort: *Zombie* Drag Queen." From life to death to undeath to, well, *this*, what you see standing—well, somewhat teetering—before you today.

As for my dragged-up friends, they headed for New York, while I opted for the confines of that aforementioned salt factory in Utah. Sure, I could've gone with them, taken a chomp out of that Big Apple core, but even then, neophyte zombie though I was, I knew that I would outlive them (to use the term loosely) by eons. And being a zombie was bad enough without being a zombie who also had to watch her friends die, one by one by one. As in really die. As opposed to what the rest of the world did. As opposed to what I did, me and those zombies I took with me back when all this began, back when one world ended and another began, all of us sustained by the salt, plus the dozen or so salt-administering humans that were with us at the time, now totaling, many generations later, that also aforementioned couple of hundred.

But what of my friends' fates? Honestly, I hadn't a clue what happened to them once we parted ways. After all, my ragtag little group was out in the middle of nowhere, surrounded by mountains, and if there were cell phones still working at that time, they certainly weren't doing so in the confines of Utah. Also, Yahoo froze the minute the blast blasted, and that was my only email account. Ditto for Facebook, forever on the fritz, just like me. In any case, within fifty years, give or take, the electricity completely stopped and by then I assume so had they. Sad but true.

So there we were: New San Francisco, we called it. Or at least I did. And what the queen says, goes—because, yes, in terms of perks, it was pretty much the only one I had. The cognizant zombies in my care, all as old as me now, all friends of a sort, stayed for the salt, the humans for the protection. After all, they were surrounded by human-hungry undead monsters. And by surrounded I mean, quite literally, *surrounded*. Wait, to put it a better way, *SURROUNDED!* Yes, that's about right. As for the protection I offered, well, at the very least, all of those monsters I mentioned obeyed my commands, what with me being a conduit, if you will, between life and death, a connection to what they once were and would never, ever be again.

In any case, the factory was well protected, the fences sturdy and tall and, thankfully, a great distance from the cement buildings we called home. Sure, we could hear them out there, forever groaning, day in and day out, eager to enter and devour the humans, but at least we couldn't easily see them or, better still, smell them. Because a zombie tends to stink pretty awful after a few centuries. Not us, however, those lucky few with memories and feelings. No, we take dust baths, much like a rutting pig would do, aided, of course, by the humans. Because the undead are many things, but limber, unfortunately, is simply not one of them. Picture, if you will, the Tin Man minus his oil can, and you wouldn't be far off the mark.

Anyway, in return, like I said, we gave my human minions protection. They had ample shelter, seeing as the factory is huge, and plenty of food and water to sustain them. Though none of that was easy to come by, at least not at first. Took a generation or two before New San Francisco was properly up and running, you see.

Fortunately, a generation or two is also how long it took after the solar flare for the rains to return to good old Mother Earth, for the dust storms to die down, for the incessant heat and winds to abate. Fortunately for us zombies, that is to say, because a good rain storm would've taken out millions of zombies within seconds. As it happened, by the time the drizzling drizzled, our flesh was waxy as the best Madame Tussauds had to offer and completely non-absorbent. Meaning, about the only thing that could rekill what was clearly already dead was a really strong blow torch or a lopping off of the head. Or so I'm speculating. Not like I'm all that eager to find out for certain. I mean, I might be dead, but I'm certainly no glutton for punishment.

Also, aside from the solar flare wiping out nearly all of humanity, plus every other living animal on the planet, the ensuing radiation, which gave us zombies, uh, *life*, also made fresh water undrinkable and the soil infertile. So for the first hundred years or so, the humans were forced to drink anything already bottled and to eat anything prepackaged, which meant a hell of a lot of Ramen Noodles after the cans of most everything else expired. Luckily, as humans, we (or at least they) were quite accustomed to that by then already. And so, over time, we amassed, through various forays into the city, enough potting soil and supplies to build adequate greenhouses. Plus, the rain water, once the rains resumed, was radiation-free, so, like I said, their needs were met. Sure, existence was bleak, but it was still existence nonetheless. Take what you can get, sweeties, and leave your bellyaching at the front door.

But what of our needs, we zombies? Well, we don't eat and we don't dare drink, not without dire consequences, and sleep is but a distant memory, seeing as we no longer need to recharge our batteries, so as to needs, nope, just the salt and the dust baths, thank you kindly. Well, that and the occasional mending of clothes, combing of hair and, for me, application of makeup, which, truth be told, I need quite a lot of. Really, a lot. Like spackling. Heck, my foundation could give a skyscraper's a run for its money. Such is the price of drag-queendom though. And, trust me, if I could heavily sigh, I would.

But why bother, you might ask? Why bother to shimmy into a dress and layer on the war paint? I am, after all, quite dead, right? Or at least dead*ish*. So why gussy up an already plucked hen? Well now, seems like my being a drag queen died a lot harder than I did. Plus, I'd given up pretty much everything else—like eating, drinking and sleeping, not to mention a last season or two of *Mad Men*—so why not keep one last vestige of my past, the one thing that defined me more than anything else? Also, didn't the troops deserve a little entertainment, even if was from a rickety old (seriously old) drag queen, lip-synching to long forgotten (again, seriously long forgotten) songs played on a solar-powered CD player?

Well, we'll go with yes on all that, because, like I said, I'm the queen, and what the queen says goes. Again, it bears repeating. And usually to my minions. Who, by and large, could've gone without the so-called singing skills of one Miss Britney Spears and the lesser talented (if humanly possible) J. Lo. Yes, like I said, bleak, but better than being ripped apart by the zombie hordes.

"This is what people listened to back in your time?" one of the humans always tended to ask me just after one of my shows.

"Um, well, Auto-Tune was at its peak back then," I generally replied.

Their head would then further tilt. "Auto-*what*?"

At that I'd simply turn and start my encore: Cher, always Cher. And, no, no Auto-Tune for the likes of her. At least not for her first thirty years in the biz. Plus, I'm fairly certain that she ultimately survived the solar blast. Mainly because after a nuclear attack the only things left, or so it was prophesized, would be cockroaches and Cher. Though, to be fair, I hadn't seen a cockroach in well over several hundred years. Go figure.

Anyway, at least it broke up the monotony. That and if I didn't regularly use my muscles, rigor, with a great deal of mortis, would settle in for a long winter's nap. Truth is, it's hard enough to speak let alone lip-synch, but far be it from me to withhold my, um, *talents* from the masses, slim though said masses were.

Funny thing is, it was the zombies who really enjoyed my show. And not the New San Francisco zombies either. No, I mean the ones outside the fences. Now they were an attentive lot.

See, once I began my act, and if I so deemed fit to set up the stage up in front of them, then, wouldn't you know it, the groaning would stop and all eyes would be on me. Or at least that's what it seemed like. Though since they couldn't blink and their heads were already turned my way, it might've only been wishful thinking on my part. But, to be honest, I truly think not.

The zombies, I figured, were simply drawn to life. Which is why they groaned when presented with a human, of which, it appeared, I had the only remaining ones left. But the undead were drawn to me as well, seeing, like I said, as I was a connection to them, to life, that I could still think and feel and communicate, that I was both like them and like the humans. It was, I assumed, why they heeded my commands and no one else's, not even the other zombies of my cognizant ilk. It's why they still do, in fact, but for other reasons I now well know of.

In any case, throw in a little Britney or Madonna or Pink into my repertoire, and, voila, I had one hell of a captive audience. Silent though they were. And, trust me, no drag queen worth her Jimmy Choos likes the sound of one hand clapping. Still, beggars couldn't be choosers, and at least they ceased groaning, if only while the music played and my lips and hips managed to swivel. No easy feat for my feet, mind you. Kudos to *moi*.

"They do seem to worship you," one of my minions would, and rightly so, whisper in my ear once my set was over.

"Guess even the dead know talent when they see it."

The minion would then nod—again, and rightly so—or face the consequences, namely the thousands of rows of yellowed teeth facing our way. Not that I was that kind of ruler, mind you, but a little bit of threat of being torn limb from limb does indeed go a long way. And since I was no longer getting tipped for my talents, nor drinking frosty libations afterward (sob), I might as well have been bathed in compliments, even if they were a tad forced. Not like I had anything else to bathe in, right?

Well, not exactly.

Like I said, I didn't eat or drink or sleep, but there was just enough human left inside of me to enjoy life, for lack of a better word. To rephrase all that, Creature Comfort, zombie drag queen, could still pop one serious boner. And when radiation is powering your turgid tool instead of blood (mine being quite stagnant), then watch out, because if you think Three Mile Island blew her stack, you ain't never seen a long dead zombie do the same.

I had my pick of the litter, too. After all, there were teeming masses of undead surrounding us on all sides, a sea of them, an ocean, in fact. All I needed to do was point my miraculously well-manicured fingernail (and, yes, those still grew, even in death) and issue a command, and I could've had a veritable harem of hunky He-Men by my side.

Though that's not what I did, tempting as it was to do so. Because talk about your hollow victories. I mean, yes, it was nice to have my minions fawning all over me, but a lover should always be an equal—well, maybe not equal so much as one notch down. Same thing for a friend, which, after those first few decades, I sorely needed. And by friend, I mean friend of Dorothy, if you get my drift.

Sadly, there were no gay dudes among my humanized, salt-swilling brethren to choose from on that front. They were a meager lot to begin with and small town hicks at that, so, no, not an option. Which meant that I inevitably had to pick—to change, to *turn*, as it were, a la the salt cure—just the right one from the horde outside the fence.

Just one, though, because, though queen, I wasn't God, and didn't feel the need to lip-synch my way through that role either. You see, I could've turned dozens of them, hundreds, but to what end? What gave me the right to inflict consciousness on the unconscious, to breathe life, or at least the next best thing, into the dead? I mean, think about it: yes, they were trapped out there, trapped in their own skin, unthinking, unfeeling, but what was so great about living in a salt factory for presumably thousands of years, your friends and family all gone, life as you know it equally as kaput?

And though I could've easily sent a great many of them to their maker as well, to put them out of their misery, that wasn't my job either. Plus, it's not like shooting ducks in a barrel. These were still humans, undead zombies though they were. And killing someone, and/or rekilling, even an undead someone, was never fun and only to be done out of dire necessity. Like when a horde of them was chasing after you, eager to rip into your flesh. Gives me the chills to think about it. Or at least would if my body wasn't already as chilly as a San Francisco summer, minus, of course, that oddly sizzling power plant of mine, which never seemed to warm the surface of things, nice as that would've been.

So, yes, I had to choose well. This was, after all, an important decision. And, okay, I'll admit it, a rather selfish one, but, come on, I had been through an awful lot—emphasis on the awful—and deserved at least an iota of comradely from someone who enjoyed a little Britney from time to time. Heck, I would've settled for a Celine fan by then, shudder the thought.

In any case, thirty odd years into my reign, I began to circle the perimeter of the fence, seeking that special someone out. And, yes, staring into the face of death, thousands of faces of death, in fact, is enough to turn any stomach sour, even my long-still one.

The groaning would amp up as I passed, dead eyes fixed on me. The fingers and hands poking through the fence, purple from death and red from the sun, would cease gripping for nothing but the air in front of them, only to start up again as I eventually strode by. And to each of the undead I would give the once-over, eagerly looking for a *tell*, something, anything that would give them away.

But guess what? After thirty years or so, pretty much every zombie looked alike. Death, of course, isn't pretty, but even less so when you're standing in the sun for that long. Kind of like an undead Republican convention: all one color, all with the same flicked-off minds.

Still I looked, circled, one day after the next, hunting for any new face that would manage its way to the front of the line. Weeks on end went by, months, one year, two. Yes, fine, it filled the monotonous void, but also had me growing ever more despondent. What if I was forever to be alone, just me and a handful of zombie brethren and a couple of hundred somewhat-fawning humans to keep me company? It was sort of like being able to watch TV, but the only station you could get was Fox News.

And then two years, ten months and fifteen days later—fine, I was counting, so sue me (and good luck finding a lawyer)—there he finally was, at long last.

My heart would've stopped beating had it not done so all those years prior when the sun suddenly went *kerpow* on my ass. I froze in place, my eyes on his, his on mine. He was about my age—or at least the age we were when we, you know, *died*—my height and slim build, sandy brown hair and eyes the color of a summer sky (minus the ever-present bloodshot streaks). And then, glory be, I scanned downward.

"*Britney*," I whispered, reverently, barely managing to squeak it out. A grown man wearing a Britney T-shirt, and vintage Britney at that, could only mean one thing. Unless he was merely being ironic, which I knew straight boys sometimes did, but prayed against it just the same. Plus, I felt something else, a twinge if you will.

I walked up to the fence, loud groaning enveloping us for fifty feet all around, less boisterous groans at the periphery and even more groaning, of course, beyond that. His hand had already been poked through the hole, fingers instantly coming to rest on my shoulder, a spark running through me as sure as any bolt of lightning. He was the one; I felt it, knew it down to my very soul, tamped and stomped down as that sucker might have been.

"Follow me," I commanded, ever the queen.

I moved down the fence, heading for the main entrance. He followed, step for step, snaking through the undead horde as he did so, his face but a blur as it came in and out of sight. When I reached the gate, I bellowed, "No one is to enter! All zombies stay put!" Then I raised my hand and aimed my index finger his way. "Save for you. You, my dear, may enter."

We hadn't left the compound all that often over the years. Our raids into Salt Lake City were few and far between, you see. It was, after all, exhausting work to make our way through the zombies and into the city, keeping the undead at bay the entire time as the humans grabbed what they needed, occasionally meeting a horrible fate when my back was turned. Still, when I unlocked the gate this time, my spirit soared. This felt different somehow—like, well, *freedom*.

The zombies moved in reverse, as I'd bade them to do, all save one. I stood and stared at him; he stood and stared at me. It meant nothing, I knew, simply a robot following orders, but it was the first time in a very long while that I felt something akin to hope fill the void inside of me. "Enter," I managed to say, my bony finger aimed his way.

Slowly, he trudged inside, while I, in turn, locked the gate behind him. I then led us away, while he obediently followed, the groaning behind us still piercing the air.

One of my minions quickly approached us. "Well now, who's this?" asked Glenn, the eldest of the humans and my frequent right hand (and left hand) man. He eyed the newcomer suspiciously, then did the same to me. "You've never let one of *them* in before." He said it with disdain. I couldn't rightly blame him.

I stopped and sighed. It was and will always be a forced gesture on my part. After all, it wasn't like I needed to inhale or exhale. Still, it felt like the right thing to do. "Guess it's about time then, Glenn."

He looked from me to the zombie and then back my way. The slightest of grins rose northward on his wizened face. "The T-shirt says it all, you know." The smile widened. "My company isn't enough for you, Creature?"

I shrugged as best I could. "Not the same, Glenn, is it?"

He closed the gap between us and placed his hand on my shoulder. Most humans never touched me, never touched one of us. Our association, for the most part, was simply out of necessity. Glenn, however, saw beyond what I'd become. He'd been a friend to me, of sorts. And that is what he was at that very moment when he told me to stay where I was, that he'd be back in a few minutes.

And so I stood in the middle of the barren parking lot staring at the undead stranger, everything silent save for the peripheral groans. His hair blew in the warm breeze, highlights catching the sun, but, apart from that, he didn't so much as budge. It was just him and me, me and him, a swarm of undead butterflies taking wing inside my belly.

"Please forgive me for what I'm about to do," I whispered his way. I then turned, watching as Glenn raced back to us. In his hand he held a funnel. It was how the salt was administered. One full funnel equaled a one-week's dosage. Miss the dose and we'd quickly revert back.

"Ready?" he asked, winded but smiling just the same.

I nodded. "Head tilted back," I commanded the zombie. "Mouth open."

He did as I instructed, with difficulty, of course, seeing as he'd obviously done neither in a very long time, but his head did eventually tilt and his mouth did pry open. Glenn placed the funnel inside, the tip down the zombie's throat, and then poured the salt inside. I watched as the white crystals slowly drained through the plastic—like sands through the hourglass, so were the days of our unlives—then I stared at the stranger, waiting for the inevitable result once the funnel was removed.

A minute ticked by, two. It felt like hours. And then, all of a sudden, *blink*.

"Here it comes," said Glenn, sounding giddy as he stood by my side.

Again I nodded. "Yep." Then *blink, blink. Blink, blink, cough*. "Hello?" I managed to croak out. "Can you hear me?"

Cough, blink, blink. "Yes," the stranger replied, slowly, his voice sounding jagged, creaky, like a rusted hinge. "What . . . happened?"

I turned to Glenn. He turned to me. It was a hard question to answer. I mean, how do you tell someone that they're a zombie and have been for decades, that their family is long dead, or undead, that all he knew was gone, that this factory we stood outside of was all that remained? I remembered what it was like, the realization of what I'd become, even all those years later. Which is why I'd begged his forgiveness to begin with.

"You're safe," I replied, simply. It was the best I could do for the time being.

He looked down at his purpled, vein-riddled hands, then at my own. "Safe . . . from . . . what?"

Glenn's smile disappeared. He moved in and gently helped the stranger turn around. "From them, son," he replied as soothingly as possible. "From every last one of them."

***

That was just about three hundred years ago. Hard to know exactly. Not like we had calendars anymore. Nope, all we had were the humans, who came and went, generation after generation, Glenn was replaced by a son, a grandson, and on and on and on, while we zombies stayed the same, locked in time, locked inside a fence.

Though things had indeed changed after the stranger came into my *life*.

Hard to think of him that way now, a stranger, to remember how I'd found him, my Dara Licked. Yes, his drag name. Because, thank goodness, I had indeed picked well that day so long ago. Guess it took one to know one, right?

Dara, I simply called him—well her, really, because even after all those centuries, I still hadn't got my pronouns right. I mean, come on, how do you call someone named Dara a him? Anyway, she had in fact become my soul mate, my raison d'etre, even when I had little reason to etre left in me. And if you think one drag queen put a spring into those zombie's steps, you should've seen what two did. Though, yes, *spring* might've been pushing it when it came to likes of them, but at least it was a far better cry than staring at a rusted fence year in and year out.

"I wish we could do something for them," Dara said to me that particularly fateful afternoon as we stared at the milling horde. We strolled hand in hand, him and I, side by side. He'd become the yang to my yin—and, yes, he had one mighty fine yang as it turned out. Like I said, I certainly knew how to pick them.

"I know, hon, I know," I said in return. "But to what avail? The more zombies we allow inside here, the more there will be out there to take their place. It would, I'm afraid, be a Sisyphean task." We'd had this talk before. It never changed. After all, how could it?

He giggled, as best as any zombie could. "I used to know a drag queen named Sisyphus." He scratched beneath his platinum blonde wig: a treasure from a recent foray into the city. "No, wait, it was Syphilis." Then he leaned his head on my shoulder. "Anyway, it's still awfully sad to think of them all that way." He pointed at the distant groaning throng, a hot breeze washing over us all the while.

I squeezed his hand firmer in my own. "Just their destiny, hon." I kissed his bewigged head. "And ours, sad to say."

Though ours, and theirs, really, was about to take one hell of an unexpected turn.

CHAPTER 2
DEAD RINGERS

The humans heard it first. I suppose their hearing was better than ours, that their synapses relayed faster or something along those lines. In any case, they went running out of the factory before us, their faces all pointed to the cloudless sky, hands placed over their eyes like makeshift visors. Me, I ambled out a moment later, the only one among the throng to recognize the sound. I was stunned—a gross understatement—to actually be hearing it.

Another of my zombie kind, one that had been with me from the beginning, just like all the others on our side of the fence, made his way from a different building, standing behind me not two minutes later, several others a few seconds after that. He pointed to the fast-approaching object, his mouth agape—which, for a zombie, was pretty much par for the course anyway, but this time it was certainly well-deserved. "Plane."

The word was repeated, round and round she goes, until it was on everyone's lips, both zombie and human alike. I turned around just as Dara appeared by my side. Yes, our faces were pretty much locked in whatever expression was on them when we died—usually terror— but, even still, I could detect something else there all of a sudden: surprise. And even I found it ironic that one gross understatement was followed with an even grosser one. Because *surprise* couldn't even begin to cut the Grey Poupon right about then.

"But how?" asked my partner.

I squinted into the sky, the plane almost directly overhead, flying low. And, suddenly, it felt like I'd been sucker-punched. And to feel anything, let me tell you, was tantamount to a miracle. Like finding a life-partner in a sea of death or surviving(ish) a solar apocalypse. And since those two miracles had in fact occurred, I was inclined to believe that this one was doing the same, that it wasn't just some sort of mirage we were all witnessing.

"How indeed," I croaked out. I turned to Dara and placed my hand on her shoulder, her eyes of blue offset by the shimmering green she was wearing on her generally gray-tinged eyelids, blonde wig flowing in the breeze. "I . . . I think I know that plane."

She stared at me and then at the plane in question as it banked and flew back in the opposite direction, clearly looking for a place to land, which, also clearly, had to be within the fence. Otherwise, it'd be landing on top of a whole lot of groaning, stinking zombies. "How, exactly, do you *know* that plane, dearest?" she asked.

I gulped. Or, that is to say, my brain told my throat to gulp and my throat promptly ignored the transmission, as per usual. "I believe that it's the same one my friends left in before heading to New York."

"But they're—"

"Dead." I finished her train of thought. "Obviously. But the plane is still very much, shall we say, *alive*"

She nodded. "And landing."

Which wasn't as difficult as it sounded. The plane was a private number, perhaps six seats at most, and the factory parking lot inside the gates was fairly long and devoid of cars along the perimeter of the fence. In other words, it'd be tight, but not impossible. Especially since, given that several hundred years had passed since last I'd seen it, in the realm of possibilities, landing was more likely than seeing the damned thing in the first place.

Again Dara turned my way. "You're looking awfully pale, Creature."

My eyes further squinted. "I'm dead, Dara." And, yes, gross understatements always travel in threes.

Again she nodded. "Pal*er*, then. Like you've just seen a ghost."

I pointed to the plane as it finished its landing, the engines temporarily drowning out the constant groaning hum of the surrounding undead multitudes. "Perhaps I have, Dara," I replied. "Perhaps I have."

But would that be a literal statement? Could my friends—Destiny St. James, Blondella Bombshell and Kit Kat—somehow have survived? They were, after all, still human when last I'd seen them. Could they have turned in the interim? And, if so, why the three hundred plus year gap since that time?

In any case, I didn't have all that long to wait for the answers to those questions. The plane was now taxiing our way, all eyes and ears and gaping mouths faced its way. It came to a stop a dozen feet away, the engines cut, the enveloping silence, minus the ever-peripheral groan, very nearly deafening.

"Should we have brought a fruit basket?" asked Dara, her hand suddenly in mine.

"Sweetie," I replied, "ain't no bigger fruits than us for miles and miles around."

Or so we thought.

See, when that plane door opened and the stairs folded down, out came three of the most fabulous-looking drag queens I'd ever laid eyes on.

"Is it . . ." Dara whispered my way.

I shook my head, if just barely. "No, hon. Close, but no cigar."

Down they clicked and clacked, mega-high heels soon crunching the gravel as they quickly closed the gap between us, until, shut the friggin' door, there they stood. Though *towered* would've been a better world for it.

The middle one spoke first, a dead ringer—and, trust me, I know dead when I see it, though these broads were anything but—for Miss Destiny St. James herself. "Oh, thank goodness. Creature Comfort. At last."

"You . . . you came looking for *me?*" I squeaked out.

"Yeah," said Dara, eyes so wide they could've just about popped out of her head. "For *her?*"

I poked her in the ribs and again gazed their way. "Who . . . who are you?"

Again the middle one spoke. "Oh, forgive my manners. It's been a frightfully long flight."

The one on her left, a rather rotund, mahogany-tinged queen with a train of jet-black hair, gazed down at us. "Emphasis on the frightfully." She got poked in the ribs next.

The middle one, a fetching beauty with a flaming red wig and a matching red mini-dress, held out her hand—or at least limpish wrist—and said, "Ginger St. James, of the House of St. James. A pleasure."

The queen on the right, the tallest of the three, bedecked in shimmering silver and crowned in blonde, at last spoke up. "For the first two minutes anyway. But then the pleasure fades. And quickly, I might add." And then so many ribs were getting poked that it suddenly felt like an outdoor barbeque.

"The House of St. James?" I thought to ask. "As in Destiny St. James? Since when does she get a house? Outhouse of St. James, fine, but a whole *house*?"

All three shut their eyes and put their hands up in silent prayer at the mention of her name—as opposed to fingers plugged in their ears, which, last I checked, was the usual response. But I didn't get an answer to my question. Instead, the one on the left stepped forward and said, with a belch, "Aflo Sheen, but you can call me Flo." She then looked around. "I don't suppose you got any candy bars around this place. My sugar level is lower than a hound dog at a funeral."

I tilted my head in confusion. "You have a hound dog?"

She sighed. "It's just an expression, hon."

Dara spoke up next. "And, no, no candy bars." She pointed to the fence. "*Those* are the only bars we got around this place."

"Poor you," said the one on the right, cringing all the while.

"Yeah," said I. "Poor us. And you are?"

Her ginormous blonde wig pitched forward just before she did, her hand daintily held my way, a rhinestone adorning every nail, each one sparkling like the real deal. Beautiful, if not a smidge gaudy. In other words, or word, perfect. Meaning, I would've died from envy had I not already . . . well, you know the drill. "VaVa Voom, at your service," she informed.

Flo snickered. "Yours and everyone else's, sugar."

"Bitch," said VaVa, her hand wrenched out of my own.

"Ladies!" belted out Ginger, the apparent referee. "*So* not the time."

I raised a bony finger in the air. "Um, not that I don't love a good floor show, but . . ."

"Ah, yes," said Ginger as she dabbed a fresh coat of lip gloss across her already glossy lips. "I suppose our appearance here must be a bit confusing."

Again Flo snickered. "That skirt matched with that top is confusing, sugar. This here is a walk in the park compared to that."

"Actually," said I. "No walks. No parks. Just fences and zombies and salt. So, yes, confusing. Very."

"Very," echoed Dara. "But a little lip gloss might make it *less* so."

VaVa smiled and handed over the small tube, dropping it into my partner's hand. "Keep it, hon. On me."

"Like every other man in town," muttered Flo.

"Town?" I asked. "What town? Sorry, I'm lost here. There are others out there? Other humans who've survived? Besides ours, I mean?" I pointed behind me, to my humans, who were now ringing the area around us, keeping a safe distance. And who could blame them? These three must've seemed like aliens to them, landing in their U.F.O. And, for all intents and purposes, that's just what they were.

The trio stood there, looking rather pensive—that is, if you were able to see beyond the gallons on makeup, chiffon, silk, synthetic hair, fake eyelashes and heels. So, yeah, um, *pensive*, but with a certain, shall we say, *flair*. "It's a long story," finally replied Ginger.

I couldn't help but laugh. "Funny, I have all the time in the world. Seriously. All of it."

"Ditto," said Dara, head nodding in agreement.

The three of them shrugged in sync before VaVa replied, "Um, well, that is to say, it's a long story and we don't have a lot of time to tell   it."

"Yes," interjected Flo. "You see, we need to get back."

"Wait," said I. "Let me get this, for lack of a better word, straight: you came looking for me, three hundred plus years after we arrived here, and you already need to get back?"

Ginger smiled, her nodding now in overdrive. "See, you're not as lost as you thought you were." She reached down and patted my shoulder, if just barely. "Now get your things and let's get a move on. Time is money, after all."

Before I could inquire, yet again, Flo raised her perfectly manicured hand up to stop me. "Again, just an expression, sugar. After all, money is only used for tips these days. And you haven't even seen our act yet."

To which Dara grumbled in response, "Not so sure about that."

Still, we weren't budging. "Uh, where exactly are we getting a move on to, if you don't mind me asking?" I held off asking the why, seeing as this merry threesome seemed to have a hard enough time answering one question let along two. Or six. Or the ten I had lined up.

Three pairs of fabulously painted lips cracked three beguiling smiles. "Why, Liberty Island, of course."

"Of course," I echoed. "And where, pray tell, is Liberty Island?"

They looked at me as if I was crazy. And spending any more time with these queens would probably make me as such. Still, Ginger replied, "East of New York City. Just."

"Just what?" tried Dara.

"Just east," replied VaVa.

I turned to Dara and pressed my lips to her ear. "Please stop asking questions, dearest. I have a feeling they're not going to get us anywhere."

She nodded and then placed her lips to my ear. "So what are you saying, that we go with them?"

I paused, letting the thought sink in. Then I pointed to the thousands and thousands of zombies on all sides of us. "Sure beats the alternative."

She squinted her eyes. "I see your point." She then turned and stared at the impatient-looking mess of drag aimed our way. "Think they'll loan us some of those outfits of theirs?"

I too turned. "Do you have any clothes for us?" I asked, pointing their way. "Like those?"

"Hundreds," they instantly replied, in unison.

"Huh?" squeaked Dara.

"Hundreds," repeated Ginger. "And just as many wigs and shoes and boas."

"Boas." Dara was suddenly holding my gaze. "She said boas, Creature." And if my after-life partner could drool, a pool of it would've already formed on the gravel below.

I grabbed her hand in mine. "I heard, hon. I heard." Again I turned their way. "Okay, we're ready. All we need is a few bags of salt."

"But what about your personal things?" asked Flo. "Toothpaste?"

"Makeup?" added Ginger.

"Clothes?" asked VaVa.

"Makeup?" repeated Ginger.

"Shoes?" tried Flo.

"Makeup?" Yep, Ginger again. Seems she had a one-track mind. Luckily, it was a rather nice-looking track.

Still, I held up my hand to stop them. "We'll borrow yours."

Again Dara squeaked. "Or just, uh, *take* them. Seeing as you have hundreds, right?"

"Hundreds," agreed VaVa. "And you can have as many as you like, just, please, hurry."

And it was then that I spotted my human minions, all of them clearly listening to the conversation, not a smile to be seen among them. After all, without me they were completely trapped within the fence, vulnerable. No forays into Salt Lake City. No protection from the zombies. No Britney medleys.

I frowned and turned to Ginger. "We'll go, but only for a short while. A vacation of sorts."

They seemed to not like the sound of that, but nodded just the same. "Fine, we'll bring you back," said VaVa. "Promise." She crossed her padded heart. "Just get on the plane. Please. Now."

I moved to the nearest minion, his frown practically dragging the pavement. "Don't worry. There's plenty of food, the fence is sturdy and we'll be back in no time."

"How soon?" he asked, clearly nervous at the prospect of my leaving.

I looked over at Ginger. She nodded and replied, "Soon. She'll be back soon. And with a whole new wardrobe."

"And boas," Dara quickly piped in with.

"And boas," agreed Flo. "Now on the plane with you."

My eyes moved from my minions to the drag queens to Dara. Her eyes were doing the same. She then took my hand and moved us a half dozen feet away, out of earshot. "They sure seem awfully desperate, Creature."

"My lip-synching abilities must've preceded me."

"Though it seems to have taken quite a while to do so."

I reached my hands out and pulled her in tight, my chin resting on her shoulder. "I know how it sounds, Dara, how they sound, but we've been here hundreds of years now; do you want to go hundreds more without a little, I don't know, *adventure.*"

She sighed. "Yeah, but just how *little* are we talking about here?" The sigh repeated. "Plus, the humans are counting on you. Our zombies would be fine, could even blend back in with the throng, but your minions, they'd be, well—"

"Lost without me?"

She patted my back. "I was going with eaten, Creature. Torn to shreds and eaten, should the fence give way or if they had need to visit the city, which you know they do, from time to time."

She was right, of course. But, then again, so was I. Even a queen deserves a break every once in a while, every century or three. "Look, Dara, VaVa promised we'll be back, and we will be back. But for some odd reason, these queens came looking for me and also seem to need me; might as well find out why. And maybe get some fabulous new clothes in the bargain. Not like they have any back in Salt Lake City, right?" Trust me on this one: the answer is a resounding *no*.

In any case, I knew that last bit would be the nail in the coffin, so to speak. "Fine. Besides, what's the worst that could happen?" She laughed. "We die?"

Not likely.

At least not again.

But close. Oh so very, *very* close.

***

After we filled the plane with a few sacks of salt and a couple of funnels, we took our seats: me on one side, Dara on the other, Ginger and Kit in front of us, VaVa, *gulp*, in the cockpit.

"Um, excuse me," I shouted toward the front of the plane. "But how, exactly, could you possibly know how to fly a plane? Do they have lots of planes on this Liberty Island of yours? Some sort of flight school for wayward drag queens?"

She revved the engine and then turned back our way. "This is our only plane. And, as a result, the only one I've been trained to fly. Just like my mother before me was trained to fly it and hers before her, going all the way back."

"Back to what?" asked Dara.

"To the beginning," replied Flo from catty-corner to me, a candy bar suddenly in her hand, ruby red lips now dabbed with chocolate brown. I was surprised to see the bar there. It had to be as ancient as, well, *me*. As to its origins, I'd learn of that soon enough.

"The beginning of what?" asked Dara as the plane began its way across the parking lot, picking up speed as it did so, VaVa's head again facing forward.

"The beginning of the House of St. James," replied Ginger.

I nodded, ruefully. "The beginning of the apocalypse, you mean."

"We do not speak of that," all three of them replied, the plane suddenly lurching—it and my stomach both.

I stared out the window and down, my minions staring up, my fellow zombies doing their best to do the same. The factory looked impossibly small from up there, the undead horde impossibly large. So I gazed into the approaching cloud bank instead. "You don't speak of it? You're joking, right? It's all around you."

Flo was now on candy bar number two—or two thousand, it seemed. "We never joke, sugar. At least not without the promise of tips."

Dara rested her head back into the seat. "But why do you need tips if you don't need money?"

"It's the thought that counts," replied VaVa, the plane banking to the east as it slowly gained altitude. "Besides, we look at it as a tithing."

I scratched beneath my wig. Not because it itched so much as I was confused. Yet again. "A tithing? But isn't that a religious term? Like paying taxes to a church or something?"

"Exactly," said Ginger, as if it was obvious. Though, it seemed, with these three nothing was in fact obvious.

"Okay," I said, moving on to a different topic, seeing as I was clearly missing something here. Or they were. And I was betting it was them. "Just out of curiosity, how did you find us?"

Ginger turned around, confusion blanketing her face. And with so much makeup on, it was more like a tarp than a blanket. "What do you mean *how did we find you?*"

"Well," I replied. "Not like you could Google us, right?"

"Goo . . . *what?*" said Flo.

"Never mind," I replied. "Just tell me. How exactly did you locate us, all the way from Liberty Island to Utah? In fact, how did you even know about me in the first place, about us?"

Ginger was still facing my way. "You're joking, right?"

"Not without tips," deadpanned Dara. Emphasis on the dead.

"Um, just humor me, please," I said to the lot of them.

It was again VaVa's turn to answer, her face now forward as she flew us ever higher. "The factory is the only place we could go. It is where we knew you would be. Must be."

"You lost me," I freely admitted.

"No," said Flo. "We found you. Sort of."

21

"Sort of?" said Dara.

"Well, one cannot find something that is not missing," she replied. "We knew where you were. The plane knew where you were. This is the only place the plane can go. Are you now, as you said, *humored*?"

Not even close. Not even fucking close. Still, a lightbulb did pulse above my head all of a sudden, dim though it was. And so I unbuckled my buckle, asked Flo to help me from my seat, and then trudged the few feet to the front of the plane. "Show me," I said to VaVa. "Show me why the factory is the only place the plane could go."

She pointed to the screen that was embedded in the dashboard. Instantly, I knew what they were all getting at. "Destiny and Kit and Blondella," I said. "They flew from Utah to New York."

Suddenly, upon hearing their names, Miss Voom's hands again went up in prayer.

Dara yelled from behind me, "They're doing that back here, too, Creature."

I nodded. "Those are coordinates there," I said, pointing to the screen. "The very last ones."

"The first ones," she corrected me. "From the beginning."

I didn't argue. By then, it seemed pointless. "So if this plane can only go from Utah to New York and back again, and you've never been to Utah before . . ."

"No fucking way!" hollered Dara.

"Way," I uttered, if just barely. Then I tapped VaVa on the shoulder. "So, just to clarify, this is the first time you've ever flown this plane?"

She looked up and smiled. "Any plane. Seeing as this is the only one."

Hard as it was, I managed to take a seat next to her, then once again buckled myself in. Tight. "So you've been trained to fly, but never flown."

She nodded. "As was my mother before me and hers before her—"

"Back to the beginning," I interrupted.

She touched fingertip to nose. "Exactly. See, not so difficult."

"Says the drag queen flying us cross-country for the first time."

"And hopefully not last," said Dara, now chiming in.

"But I'm not flying," VaVa replied. "The plane is."

"Huh?" huhed Dara.

My face craned right. "Auto-pilot, hon." Which explained a lot. Or just enough. For now. Because suddenly I'd had my fill. And so I simply stared out at the passing clouds, glad, at least, that there were no groaning zombies within thousands of feet of us.

For the time being, that is.

CHAPTER 3
LADY LIBERTY

It was a long flight, several hours, and when you can't sleep or eat or drink and the nearest Kindle fizzled out hundreds of years earlier, several hours ticks by like molasses off a turtle's back. Still, the girls had plenty of makeup on them, so while we didn't get any answers to our innumerable questions, at least the confusion on our faces was dressed to impress.

And then, all of a sudden, we saw it. Or *her*, that is to say. And, no, she didn't look at all like she used to. Not unless I was remembering her all wrong, which seemed highly unlikely. I mean, not like Lady Liberty had been a drag queen several hundred years ago, right? Butch, okay, but a drag queen? No way.

"Liberty Island," said Dara, her newly made-up face pressed firmly to the glass. "I forgot that's what it was called."

VaVa banked the plane and made a wide arc around the emerald-colored statue, her face now adorned much like our own, her toga painted a shimmering gold. And that, in and of itself, was reason to give me pause, had the rest of it not been equally as surprising to see. Because where once there had been churning water between her and Ellis Island, there was now a makeshift city, all built, it appeared, on pontoons, hundreds and hundreds of them that connected the two islands, thereby creating one giant one.

"Look at all the people," I managed, my eyes wide, mouth agape as, necks craning skyward, they waved up at us.

"Libetians," said Flo.

"We don't drink," commented Dara.

Flo shook her head. "Not libations—and too bad for you, because we make some fierce cocktails, girl—Libetians, the people down there, huddling and amassing below Libby."

I chuckled. Seems Lady Liberty got a new name *and* a makeover. Goody for her. No one should have to wear the same dress for five hundred years. Trust me, I know.

As to the runway, there was a now-ancient bridge that connected Ellis Island to the mainland. It had, thank goodness, been widened for takeoff and landing. Beyond that, a narrow band of fields and crops hugged the coastline, all of them clearly converted from parks and parking lots, and all of it ringed with a dense copse of trees, obviously hundreds of years old. New York City lay in the not too distant distance, still as magnificent as she once had been, if not a tad bit more ivy-covered, slightly cracked, off-kilter. Then again, I'd always so loved all things cracked and off-kilter. In fact, I was just as cracked and off-kilter myself these days.

But what of the zombies? With this many humans so nearby, there had to have been millions of undead clamoring to get to them, even if the watery barricade would forever keep the two races separate.

"Where are they?" asked Dara, now turned my way as the plane began its descent.

"Who?" asked Ginger.

"The zombies," came her reply. "People like me and Creature."

Behind the façade of makeup, of rouge and lipstick and eyeliner, I could still detect the cringe, faint as it was. "We . . . we do not speak of them."

"Of *us*," I reminded her.

Flo turned our way as the plane at last skidded on the pavement, the engine quickly revving down. "You are not like . . . not like *them*."

"Semantics, sweetie."

The plane stopped. There was now silence in the cabin. Almost. "They're out there," I whispered, squinting as my eyes scanned the horizon. "Not nearly as close as ours are in Utah, but they're there all right."

"I don't hear anything," said VaVa as she reemerged from the cockpit, hands primping her towering blonde wig, her tight silvery dress readjusted.

"But we can," said Dara. "After all, it's all we've heard for hundreds of years now. Like a buzzing mosquito, unseen but there just the same, ready to sting, to suck."

The queens looked at one another and shrugged before VaVa unlocked the plane's door and lowered the stairs. Her manicured index finger instantly pointed outward. "Listen to *that* instead, girlfriend."

Once we were helped out of our seats, Dara and I, hand in hand, poked our heads out the door, our ears instantly greeted to the uproar, to the din of the cheering crowd. To the thunderous applause of—steady yourself—a *sea* of drag queens, a flock of fawning fans, the likes of which I could barely imagine in my mind's eye.

"What the—" croaked out Dara.

"Fuck," said I, finishing her train of thought. My head turned this way and that, trying to take it all in, to take them all in, to wrap itself around this vision of quantum queenliness. "Fuck," I repeated in one long, deep exhale. And with lungs as long dead as mine were, that was no easy task, let me tell you.

"You already said that," said Flo as she led me down the stairs. Well, carried really, because zombies can do many things, but climbing down isn't generally one of them.

"It merits repeating," said I as she set me down, Ginger doing the same to Dara, until we were both standing on pavement, the sea of humanity now a tidal wave, surging toward us. Suddenly, I knew what Dorothy felt like when she emerged from her twister-riding, black and white house into Technicolor. *BOOM!*

"I don't get it," Dara said, her hand again gripping my own. "Every man and woman and child, all drag queens. Did we die and go to heaven?"

"Technically . . ."

"Yeah, yeah, I know, hon," she said. "But it's either that or one hell of a dream."

Ironically, neither one was still possible: dying or dreaming. "Technically . . ."

She squeezed my hand. "*Technically*, we shouldn't be three hundred year old zombies, so please stop saying that."

By then, the sea had parted, and we, like Moses, proceeded to amble through it, hands lifted up on all sides of us in cheer, voices as well, like we were the prodigal, um, *sons* (yes, more irony) returning home.

I looked to my left. VaVa was by my side, waving at the throng, her smile so big and bright that it looked painful. "They adore you," I made note.

"*Us*," she retorted. "They adore *us*. As well they should."

Again she lost me, but with all the hubbub and ado, now, I figured, was not the time for more questions. Save, that is, for one. "But how . . . how can an entire population be, well, *gay?*"

She stopped, I stopped, Dara stopped, and Ginger and Flo kept right on walking. Guess they were too swept up in the moment—go figure, a drag queen who lives for applause. "Gay?" said VaVa, sotto voce. "It is not a word allowed here."

My face froze—uh, well, froze even more so than usual. "Huh?"

"Yeah, what she said: huh?" said Dara. "But you're all drag queens."

She shook her head. "We are Libetians. It is what we have always been, back to the—"

"Beginning," I said, with an ever-growing frown. "Yes, we got that." And it was then that I understood, finally. "My friends, Destiny and Kit and Blondella . . ." Again she seemed to pray at the mention of their names. "You, you *worship* them?" I stared at the torch-bearing drag queen that rose high above us, then back to VaVa. "But they weren't gods. They weren't even all that talented entertainers. Though they could certainly drink a sailor under the table, but that's no reason to worship someone, is it?" Admire, maybe, but worship? I think not. A whole boat of sailors, okay, but not one measly sailor.

She stared at me as if in a daze, but then seemed to shake it off. Or forced herself to. "Please, just follow me. Your room is waiting."

Dara again gripped my hand and pulled me toward her, her mouth up to my ear. "Watch what you say, hon. Might not be in our best interest to mock, just yet. Fun as that usually is."

I nodded my head. "Good point." Then I again turned to our hostess. "Please, do lead on."

And so she led while I stared at the adoring masses, each one dressed, if my eyes did not deceive me, in, what I could only assume, was now vintage Donna Karan and Stella McCartney and Versace and a host of designers I had knock-offs of a few hundred years prior. Plus, they were all in towering heels and equally towering wigs, with enough makeup to spackle all of Hoover Dam with. Beguilingly beautiful, yes, but just as unnerving, too. I mean, back in the day (like way, *way* back) it was great being a big fish in a little pond, but now, suddenly, all the people were the same, everyone and everything, well, *fishy.*

"Are you as lost as I am?" shouted Dara above the din.

"Loster," admitted I. "Guess it's best to just go with the flow for now."

She shrugged. "Hell, for one of those Bob Mackie gowns we just passed, I'd flow like a simultaneously menstruating school for girls."

"Gross," said I. And this coming from a seriously crusty, old zombie. Meaning, I knew of gross. And then some.

In any case, soon enough we were driven across the pontoons, through the center of town, and lifted up, up, up the stairs and into Lady Liberty herself before we were shown to our quarters. I didn't ask why we were given these accommodations; it was, after all, obvious in just about two and three-quarter seconds—the three-quarters needed to get over the initial shock.

"This is where they lived," I said, reverently, the last word, *lived*, very nearly breaking a heart that had long ago shattered into brittle, little pieces.

By then, it was just the five of us again, the crowd silenced once the front door to the statue was shut behind us. "The House of St. James," informed Ginger, that prayer thing again taking place. Creepy. *Very* creepy.

"And the other houses?" I asked. "The House of Kat, the House of Bombshell?" I was only joking, of course.

Suffice it to say, it wasn't taken as such. "Down the hallway," said Flo. "The House of Kat is on your left."

VaVa spoke up next. "The House of Bombshell on your right."

"All sacred," said Ginger.

"Sacred," echoed Flo.

"Sacred," echoed VaVa.

I scratched beneath my wig. "Uh, right. But we're tired now, from the long flight. Maybe you can come back for us in a couple of hours."

The three queens nodded, smiled, and then promptly left, their high heels loudly clanking down the hallway before they exited the building, pooped out of Libby herself. It was then that Dara turned to me. "We don't get tired, hon."

I grinned. "I know, but a little of those three goes a hell of a long way. Now I know why the guys at the drag bar were always so drunk: out of necessity."

Dara chuckled. "I used to know a drag queen by that name: Nessa Titty. Or was it Messa Titty?" She shrugged. "Anyway, point taken, girlfriend. One and one doesn't seem to be adding up to two around here."

I nodded as I had myself a look around. This had clearly been Destiny's room, a one-time office converted to living quarters. Even after all these years, I recognized her taste (or lack thereof). But what most caught my interest were the Polaroids, all clearly taken post-apocalypse, all of my friends. Oh to be able to cry again, to feel the bursting of my heart upon seeing them after so long.

Dara trudged over and patted my back. "They were . . . beautiful."

I laughed. "Nice try."

"They were your friends."

I nodded. "Better. And, yes. In fact, they saved me, turned me, even at their own peril. I could've just as easily eaten them."

She pointed at Kit Kat, a Snickers Bar in one hand, martini in the other, her smile blinding. "Well, maybe not all of them. At least not in one sitting."

I turned and rubbed our foreheads together, a kiss added to the mix. Thankfully, though I couldn't cry or pump my heart's now stagnant blood, I could still very much love. "I wish you could have met them."

She smiled and kissed me in return, her purpled lips lingering on my own. "It looks like I have, though, right? Ginger and VaVa and Flo: they emulate them down to the clothes on their backs, their wigs, their makeup. Like I used to dress up to look like Britney, they do so to your friends. But why? And all these years later? All of them doing it, too. Every man and woman and child on this island of theirs."

"Back to the beginning, as they so frequently put it." I set the picture of Kit back down and touched my fingertip to the glass. I sighed, if only in my head. "My friends survived the solar flares and headed to New York. Makes sense that they'd end up here, surrounded by water, safe from the zombies. Others would have done the same, created a community out here. Plus, they had the ferries at their disposal, so they could've made excursions to New York, hence the clothes, the makeup, anything else they would've needed until they could plant some crops and barrier trees, once the radiation levels diminished enough. But, by then, my friends would've been long dead (it smarted even to say it), so why the cult following? This House of St. James we're in, it might as well be a church, or at least the reliquary of one."

"And why us?" she added. "Here, now, I mean? What could they possibly need with us, or, more than likely, *you?* Everything appears normal enough."

I couldn't help but chuckle. "Apart from an entire race of drag queens, you mean."

She shrugged, grinned. "It could be worse, though."

I nodded my head. Worse indeed. I, after all, intimately knew of worse. "Funny thing is, I literally saved all of our humans. Their ancestors owe their very existence to me. But they don't worship me, minions though they are. In fact, they keep their distance whenever possible, the forces of life and death at odds with one another. So why my friends, why worship them?"

Dara walked around the room, admiring the furnishings. We were so used to the bare minimum, to an existence in a salt factory, to concrete and rust. This, at least, reminded us of what we once had, what life had once been like. "Well, your friends weren't zombies, for one. Have you noticed how these queens are nice to us, but still don't much like to look at us too closely, to touch us, to even acknowledge what we are beneath the dresses and makeup?"

I nodded, frowned. "Well, we are zombies, dearest. The walking undead. Like I said, opposing forces to them. If the pump was on the other foot, I would feel the same way, I suppose."

"But yet we're here just the same," she replied. "Three hundred plus years later. Even though they seemingly knew about you this entire time, knew where you were, had the ability to visit you whenever they liked."

My nodding continued, the frown on my face hanging even further south. "Despite my being friends, at one time, with their apparent, well, *gods.*" Oh the bitter irony in that. Heck, they weren't even the best-loved drag queens at our bar, back in the day. Certainly not the most tipped on your average night. Now they were practically enshrined in this place. Though, with me here, entombed seemed more appropriate.

I walked over to Dara, who was now admiring Destiny's wardrobe, and took her frigid hands in my own. In the silence I could hear the radiation inside of me, inside of her, what made us what we were. "But you're glad we're here, aren't you?" My frown quivered, inched up a notch.

She nodded, bloodshot eyes sparkling beneath the fluorescent lights. There was some sort of generator obviously nearby, something powering the entire island. Heck, if these queens had Gucci and Pucci at their disposal, what were a few gas-powered generators? We had the same thing back in Utah, minus, *groan*, the fabulous clothes. Because good luck finding a Mormon who would've known who Gucci even was, let alone Pucci. "Yes," Dara replied. "I'm glad we're here." Her own grin widened. "It is sort of fabulous, isn't it?"

"Odd but fabulous, yes," I admitted. "And a nice break from the monotony of a salt factory, safe though we are out there."

She paused, then asked, "Think your minions would like it out here?"

It was a rather pointed question. "Highly unlikely. Hundreds of years later, they're even more backwoods than they were when we started. As to wearing dresses and makeup, they barely tolerate us doing so, and only because they owe their safety to me. Plus, how would we get them here? Six people at a time? On a plane? They never even saw a plane before today, let alone flew in one, cross-country, piloted by a drag queen, in heels no less."

She nodded. "Right. You're right of course. Just, well, wishful thinking, I suppose. But maybe we can at least plant trees along the fence-line, tamp down the noise a bit, if not the infernal sight beyond."

I kissed her, something akin to warmth spreading through me. "Good idea, Dara. Good idea." I kissed her again. "But first, let's find out why we're even here to begin with."

"After you help me try on some of these clothes, though, right?"

I giggled. And a zombie giggling is quite a sight, let me tell you. "Goes without saying, dearest."

"Mhm," she replied, hand already on something silky. "Just don't go without saying it."

***

After we helped each other change into something less comfortable but way more satisfying to the eye, we waited for our newfound friends to join us. Though that's not who arrived exactly two hours later, as planned.

There was a knock at our door. "Come in," I said.

And in she walked, easily six and half feet tall, in towering stilettos, wearing a platinum blonde wig and a platinum-colored gown that shimmered as she sauntered up to us. Her lips and eyelids were painted in the same shade, her fingernails as well. "Hello," said the strange-looking stranger, her smile bright and beguiling, inviting even. "I am Topaz, high priestess."

My neck craned up to take her in. "High is right. There even enough oxygen up there?"

She ignored the comment. Or perhaps heard it a lot. Or simply didn't understand my humor, centuries old as it was. "Thank you for coming," she said instead.

"About that . . ." said Dara.

Topaz nodded, sagely. Or at least as sagely as anyone could who looked like a bright, shiny, new lamppost. "You have questions."

I nodded. "Got any answers?"

Her nod echoed my own. "Care for a walk?" She clearly remembered that walking wasn't exactly our forté anymore and quickly rephrased the question. "Or a drive?" Better. Much.

"That would be nice," I replied.

She led us outside, carried us each down the steps and helped us into a golf cart, a throwback to the Ellis Island tour days. "Ready?" she asked.

I looked at Dara, who nodded my way. "Ready," I replied.

We drove from Liberty Island and headed through the tangle of small houses that rode the water atop the pontoons. They were strangely sturdy, anchored as they were to the two islands and weighed down by the buildings that sat atop them. Plus, a road had been paved over them, so our ride, at least, was a smooth one.

As we drove by, the inhabitants smiled and waved at us and bowed to Topaz. "You said high priestess," I commented as I gazed at the brightly-colored homes, reminiscent, to a degree, of what I remembered of San Francisco. "High priestess of what? To the House of St. James?"

"No," she replied. "To all the houses. Though I, in fact, was born to the House of Bombshell. I therefore emulate the goddess in my attire."

I coughed. "Blondella is a goddess?" Which, in my head, sounded like *no fucking way*.

She paused, praying, it seemed, upon hearing her name. In a

whisper, she replied, "You . . . you knew her, yes? Was she as beautiful as she appears in her pictures?"

"You've got to be k—" Dara kicked me, a clear reminder not to speak from the top of my head, as was my way. "I mean, yes, beautiful. Sure. We'll go with that." I mean, in bar light, dim as it was, she was, well, pretty. From a distance. And after a few strong drinks.

Soon enough, we arrived again on solid ground, on Ellis Island. Here the buildings had been converted to apartments, the gardens to crops, a veritable city springing up from what was once a museum. Funny, because here now were the last remaining immigrants on an island that had once been dedicated to just that. It was, I thought, a testament to humanity. We did seem to cling to life. Even I did, however much you could call it that anymore—life, I mean. Then I turned to Dara and smiled. Guess we clung to love as well, I quickly realized. And hope.

Dara tapped our hostess on her silvery shoulder. "Why did we end the tour here?"

Topaz nodded. "You wanted answers; here is where you will find a great many of them."

She pointed to one of the main buildings, its façade now painted in a rainbow of colors, much different how I remembered it from my one and only visit during a trip out east for Gay Pride. My stomach suddenly knotted. Something about this place sent a wave of foreboding through me, despite its cheerful appearance.

Topaz helped us out of the golf cart and led us up the short promenade to the entrance of the building, those knots in my belly tightening, strong enough to dock a tanker with. She opened the door, and we entered. The room was large, with high ceilings, window-lined and bright. The purpose it had originally served, either for the immigrants themselves or the museum that followed, had long ago been forgotten, altered.

"Wow," said Dara, craning her neck to take it all in.

"*No*," I managed to squeak out, so much dread running through me that it was a wonder I was still able to stand, despite the rigor mortis keeping me locked in place.

From one end of the great hall to the other, a mural had been painted in the same rich and vibrant colors as the building itself, reading from left to right. I had started from the right, hence my *no*, while Dara had started from the left. A heavy groan rumbled through her once her neck finished moving across.

I knew it before I saw it. Felt it before we even entered. Perhaps, as someone who had been long dead myself, I was connected to it, to death. Though, for some, it appeared to have been more final.

"The goddesses," said Topaz, her voice barely above a reverent whisper, her index finger moving in an arc across the great expanse of the room, our eyes following, the mural recounting the story.

"So this is why you worship them," said Dara.

Topaz remained motionless. This, I knew, was holy ground. You could feel it all around us. It was as if the air itself was charged, like you were standing in a great cathedral. "To a degree," she replied. "In and of itself, what they did was enough to be venerated."

And, as I looked from left to right and back again, as I played the scenes out in my head, almost imagining them turning from paint to flesh, I understood—understood why this place was the way it was, why the Libetians were the way they were.

"My friends," I said, my face again turned to the left side of the room, to the beginning of the mural. "They overcame great obstacles to arrive here. They helped build a new civilization, one of equality, it looks like, of peace and beauty, until—"

Dara took up my story, the remaining words suddenly lodged in my throat. "The zombies, they attacked this place. Destiny and Kit and Blondella fought to save it, and, as a result . . ."

She couldn't finish it, so Topaz did it for her. "Yes," she said, the word like a prayer, or like an amen at the end of one. "They gave their lives to save us all." She pointed to the glass cases that were spread around the room. "From what I know of this room, it once contained the clothes of the people who came here long ago. The early Libetians wore these clothes. It was easier than raiding the mainland in those early years."

The cases now contained my friends' clothes, the ones they apparently fought in, ratted and tattered, the rhinestones still sparkling though, beads and sequins gleaming as the light flickered over them. I smiled, remembering my cohorts as they looked in these impossibly old outfits. "But now you dress like . . ." I pointed to the remains. "Like they once did."

She nodded. "They were brave, your friends. My ancestors honored that and still do so today."

And, in a way, I suppose they were brave. They certainly lived lives outside the norm. They were, in fact, larger than life. And now they were even larger than that.

Dara smiled. "By dressing like them, by taking on their, well, *affectations.*"

Topaz also smiled. "I do not know of the old ways, of what life was like before the goddesses. That life didn't seem to work anymore, not in this place. It's not taught, never spoken of. All I know is what you see today: *fabulousness.*"

Hence that word they all bandied about: the beginning. For them, my friends were just that: Adams dressed like Eves. And now all there was were Eves. Nice work, if you could get it.

Dara held my hand while her free hand pointed again to the left side of the mural. "There you are, Creature, also at the beginning."

I'd failed to notice it. After all, my friends were painted much larger. Me, I was already a zombie by then, left in Utah, a relic, barely worth a mention in their herstory.

"Saint Creature," commented Topaz.

I chuckled. "You've *got* to be kidding."

"Not without tips," replied the priestess. It seemed to be the standard reply around these parts.

"And, yet, no one's come looking for me in all this time." It wasn't a question. After all, I already knew the answer. I was a zombie, after all, saint or not. And these people avoided zombies, and wisely so. Until now, that is. Still, there was one thing that puzzled me, and so I pointed to about three-quarters of the way through the mural. "There's no way for the zombies to have attacked. Back then, we weren't as waterproof as we are now. Plus, apart from me and my ilk, we're unthinking and certainly unplanning, unscheming. So how could there have been an attack, a raid, all the way out here?"

At this, Topaz's demeanor changed, her peacefulness, her solemnity, replaced by an obvious unease. "We . . . we do not know."

"But they did attack?" said Dara.

Topaz nodded, the frown low on her otherwise beautiful face.

And that unease I'd been feeling, even before we entered this place, where my story ended and theirs began, grew and spread through me, the radiation suddenly sizzling down my spine. "And are attacking again?" I thought to ask. And still the priestess nodded. "Which is why you brought me here, *us*?" I gripped Dara's hand even firmer in my own. "It's not a homecoming; it's a home *saving?*"

Her nodding ceased. I wished I could say the same for that sizzling unease of mine.

CHAPTER 4
THE QUEEN MEGA-MARY

We were taken to a ferry landing after that; the ferry waited there, moored and bobbing. It was newly painted and very much reflecting the island's current inhabitants. In other words, as Topaz had said, *fabulous*. In fact, it was the gayest-looking boat I'd ever seen, a Carnival cruise on steroids—or maybe make that estrogen—like someone went berserk with a rainbow-colored brush and cans of glitter and reams of chiffon. Then again, with all those things, berserk really is the only way to go, right?

"If my teeth hadn't already rotted," commented Dara, finger pointed seaward. "I would've instantly gotten a cavity looking at that."

"It is beautiful, is it not?" replied Topaz.

I shrugged. I was leaning with *not*, but said instead, "Well, it's a, um, a boat alright."

Dara patted my back. "Good girl."

Still, this is not why she brought us here, to this spot. We knew it without her even having to say it. After all, though we could no longer see it, we could in fact smell it: blood and lots of it, from many humans, I was certain.

"There was some sort of skirmish here recently," I made note.

Topaz nodded, her face sad, eyes cast downward. "They came in the middle of the night, we figured, then hid among the nearby buildings, behind trees, anywhere out of sight. Come morning, we were defenseless."

"Your people have no weapons?" asked Dara.

"We have a modest supply of guns, but those we keep locked inside of Libby." She sighed. "By the time we dispatched the zombies, many of our people lost their lives."

37

I scrunched my face and stared out to sea. "Doesn't make any sense. Zombies can't swim, that's for sure. And they certainly can't steer a boat or land a boat, not without adequate help. It's just not possible. And even if they could attack, it would still be a fool's mission, slow as they are and all, with so many of you as there are."

"And yet it happened," said Topaz. "I saw it with my own eyes, saw my friends murdered. I even took down a great many of the zombies myself, once I made it to this spot."

"How do you think they got here?" Dara asked the priestess.

Topaz shrugged. "Not a clue."

"And has this happened before?"

Topaz looked to Dara—well, to and down quite a bit. "You saw the mural."

I tapped Topaz on the shoulder. Or at least would have if I could have. I settled for her elbow instead. "So just over three hundred years ago there was a zombie attack, and then nothing until recently?" I failed to mention that her people had waited the same amount of time to reach out to me. Why rub salt in the wound? Especially when the wound was solely my own.

She touched fingertip to button nose. "Exactly."

I squinted up at her, the sunlight forming a halo around her head, an errant beam momentarily blinding me. "Um, mind if Dara and I check out the ferry?"

"Suit yourself," she said. "Do you need help?"

I shook my head. "The dock isn't too steep; I think we can manage it. Thanks."

Dara took my hand and ambled seaward with me. We boarded easily enough and disappeared around the corner, both of us staring out at the Manhattan skyline. The Big Apple had aged well, minus a few noticeable bite marks taken out of her, that and all the green that had sprung up where once there had obviously been cement-tan and steel-gray.

"Why the need for distance from Drag-daddy Long Legs?" asked Dara.

"Why did they bring me here, hon?" A question for a question.

"Your dashing good looks and razor-sharp wit?"

I grinned. "More like razor-sharp looks and dashing good wit, but thanks. And no."

She sighed. After all, she knew the answer as well as I did. "You can communicate with other zombies, control them."

I nodded my head, my neck bones creaking and grinding as I did so. "And yet, my abilities began before *the beginning*, as they put it. And if they have no oral history, if they don't talk about their past, talk about life before they were Libetians, how would they know about my, uh, *skills*?"

"Word gets around?"

"Again, nice try. But, barring some sort of rampant zombie fan club of mine, the only word for miles and miles (and miles) around is *grr*, and that's not even a word."

"So what you're saying is—"

I stopped her. "I'm not saying anything. Yet. Just, we have to be careful around these people is all. Clearly, they have no love of our kind and the only reason I'm here is to help them. Plus, I have a sinking feeling that they're not telling us everything."

She cringed. "Please don't say *sinking* when we're standing on a boat, my love." To which she added, "In any case, they do call you Saint Creature."

I shrugged. "An homage to my past, not my present. They'd just as soon look at me in that mural than in person."

She closed the small gap between us, a perfect kiss placed on my lips. "Well, *I* like looking at you. Past, present *and* future."

"Ditto, girlfriend," I purred—though, coming from me, it sounded more like a soft roar mixed with crunching gravel.

"So what do we do then?"

A shrug joined with a sigh. "Guess we help. If nothing more than in deference to what my friends created here."

"It is beautiful," Dara said.

"But is it only skin deep?"

Ah, now that was the question.

***

A short while later, we found ourselves back in the golf cart. "So, will you help?" asked Topaz.

I turned to Dara. She smiled and nodded, ever so slightly. I mimicked the gesture. "We'll help," I replied. "If we can."

Topaz left it that. And then she left us to our own devices, back at the base of Libby. She pulled away, shouting over her shoulder, "Let me know if you need anything." And with that, and a honk that sounded like a sharp squeeze on a clown's nose, she was gone.

I turned to Dara. "So much for our vacation."

"Better than Utah."

She had me there. "Well then, first thing we need to figure out is how they're attacking, then why after all this time. Any ideas?"

"They came by water, so they must've had some sort of vessel that took them here. I didn't see any other boat besides the Queen Mega-Mary back there. And they couldn't have used that if it's still docked on this side of things, right?"

"Right." I knew what she was getting at and added, "But, besides being such a pretty face, the kind that only a zombie mother could love, I can't drive a boat, which is the only way for us to investigate the mainland, where they had to have originated from."

"Still," she said, "someone knows how to steer that thing, right?"

"What thing?" we suddenly heard from behind us.

We turned. VaVa and Ginger were headed our way and closing fast. "The ferry boat," I replied.

VaVa, who'd since changed and was now in a rather fetching pantsuit and flowing amber wig, smiled widely. "Plane, car, cart *and* ferry boat captain, at your service."

"You're joking," said Dara.

And before the two of them could respond, I needlessly replied, "Not without tips."

"Exactly," said VaVa. "It's my job to know how to operate all working crafts on the island, as it was my mother's job and her mother's before her, back to—"

"The beginning," interrupted Dara. "Got it."

"So can you take us to the mainland?"

Her grin faltered. "Um, I said *could*, not *would*."

"But you said 'at your service,'" said Dara.

"I thought you meant something like a booze cruise around the harbor."

"We don't drink," I reminded her.

"Sucks to be you," said Ginger, her hand placed reverently just above her liver.

I shut my eyes and counted to five. "You brought us here to help. We can't help without investigating. And the zombies had to arrive via some sort of water craft. Since there's no such craft docked where the slaughter took place, we must assume that said craft is back on the mainland. So to prevent the next slaughter—"

"She'll take you there." It was Flo, who walked in from our left side, a chocolate bar in her hand, a smudge of brown against her emerald-painted lips.

"Um, if you don't mind me asking, is that candy bar you're eating more than three hundred years old?"

"Yuck," said Dara.

But Flo shook her head. "The island has enormous working freezers."

I knew where she was going with that, mainly because she reminded me so much of my long-dead friend, Kit. "Let me guess," I guessed. "The goddess of the House of Kat stocked a great deal of chocolate in those freezers."

Flo smiled. "How did you know that?"

My smile mirrored hers. "It's the first thing she would've done. And the concession stands on the island back then must've had hundreds of cases of chocolate."

"Hundreds," she agreed. "Plus the hundreds and hundreds more we have stored at the stadium on the mainland, where we have just about everything we store, everything we could possibly need."

VaVa joined in, but she wasn't smiling along with us. "Two birds, one stone?"

Flo was already headed to a nearby golf cart. "I'm out of Snickers; our guests need to get to the mainland. As to two birds, good luck finding any."

"It's an expression," glumly replied VaVa, now following close behind, the rest of our posse doing the same.

"So is *take us to the mainland or else*," replied Flo as she hefted herself into the passenger seat, Ginger helping me and Dara into the back before joining us.

"That's not an expression," said VaVa as she cranked up the engine.

Flo finished her candy bar and smiled. "Wanna make a bet?"

***

After a quick stop inside of Libby, guns soon in our possession, we found ourselves aboard the ferry, which chugged us steadily out into the harbor, our green-tinged, gold-robed friend quickly shrinking into the distance as Manhattan loomed ahead.

"What can we expect out there?" I hazarded to ask Flo, my face pointing ahead.

"Zombies," came the reply. "Lots and lots of zombies. They probably already smell us; the wind's carrying our scent their way even as we speak."

"Any way to sugarcoat it?" asked Dara.

Flo shook her head. "Trust me, that was sugarcoating it. And I do so love things sugarcoated."

Which was about as duh a comment as I could imagine, but failed to say so, seeing as we were quickly heading into the belly of the beast. "Steer us east," I said, because I too had a keen sense of smell, and something was telling me that our prey came from that direction.

"Perfect," said the captain. "That's where we need to head as well."

The waterway split, one going up the east side of Manhattan, the other west, with Brooklyn now off to our right side as we headed, as asked, east, the stunning New York skyline on our opposite side. It shimmered in the light of day, magnificent despite the ferocious sounds of moans and groans crescendoing all around us. I would've covered my ears if it'd done any good.

"Millions of them," commented Dara, her voice leery. "Everywhere."

I nodded. "And every last one of them eager to rip our newfound friends here to bits." I looked over at Flo and Ginger, who were sitting on a bench in the middle of the boat. They'd smartly retrieved two sets of furry earmuffs from some storage area and were trying their bests to ignore the surrounding ruckus. Again I looked at Dara. "Seems they're quite popular around these parts."

She grinned. "Seems their parts are quite popular around these parts."

My grin mirrored hers. "Still, it explains why they don't talk about the zombies, why there's a wall up, a veneer, smiling on the outside, cringing within. I can sense it, even without seeing it."

"Same with our humans back in Utah," said Dara.

I nodded. "Exactly. Kindness out of necessity." My smile flatlined as I stared out at the skyscrapers. "Still, I suppose I understand. It's like repelling magnets. Life forever fighting against ever-present death, and here we are—"

"Death warmed over."

And still I nodded. "Heated over. Boiling over. Sizzling." I looked up at our steering captain. She was pointing into the distance. I squinted but couldn't as yet make out where we were headed.

Dara and I walked over to Flo and Ginger. They removed their earmuffs, their shoulders instantly bunching up at hearing the piercing din, like millions of mosquitoes buzzing from all sides, the sound carried on the wind. "Where are we headed?" I asked.

At that, they both managed a smile. "Queens," replied Flo.

"Figures," said I. "But why there?"

"The stadium is there, just off the water."

I shrugged and looked over to Dara, the more butch of our pair, if only by a smidge. "Citi Field," she informed. "Replaced Shea. Home of the Mets."

I kissed her cheek. "You never cease to amaze me, dearest."

She kissed me back. "And, luckily, never, as in ever never, is a distinct possibility for the likes of us."

"Exactly." I turned to our hostesses. "But how do you get from the boat to there, safely?"

Their smiles widened. "Wait and see," said Ginger. "Wait and see."

Dara glanced my way, and the look on her face said it all: *these bitches scare me.* Which was saying quite a lot, coming from a centuries-dead zombie.

In any case, the waiting part of that didn't take long, the ferry chugging around the bend all too soon. As to the seeing, well, again I was amazed. And twice in a decade, let alone twice in ten minutes, was something akin to a miracle. Because, though, as I mentioned, our flesh, gray and withered though it was, was fairly water-resistant now, at least to the likes of a toy water gun or a rain shower, it was no match for a water cannon—and take a guess at what the ferry had aboard her.

Yep, all we had to do was park that sucker, aim the cannon and let the water flow and flow and motherfucking flow. And no amount of withered flesh can withstand that. Nope, cleared a path dead (pun intended) ahead, as, it seemed, it had many times before, judging by the wall of bones on all sides.

"Yuck," said I.

"Times a million," added Dara. "And there but for the grace of God go I." She grinned. "I used to know a drag queen by that name. Grace O'God. Oh the things that queen hid beneath her habit. One time—"

"Later, hon," I said, patting her back. "We have work to do."

And there again was one of those gross understatements. Emphasis on the gross. In fact, as soon as we deboarded we were assaulted by the stench of it all: from the newly rekilled right on through to all the past-kills and beyond to the zombies held in place by the wall of decay. Sadly, there were swarms of them, too, however held back they were, because, while zombies can surely trudge, we can't hop, skip or jump—at least not without tripping, falling and promptly writhing. And, trust me, writhing for all eternity would truly suck, big time. Like being George Bush. Number one or two. In any case, we pretty much had a clear path from the boat to the stadium.

Um, pretty much.

Close but not cigar. See, there were gaps in that pile-of-mangled-corpses wall. And a zombie is nothing if not determined. Literally. Nothing. Throw three juicy humans into the mix, and determined transforms into bound and determined. As in *bounding* our way.

Flo and Ginger and VaVa lifted their weapons up high as the moans and groans and scraping of feet against concrete filled our ears. "Wait!" I shouted. "Let me try first."

"Huh?" managed Flo. "You gonna wow them with a floor routine, sugar? Because, don't take this the wrong way, but I don't exactly think you have it in you."

Dara grinned. "Wanna make a bet?"

"Double or nothing," whispered I, my hands held up high, throat clearing (to whatever degree it still could). "HALT!" I then bellowed, body trembling from the exertion.

And, though it had been a while since I last commanded any new zombies, this lot of them turned out to be just like the ones back home. Which is to say, they halted.

"Holy smoke," said Ginger, eyes wide.

"Yeah," coughed VaVa. "What she said."

To which Flo added. "My bad." And then lowered her weapon.

"Never gets old," I commented, with a grin.

"Ever," said Dara. "Now let's go, before they change their minds."

44

"Or sneak in from the rear," said VaVa. "Which normally I don't mind, but—"

"Got it," I said, leading the way, all eyes now on me, just as they should be.

Sadly, though, others things were not as they, too, should be. Sure, the stadium was there, but the side door the queens usually used was unlocked, the chain a tangle on the cement floor. "How?" croaked out Ginger.

"Better question: why?" said I, a short while later.

As in, *why* were the freezers all turned off, the contents within destroyed, gas-powered generators smashed to bits, cases and cases and cases of perishables nothing but rubble now? As in *why* now, after all this time? As in, *why* do this to the few-remaining humans?

And, while we were at it, *who* was doing it all?

Though, of course, Flo had the biggest quandary to face: the what. As in, "What am I going to eat when my chocolate runs out?!"

VaVa patted her on her broad expanse of back. "There's still plenty of tomatoes and cauliflower back on the island."

Flo broke out into sobs. "Kill me! Kill me now!"

Which, as it turned out, wasn't the smartest thing to be shouting, all things considered. And, no, not because of the millions of zombies outside the stadium so much as the dozen or so within, all of them trudging our way, jaws unclenched, hands outstretched, moans at a fevered, hungry pitch.

VaVa poked me in the side. "Now would be a good time for an encore, sweetie."

I nodded and lifted my hands into the air. "Halt!" I shouted. But still they kept right on trudging, mouths even more agape, the volume of their groans notching up. I planted my feet and held my hands up higher. "Halt!" I shouted. "Cease! Desist! Stand the fuck still!" But no. Nada, nil, zilch. It was as if they had cotton in their ears. Or just didn't appreciate a good act when they saw one.

"Our turn," said Ginger, gun held up, with VaVa's and Flo's quick to follow, all three unleashing their rounds, all three taking down the zombies in about two seconds flat. Ginger looked my way and smiled. "See, we're more butch than we look."

"Damn," said VaVa, gun now at her side, free hand held up to face. "Broke a nail."

Ginger shrugged. "Or maybe not." She lowered her own gun. "In any case, care to explain why this batch of undead failed to heed your command?"

Dara moved to my side and whispered in my ear. "Yeah, hon, what gives?"

I walked over to one of the newly dead undead and leaned down as best I could. They looked like the other zombies, smelled, *blech*, like the other zombies, and, no, no cotton in their ears, so, yeah, what gave? "Not a clue," I replied. "That's never happened before. Zombies have always listened to me. Always."

"Until now," said Ginger, standing by my side.

"And," added Dara, "until now, zombies didn't attack the humans, didn't destroy their supplies, so, ten to one, the two 'until nows' are somehow related."

I frowned and started moving back the way we'd come. Because, if there was one thing I knew all too well, where there was one zombie, there were more. Lots and lots more. "Hurry," I said. "Before the backups arrive."

The others nodded, VaVa suddenly at my other side. "So, do we keep going then, take the ferry and look for the ones that attacked the island, as planned?"

I paused, if only for a moment. "Not a good idea, I'd think. Not with only three guns and no extra ammo, at least." Plus, whomever this enemy of ours was, we now knew they were well-organized, perhaps even watching our every move.

VaVa nodded. "And no extra nails either." Again she looked down at her hand. "And I just had them done."

So much for that more butch thing she promised.

Too bad, because, right about then, we sorely could have used it.

CHAPTER 5
PURPLE, BLUE, GREEN AND GRAY

We made it back to the island without any more incidents. The zombies outside the stadium heeded my commands, and there were no more zombies within the stadium to contend with. So, at the very least, we were again safe and sound—well, safe, at any rate.

By then, it was getting late, the sun just as sick and tired of this day as we were, not even bothering to turn the sky a brilliantly gay pink for us. Instead, a cold fog rolled in, the clouds gray above, Dara and I soon enough deposited within Libby's bowels. And, no, despite the humor in that imagery, I couldn't even bother to crack a smile.

"Weird," said Dara. "All of it. The queens, this place, those zombies in the stadium. Like time itself had a hiccup and all of a sudden we've been set on a different course."

I sighed. "And you know as well as I do that a zombie doesn't act out of reason, like intentionally smashing up a stadium. In fact, they only follow commands, and then, at least up until recently, only from me; they certainly don't issue them."

"Unless . . ." Dara said, eyes growing wider.

"No, can't be," I replied, knowing full well what that "unless" meant.

"But our zombies think and feel and act just as they did when they were humans."

"Aided by the salt, which is administered by the minions. And that had to have started with a human, right? I mean, I was turned by Kit and Blondella and Destiny all those centuries ago. It wasn't time that started us on this course of ours; it was them. And even that was by pure dumb luck, at the girls taking a chance that iodized salt would act like radiation sickness pills." I looked at her and sighed again. "How could the same thing have happened independently? I mean, can there be another one like me out there? Another clan of thinking zombies, of sidekick humans, all of them, for whatever reason, working to destroy what my friends started here so long ago?"

She shrugged. "Not a friggin' clue, sweetie," she replied, her attention turned elsewhere, namely to the rack of clothes in the corner.

"How can you think of dresses at a time like this?"

She grabbed a slinky beaded number and held it out for me to see, the gorgeous red outfit shimmering beneath the overhead lights. "Oh," I fairly moaned.

She grinned. "Yeah, oh."

Now, to be fair, I'd spent just over three hundred years in whatever clothes we could find in the small towns that surrounded the salt plant—in Utah, need I remind you. In other words, though there were certainly more pressing matters to contend with at the time, right then and there the only thing concerning me was pressing that beautiful beaded number against my cold, lifeless body.

Took some wrangling, since I no longer had my minions to help, but drag queens are nothing if not resourceful, and, soon enough, we were both naked and ready to try on some of those ancient outfits. Of course, it was then that we both realized we were naked and alone and equally as ancient. And, though neither red nor beaded, Dara was a delicious shade of purple, mottled with blue and gray and touches of emerald green. So, yes, suddenly I was even more concerned with pressing my partner's beautiful number against my cold, lifeless body.

"God, you're incredible," Dara said, her fingers tracing the lines of veins that crisscrossed my chest, the feel of her touch on my skin sending a shiver through me as my dangling prick began its inevitable rise upwards. And a radiation-powered boner truly is a sight to see. Or maybe that was just my boner in general. Hard (pun intended) to tell.

My hand reached out and caressed the prick aimed my way. Dara sighed and inched in closer, until we were bloodshot eye to bloodshot eye, her lips on mine in a flash, tongues doing an oral tango as we jacked one another's pricks and moaned in delight—as opposed to just moaned, which is what we zombies generally do.

Now, to backtrack just a bit, because even I, jaded drag queen though I am, realize full well that a dead(ish) zombie having sex with another dead(ish) zombie may seem, well, okay, *icky*, but one simply loves what one loves. And, to me, she (even though *she* had one stellar prick) was nothing short of stunning, purple and blue and green and gray flesh and all. Besides, it was the man (drag queen) within that I'd fallen in love with and still loved with all my (non-beating) heart all these centuries later. To paraphrase, beauty is only purple, blue, green and gray skin deep.

In any case, we're here, we're dead, get over it.

Or into it.

Because zombie love has a lot going for it: one, we don't get tired—it's tantric sex on a whole new level; two, as long as we're horny, our erections never flag—yippy for that snapping, crackling and popping radiation; and three, no sticky mess to clean up. I mean, our body fluids dried up ages ago. Ergo, no saliva, no tears and no come. Um, yes, *we* come, just not *with* come.

So I fucked her for hours and hours, some makeup remover used for lube, our bodies in perfect, if not a bit rickety, syncopated rhythm. The troubles of the day momentarily got wiped clean away, until, finally, we shot, if only in our heads, our bodies quivering and quaking in gut-wrenching and quite lovely ecstatic spasms. Not human sex, no; more like human sex 2.0, the next generation.

"Wow," Dara finally said, my cock gliding out of her stupendous ass. "That was—"

"Fucking incredible?"

She shook her head. "Incredible fucking."

I grinned. "Lord knows I've had enough practice."

Her shake turned nod. "And it does indeed make perfect."

Though none of that helped us with our mission. Ego boost, fine, but mission boost, nuh uh. So back to the investigating we went. Um, after we put on our new frocks, of course. Because a good fuck deserves an equally good frock, right? We'll go with *right* on that one.

"Too late to go tracking the invader's boat again," said Dara.

I looked at the solar-powered clock. It was, as she said, late. And there was no way for us to navigate the ferry across to the mainland. Plus, now it was even more dangerous to do so, knowing what we knew: that not all the zombies out there heeded my commands. Stupid fucking zombies.

I sighed. "Let's head back to Ellis Island, to the museum. Maybe there's a clue back there, in the history of this place."

And so, in the black of night, we strolled through town, the only sound that of the crashing waves and the wind as it whipped across us. It took us a while to make it to Ellis Island, but we had plenty of time to, pardon the expression, kill.

Inside, the museum was eerily lit, shrine-like. Again I stared up at the mural, my friends brought back to life in 1D. "Huh," I soon said as my eyes went from left to right.

"Huh what?" asked Dara, her eyes following mine.

I pointed at the mural, to my friends as they fought the zombie horde, weapons held up high: Destiny with a machete, Blondella with a pearl-inlayed pistol, and Kit, with of all things, a Snickers Bar. Bitches looked fierce, by the way. I smiled despite the inevitable outcome. Still, my "huh" was well-deserved. And so my finger kept pointing, from the mural to the cases around us. "Look again."

She squinted at the mural and then at the cases, back and forth, back and forth. "Sorry, Creature, not seeing anything amiss. Though maybe Destiny's shoes didn't exactly go with her blouse, and that wig Kit had on, well, not to speak ill of the dead, but—"

"No," I said. "And, trust, me, they heard plenty of ill in life in those regards. It's just . . ." I walked to the case closest to me. In it were Blondella's clothes, the ones she last wore. Again I pointed to the mural as Dara moved from the center of the great hall to where I was now standing, my voice slightly echoing in all directions. "It's just, this wasn't Blondella's stuff."

Dara scratched beneath her wig. Not because she itched, because zombies simply don't do that, but because she was confused. Again she looked from the mural and back to the ratted and tattered clothes reverently encased before us. "It's the same outfit that's in the mural, Creature."

I nodded. "Well, yes, it looks to be the same outfit that's in the mural, but it's not Blondella's."

"You lost me, hon."

I pointed to the pumps first. "What size are those?"

She squinted and bent down as best she could for a better look. "I dunno, maybe a nine or ten, about my size. Why?"

"And what size pump do I wear?"

She didn't have to look to know that answer because she always hated that we couldn't share each other's shoes. "Twelve, you big-footed queen."

I nodded. "Blondella and I wore the same size. Same size shoe, same size dress." Again I pointed at the case before us. "Same size pantsuit." And, yes, I could remember all of that, even though it'd been several hundred years, because every last one of my brain cells, every last memory, had been locked in place at the same time that I had in fact been locked in place.

"Huh," my partner huhed.

"Exactly," I said. "Huh. As in *huh*, that outfit might've fit Destiny, but Blondella was a big girl, tall, like me. Now, that's a nice pantsuit, but it isn't Blondella's. And it might look like the outfit in the mural, but, again, not Blondella's."

"Huh," Dara repeated. "But why make it look like it was?"

Just then, we heard footsteps approaching. I turned, Dara turned, and the approaching queen stepped into the dim light.

"Couldn't sleep?" It was Ginger.

I chuckled, as did Dara. "Um, sure, we'll go with that." I left out the three hundred plus years without sleeping thing, as it tended to make humans nervous. "And, I'm sorry, did we disturb you?"

She shook her head, flowing ebony wig swinging in sync. "We keep a fire burning in homage to the goddesses. It's my duty to tend to the eternal flame. My duty, in fact, and my mother's before her, to make sure the fire stays lit, the fuel source below ground never running low." Her smile went reverent, eyes suddenly closed, just as Topaz and VaVa had done at the mention of my friends. Funny because, in life, said friends never needed stoking; their flames were always set on high. Always. When Ginger's eyes again opened, she added, "I heard a noise and came in to investigate." The smile vanished. "What with, well, all that's happened lately, I mean."

I nodded. I knew that I could've mentioned the clothes in the case, but thought the better of it. After all, it seemed an intentional ruse. The why was something we'd have to find out on our own, though. "Can we see the flame?" I asked instead.

Her smile lit up again. She nodded and turned back the way she'd come, while we in turn followed. Dara glanced my way. I knew she was thinking the same thing I was: to keep what we'd found just between ourselves for now. Great minds, not to mention insanely old ones, think alike, after all.

Several minutes later, we found ourselves behind the museum. We saw the light as we approached. It was radiant in the otherwise dark surroundings. Sadly, it also illuminated the reason it was placed where it had been placed.

I stopped—this time no pun intended—dead in my tracks. "Is that where . . .?"

Ginger again went all reverent on our asses. "It's the goddess' earthly remains."

The light of the flame flickered on the nearby tombstones, three of them, all side by side, the trio fenced in. Had my heart not stopped pumping ages ago, it would've right then and there. It was one thing to see there clothes, beaten and bruised as they were, but this, this was something else entirely.

Like I said, my memory was locked in place, everything about me just as it was the day I, to coin a word, *zombified*. So, even though it had been centuries now, it seemed like only yesterday that we had all been together. Dara reached her hand across the gap that separated us and gave my hand a squeeze. She knew what I was feeling at that very moment.

We walked the remaining few feet and stared down at the markers. They were fairly basic, given that, I assumed, there were few tools and stones available on the island at the time of their untimely deaths. Still, it was clear who was buried there. And, yet, again something was amiss.

"Huh?" I managed, once more.

"What now?" Dara whispered in my ear as she bent down and lifted a souvenir Lady Liberty off the ground, one of many left in homage, I assumed, instead of flowers by one of the Libetians.

I turned to Ginger. "Can we please have a minute with my . . . with my friends here?"

She nodded. "Take all the time you need. If you need me, just holler." And with that, she sashayed away, hips swaying like a well-oiled pendulum.

Dara waited a moment before asking, "What's with the latest 'huh?'"

I looked from her to the graves. They were evenly spaced, headstones too, all tightly fenced in. And that was what was giving me pause. "Notice anything funny?"

She tilted her head. "Um, I know I'm a zombie and all, but *funny*? Ain't nothing funny about *that*, hon." She pointed to the markers.

"Not funny *ha-ha*; funny as in strange," I reiterated.

Her head remained tilted. There was a pause, then, "Huh."

"So you see it, too?"

She turned my way. "Aflo Sheen, she looks just like your friend Kit, right?"

I nodded. "Hell to the yeah. Could pass for her twin, in fact. Same coloring, same style of clothes, mannerisms—"

"Girth?"

My nodding continued. "If anything, Kit was just a bit, um, *rotundier*, but yes, girth. Check."

Dara again looked down at the graves. "Would've been a tight fit then. Three full grown drag queens, one *extra* grown, all of them fitting within this fence, evenly spaced like they have them." Again her scalp got a scratching. "Seems to me, the overall size would be a bit wider, but, then again, we don't know the shape they were in when . . . well, you know."

"True," I allowed, my belly suddenly in knots at the "you know," because indeed I did know. "And if it wasn't for the clothes back there in the case, I might not have even noticed, but two things off like that does make me wonder. Especially now, with the return of the zombies."

"But what does any of it mean?" she asked.

I forced a sigh and shrugged. "Beats the hell out of me." I stared down at my friends. "Sorry, ladies. No disrespect intended." Fun as it always had been to dis them in the past.

***

We walked back in silence after that. If something was indeed amiss, and intentionally so, then whom could we trust? Then again, the museum case and the graves were ages old, so maybe no one even knew the answers to our questions anymore. Maybe they were just as lost in time as my friends were.

In any case, we had more pressing issues to contend with, like the return of the zombies to Liberty Island. And if we were going to prevent that from happening again, we had to find said zombies and, more importantly, find who was controlling them. And how. And why.

"I have a headache," I griped.

Dara grinned. "You know that's impossible, my love."

My grin mirrored hers. "The centuries-old zombie drag queen is telling me about impossible?"

"Touché."

So an expedition was planned, with me and Dara, VaVa, Flo, Ginger and Topaz as the scouting party. And suddenly we had a floating drag bar, albeit one that was insanely well-armed. I stared at them all—dresses and blouses and caftans blowing in the breeze, fabulous wigs as well, and enough makeup to stamp every last pore into submission—and I couldn't help but smile, remembering my life as it once has been.

Dara held my hand in hers. "They're beautiful, yes?" She turned and kissed my cheek. "Though not half as much as you." I started to object when she touched her free hand to my chest. "Where it counts, I mean."

My smiled widened as I kissed her back. "Were you always this schmaltzy?"

She shrugged. "Just the last couple of hundred years. Like whiskey, I mellow with age."

"God how I miss that."

"Aging?"

I shook my head. "Whiskey."

The ferry pulled away from the dock, VaVa at the helm, the other queens spreading out, looking for any signs of trouble. "I could use a drink myself right about now," she whispered back. "Or six."

I stared back out to sea. "Amen to that, sister."

***

We headed the way we'd come the day before. By then, the scent trail had evaporated, but at least we knew the general direction the invaders had originated from. This time we went beyond the stadium exit, continuing around the coastline.

"There," said Dara, soon pointing in the distance.

I nodded. It was a marina, all the boats rusted, battered and beaten by age, none of them remotely seaworthy looking. None, that is, save for one. "B-I-N-G-O."

"And Bingo was her name, oh," sung Dara.

"Oh indeed," agreed I as the boat chugged us ever closer. I turned to the others. "Any of you ever seen that before?"

They all shook their heads. "No, sorry," said Ginger. "And we never have a need to go beyond the stadium, so this harbor is new to us as well."

"Still," said I, "that must be the boat that brought the zombies to your shores." I gulped, again if only in my head. "Guess we should go and investigate."

"Guess so," agreed Ginger, sounding about as thrilled as I was about it. Which is to say, not very. Or at all.

The boat slowed down as we drew closer to the side of the other craft. It was empty, that much I was certain about, no smell of death, apart from what had lingered. But that wasn't what gave me pause as we tied our boats together and went from one to the other, we two zombies lifted up by the humans.

Dara looked at me and I looked at her as all of us stood above deck. "You smell it too?" she asked.

Fear ricocheted across each of the queen's faces. "What? They're on board? Now?" asked Flo, hand trembling as she held her gun up and aimed it into the nothingness.

I reached across and lowered it. "No, we are quite alone." I heard the moans and groans from the city beyond. "Apart from, well, *them.*"

"Then what is it?" asked VaVa. "What do you and Dara smell?"

I turned to her. "It isn't what we smell so much as what we don't smell, what we thought we might smell when we got here."

She sighed. "Do zombies always speak in riddles?"

And I couldn't help but grin. "Not without tips."

Dara poked me in the side. "Good one," she whispered.

"In any case," I continued. "What Dara and I smell aboard this craft is zombies, the undead, a stench unmistakable. At least to the likes of us."

"And?" asked VaVa.

"And," I replied. "No humans. Which also have a scent unmistakable to the likes of us. In other words, a zombie somehow steered this craft and is, perhaps, steering the marauding undead, leading them, commanding them."

"Like you do," said Flo.

"Like I do, yes," I reluctantly agreed, unsure how that was even possible, that there was someone else like me out there.

Flo moved in closer. "So we kill this zombie, this supposed leader, and the rest topple over like dominos?"

I shrugged, as best I could. "Makes sense, I suppose." As much as anything did, I thought to myself, because none of it made sense, not really.

"But how do we find this zombie?" asked Ginger. "Doesn't this one smell like all the rest, like the millions upon millions on all sides of this harbor, like the billions beyond that?"

I groaned, which, suffice it to say, came a lot easier to me than sighing or gulping. "Sadly, yes."

I turned to the others, my eyes landing on the priestess, Topaz, who had, thus far, remained oddly silent. She locked eyes with me in just that instant. "So how do we proceed then?" she asked. "Wait for them to attack again and hope for the best?"

I shook my head. "No, too dangerous. Best if we strike first this time. Catch them by surprise like they caught you by surprise."

Ginger lifted her hand up. "But how do we even find them? Or, more importantly, the leader?"

The silence, apart from the distant groaning, was very nearly deafening. Sadly, though, none of them had an answer. Which meant that it was up to me. And, yes, I had thought of something, but was dread to attempt it. In any case, I turned to Dara and took her hand. "Come with me." And then I looked at the others. "We'll be right back."

All of them stared at the two us, confusion spreading across their expertly made-up faces. Still, they parted their ranks and let Dara and me walk by, until we were soon alone around the other side of the vessel and away from prying ears.

"I don't like that look on your face," said Dara.

I grinned. "Really? Isn't it the same look that's been locked on my face for more than three hundred years now?"

She shook her head. "Something new is there, something that's making the hairs on the back of my neck stand on end. If, um, I hadn't Naired them off before, um . . . well, you know."

I stroked her hand. "I know. And, trust me, those hairs, nonexistent though they are, have every right to be standing up."

"And I don't like the sound of that any more than I like that look on your face."

My grin promptly faded. "Trust me, it's about to get a hell of a lot worse-looking."

She squeezed my hand. "Fine. Lay it on me then."

"What would happen if we went out into the throng?" Before she could protest, I added, "Alone, just the two of us?"

She paused before replying, clearly thinking it over. Because, in three centuries, we'd never attempted such a thing. Then she shrugged. "Nothing, I suppose, apart from getting the willies about a million times over. I mean, for all intents and purposes, we're one of them, right?"

"For all intents and purposes, yes. And, without the humans with us, there's no reason to attack. Zombies, as far we know, don't eat other zombies."

"But why go?" she then asked. "How will that help?"

I leaned against the wall and stared out to the city beyond. I knew what was out there waiting, smelled it, heard it, loud and clear. "The leader is out there, probably nearby, seeing as the undead don't cover a lot of ground on our own. Guess it couldn't hurt to at least go look, and if we run across zombies that don't obey my orders, we know we're getting close."

"Then what?"

I shrugged. Sort of. Though it felt more like a flinch. "Play it by ear, I suppose."

She chuckled. "Sounds like a reasonably thought out plan, dear one."

"Got anything better?"

Her chuckling ceased. "Lots, but all of them involve going back to Utah. Suddenly, I miss your minions. And at least behind the fence we're not mingling with the undead hordes. Call me a snob, but . . ."

"But you're a snob, and rightly so." I turned her way. "One day, that's all. One day and then we have the queens pick us up back here. One day to do some recognizance, then figure out our next move. What could go wrong?"

"You're kidding, right."

I grinned. "Not without tips."

"You want a tip? Fine, how about don't play nice with zombies, especially ones that haven't bathed in over three centuries and that might tear you limb from limb just for the fun of it, meal or no meal."

Still I was grinning. "Are you done?"

She nodded. "Yep."

I patted her shoulder. "Good. Then let's get this over with. And no mentioning to the others what we're up to, just in case."

"Creature," she said, "I *don't* know what we're up to."

I kept patting. "See, you're doing great already."

CHAPTER 6
BREADCRUMB

The queens promised (pinky-swore and crossed every toe and finger and eye) to pick us up exactly twenty-four hours later. "Here," said Flo, her diamond-encrusted watch slipped onto my wrist. "Then you'll know when to come back." And then said watch promptly slipped right off, clanking on the deck below. "Oops, guess my wrist is a bit, um, *thicker* than yours."

"Just like your head," said VaVa, who retrieved the watch and buckled it around my arm. At least there it stayed put. "Be safe." She seemed to go to kiss my cheek, but then thought the better of it. Guess sisterhood only went so far, the boundary line clearly marked where life ended and death began.

Ginger then placed her wide-brimmed pink fedora atop my head. "To, well, to protect your, uh, brains."

Dara giggled. "Yeah, that ought to do the trick. No zombie would dare bite through that."

And then we were off, trudging down the metal walkway and not looking back—mainly because that would mean twisting our necks around and, geez, good luck with that. At the end of the plank there was a barred gate, beyond which stood the dense throng, the groaning so loud that I had to cover my ears, Dara quickly following suit.

I reached for the latch. Luckily, it gave easily enough. "Stay back," I then commanded. Once again, luck was on our side, the zombies in the front freezing in place as we slipped outside, the gate clinking behind us.

The groaning dropped several notches as the ferry pulled away, taking any vestiges of life along with it. As to our brains, desiccated as they might have been, at least they seemed, for the time being, to be off the menu. Meaning, no zombies were trying to sink their teeth into my lovely, new hat.

"Maybe they don't like pink," offered Dara.

"Or have an aversion to fedoras."

And then I stared ahead and Dara stared ahead and a few thousand zombies, milling in all directions, stared into the oblivion, none of them taking any further notice of the two of us, apart from groaning louder when we walked by. Too bad we couldn't say the same for them, that noticing part, because they were, in fact, impossible to ignore. After all, they quickly surrounded us, enveloping us in a shroud of death and decay, their stench very nearly overpowering, the sound of them making my bones vibrate.

"Suddenly I know what Jonah felt like," said Dara, her hand in mine as we trudged deeper into the foray. "Belly of the beast wise, I mean." Her hand gripped tighter in mine as the undead strode all around us, forever on the move, their lifeless bodies brushing against our own as they bumped and thrashed into us.

"Jonah had it easy compared to this," I made note as I pushed onward.

Dara nodded. "And I bet that whale's innards smelled a hell of a lot better." She then stopped and turned my way. "Still, hon, at this rate, and with so many of them on all sides, we'll never get anywhere. In twenty-four hours, we'll be lucky if we've moved a block away."

My nod mirrored hers. "That does give me an idea, though."

"Turn back and wait on the dock?"

I brushed her cheek with my lips. "Nice try, but no."

She frowned. "I don't think I appreciated Utah enough."

And I couldn't help but laugh. "Um, yeah, I believe you did, and then some." I again began moving us through the dense mass of inhumanity. "In any case, maybe there is a trail of sorts that we can follow. All we need is the first breadcrumb."

"I used to know a drag queen by that name."

"Breadcrumb?"

She shook her head. "Brenda Crumb."

"Awful drag name."

"Equally awful act."

"You're wasting time, dearest."

Her shake turned nod. "I know. On purpose. Twenty-three more hours of this witty repartee and we can turn around."

But still we kept moving. "Again, nice try. Now back to those breadcrumbs."

"Lost me."

"Watch," I replied, turning to the throng to my right. "Halt!" They halted, fifty or so of them, which was about the length and breadth my powers extended to. I then turned to my left. "Halt!" I repeated, another fifty or so stopping dead, as it were, in there tracks. I then looked at Dara. "Get it?"

She smiled. "Genius."

I nodded. "That about covers it." And our walking was made a bit easier now that the throng around us had temporarily paused. "Now all we have to do is find some zombies who don't halt."

"Breadcrumbs."

I touched fingertip to nose, missing it as I grazed my chin instead. "Exactly. And then, goddesses willing, those crumbs lead to the head crumb, the one who started this whole mess to begin with."

She grew silent as we continued pushing forward, my command going up every few minutes, but not a crumb to be found. Still, at least our journey was made slightly easier—apart from the sight, smell and infernal sound of them.

"This is how you found me," Dara eventually said, voice barely above a whisper.

I stared into the dead eyes all around me, at the lips curled into snarls, at the tattered and dusty clothes, all now centuries old. "Even then you stood out, my love."

She gripped my hand tighter. "And this is how your friends found you as well."

I paused, but then replied. "And we already know how *I* stand out in a crowd."

She chuckled, though the dread in her voice remained. For that, I couldn't blame her. Two against millions, after all, weren't such great odds. Though we'd clearly beaten odds far greater than that just by being who and what we were, and together at that. "Perhaps the goddesses are already looking out for us then."

And then I chuckled. "Um, as it's often been said as of late, not without tips." I turned and caught her eye. "But if someone is indeed watching over us, then I for one am grateful."

She smiled. "Ditto." She again looked to the dense undead throng. "Okay, crumb, come out, come out wherever you are."

"That's the spirit."

She nodded and pressed forward. "Well, at least I still seem to have one of those."

***

Hours later and we hadn't gone all that far. Heck, zombies don't move all that fast to begin with. Put up an undead barricade, and you're just adding insult to injury. And, yes, okay, every time I said halt, the zombies around us halted, and that usually would've been fine and dandy with me, but, well, nothing about any of this was *usual*, and I was finding it all that much harder to muster my dandy. Mainly because when they did indeed halt, it was then we got good looks at them. *Good* of course being such a subjective word.

"I think I need a zombie break, sweetie," said Dara as we turned a corner and came face to face with yet another teeming undead mass, another chorus of groans, another bouquet of zombie stench.

"I second that motion, hon." I looked around for a solution and spotted an open door. "There."

She shrugged. "Beats here, anyway."

And so over and in we headed, shutting the door behind us. Thankfully, we were now alone, no zombies inside. The building was an apartment complex, not large, maybe a few stories, but it was on a corner, which, as it turned out, was its saving grace. The stairs, on the other hand, not so much. And as for those stairs, well now, they were simply a necessary evil—kind of like mayonnaise or, uh, Texas, at least back in the day. See, we needed to climb them once we retrieved the weather-beaten bullhorn from outside the front door.

"Guess, by the looks of things, they were doing some kind of construction out here when the sun went all crazy on their asses," said Dara, just before we picked up that bullhorn, the company logo barely discernable across the side of it.

"Their loss, our gain," said I, because it was one thing to yell "halt" to fifty zombies at a time, but given a certain height and a certain loudness, we could cover way more ground.

Of course, then we had Murphy's Law to contend with. Good old Murphy, right? I mean, who ever heard of a couple of zombies climbing up a few flights of steps? Easily, I mean. And without one's minions to aid and abet.

So Dara and I stood at the base of the first step staring up at the dozens and dozens more. Then we looked at our nearly locked legs and frowned. "Any ideas?" I hazarded to ask.

Dara grinned, mischievously, which was my favorite type of grin, apart from the come-fuck-me one. In any case, she replied, "I always did so like your tush, Creature."

I tapped my fingertip against my hip and tilted my head her way. "Well, I suppose I did fuck you last time, so, um, I guess it's your turn to fuck me, but here, now? What, you want a built-in audience?" I smiled at the concept. "Hmm, you think you know someone. Took me almost a few hundred years to realize that my lover was an exhibitionist."

Her smile amped up a couple of hundred watts. "I used to know a drag queen with a similar name."

"Exie Bitionist?"

"You knew her, too?"

"No, just accustomed to this game by now."

She shook her head. "In any case, not what I was getting at, despite the lovely image forming in my head of fucking you on the stairs right now."

"Your loss."

"Tell me about it." She then fell backward. One minute she was standing before me, the next, she was ass-down on the third step. "Our arms work better than our legs, sweetie. Gonna take some time, but—"

"But our butts can take the abuse."

"And amply so, if memory serves."

I watched as she pushed her hands on the step, her stunning derriere rising and lowering as she slowly went from stair to stair, the bullhorn nestled in her lap all the while—lucky bullhorn. Then, once I had some room, I too fell ass-down before following her. It was slow-going, as she forewarned, but at least it was going. Plus, and this was a big old plus, the air was less stinky the higher we went.

"I would've fucked you down there, you know," she said, one flight up and a good hour later.

I nodded. "I know, hon. It's the thought that counts." Then I smiled. "Did you really know a drag queen named Exie Bitionist?"

She grunted as she moved from stair to stair. "Yep. Big old German. Had a whole routine with a hoop skirt and no panties. Very,

ROB ROSEN

uh, eye opening."

"I bet."

By the third floor, I'd learned, too, about Jackie O'Nasty, Lez S. More, and Trixie Treats, all of whom, surprisingly, had acts sans panties, which, I discovered, fairly guaranteed a packed front two rows. I was visualizing all this, at the insane amount of tucking that would've been necessary for such an act, when we finally reached the last step, a door to the roof all that remained for this part of our journey. Well, that and two zombie drag queens trying to right themselves in a narrow stairwell.

"At least we don't sweat anymore," Dara made note, her hand at last on the doorknob.

"Glass half full?"

She turned the knob, shafts of daylight temporarily blinding us. "Well, we don't drink anymore either, but, fine, we'll go with that."

We hobbled outside and made our way to the rooftop's edge. Down below we could see the streets on either side and the one up ahead, all of them teeming with the past (as in passed away) inhabitants of New York.

"You look that way," I told Dara, pointing right, "and I'll look this way." I then pointed left. "Ready?"

She held the bullhorn up to my mouth. "Ready."

And I then yelled, as much as I was physically able to, "HALT!"

Well now, given our height and the bullhorn and just the right amount of wind traveling in the correct direction, and, wouldn't you know it, but everyone down below, as far as the eye could see, halted.

Almost everyone, that is.

All but one, I mean.

Dara pointed. "Breadcrumb, sweetie."

"HALT!" I hollered, yet again, just in case.

"Nope, still moving," she said. "Definitely a breadcrumb."

"Huh," I managed.

"Huh what? That your plan worked? That we found a zombie who doesn't heed your command, like the ones we encountered in the stadium?"

I shook my head. "No, that the breadcrumb is down there and we're three stories up and away from it." I turned her way. "So much for glass half full." And so much for thinking these things through. Sort of like doing a split on stage and then realizing that there was no

64

way to gracefully get out of it. Or that you tucked your junk and doing a split on stage hurts like a motherfucker. Okay, so maybe I'm speaking from experience here. "Plan B?" I asked.

She scratched beneath her wig before glancing my way. "Got one, but you're not going to like it much."

I shrugged. "I wasn't too thrilled with Plan A either, but try me."

She pointed to the street below. "Think landing on a few dozen of them will hurt?"

"You're kidding."

"Not without—"

"Never mind. In any case, we'll kill them."

"Technically speaking . . ."

I sighed. Then I looked at the breadcrumb, who was, thank goodness, somewhat trapped by all the halted zombies, and they, I figured, wouldn't remain halted for all that long. "Technically speaking, they're already dead and we're already dead, so no one, technically, is going to get hurt," I said, finishing her train of thought.

"Technically, no."

"And not so technically?"

"The breadcrumb and his ilk will kill more of the humans on Liberty Island."

"You don't play fair, dearest."

She smiled. "Never have, never will. Now then, care to do the honors?" Again she held the bullhorn aloft, my lips soon pressed upon it.

I groaned, and not the good kind of groan either. "Everyone directly down below, fall on top of one another!"

Lo and behold, *topple, topple, topple,* and we had ourselves one instant zombie mattress. Take that Sealy.

"Ready?" she asked.

"Not even close."

In any case, I leaned over and fell and she leaned over and fell, and mid-flight I realized that this, too, wasn't such a swell idea—which Plan B's rarely are—but the laws of gravity being what they are, well, we kept on falling before we heard a few dozen brittle bones crunching and breaking beneath us, our own bones, miraculously, all still in one piece.

The rest of those next few minutes I chose to wipe clear from my memory as best I could, which, suffice it to say, wasn't as successful an endeavor as I would've liked, but at least we were no longer on the roof and the breadcrumb was barely a block away.

So, newly righted, which wasn't nearly as easy to accomplish as simply falling three stories down, we again picked up the trail.

"Well then," said Dara, when the crumb was again in sight, roaming ever onward, "do we simply follow?"

I paused and considered the question. "He's probably just ambling nowhere in particular. Doubtful he has a destination in mind, such as heading to his master. But he also doesn't heed my commands, so following might be all we have for now."

She nodded her head. "And maybe they congregate with one another. Maybe they're told to report back. Who knows?"

Once again I touched fingertip to nose, which took a few minutes, and still I missed, but made the point just the same. And then we picked up the pace, which was about like adding grease to a slug's, um, feet. *Foot?* Well, whatever. At least, slow as we were, we were gaining ground, especially since he had just as many zombies to contend with as we did. Plus, we could sidestep, while he, in turn, got slammed like a pinball on one bumper after the next.

Thirty agonizing minutes later, give or take, and we were right up on his ass.

"Any ideas?" Dara asked.

"Well, we know when we have to be back at the ferry and we know, approximately, how long it'll take to get back there, so, just to cushion it a bit, let's follow for another few hours. If this turns out to be the only crumb, then no harm, no foul. But, fingers crossed (as if we could manage something like that), he leads us, as we said, to the bakery from whence he sprang or, better still, to the baker him- or herself."

"Sounds like yet another plan."

I shrugged. "*Sounds* like all we have."

And so we followed. Every so often I'd bark out a "Halt!" to see if the crumbs were amassing, but all we came across were halting zombies and our lone ambling one.

"What do you think his name is?" asked Dara, a couple or so hours later.

"I don't know. Charles?" She shook her head. "Max?" The shake repeated. "Lester?"

The shaking stopped. "Mmm, how about . . . Ricky."

The zombie was mostly gray with a bit of mottled purple and a hint of green. His clothes were tattered, dusty and considerably torn, his shoes mere straps of leather barely hanging on to his shuffling feet. In other words . . . "Sure, why not."

"Ricky Shea it is then!"

I grinned. "Another drag queen you used to know?"

"Nope," she replied. "Sometimes you just gotta go original. Besides, look how well he bumps off the other zombies like he does."

I tapped Ricky on the shoulder. "That work for you?" Suffice it to say, he continued ambling. And groaning. And stinking. And, sadly, not amassing. "I hate to say it," I hated to say, "but I have a sinking feeling that he's not leading us anywhere, apart from away from the water, which, I'm afraid, doesn't bode well for us. That, and it's starting to get dark out, and if we get lost, we're screwed."

"I know," Dara said. "I've been thinking the same thing. Which does leave us one other option."

I was already thinking the same thing, but was loathe to mention it. "You know I hate turning them, Dara." In fact, she was the very last one I'd turned in nearly three hundred years. "And then what, we take him with us forever? Or do we just let him eventually revert back?" Even the thought of that made my non-beating heart break. "Plus, once he's, well, *back*, there's no telling if he'll even help us. Because then he'll have his own free will again."

She nodded and kept on following. "When you were turned, did you remember your zombie existence?"

And then I nodded. "Bits of it, like a hazy dream. You?"

"Sadly, yes. Days and weeks and years of nothing but walking and standing and groaning. But I did remember it, awful though it was, and hazy, like you said, though it was."

We kept on walking and following, both of us obviously considering the consequences of what we were planning on doing. "What if he doesn't remember his encounter with whomever commanded him, this person that he obeyed at one point in time, the reason, seemingly, he doesn't obey me now."

"And what if he does? What if he can lead us right to this person? Then we're almost there, right? Then all we have to do is gather the troops and attack. Or, better still, aim the troops, let them attack, while we try on new clothes."

I forced a sigh. "I hate this, Dara."

"I know you do, Creature. But what choice do we have? Wait until the island is attacked again and hope for the best? Plus, what if they attack and get to us next time? What will happen to your minions then?"

"Ouch," I replied. "Hitting below the belt now."

She chuckled. "Well, I do so normally love your below the belt."

"Not helping."

"But trying."

My sigh repeated itself. "Did you bring any salt?"

She nodded. "I never leave home without it." She reached into her front pocket and removed a satchel. "Just in case." She swung it his way, my stomach lurching at the sight of it.

Still, as we'd come to the conclusion, what choice did we have now? There was simply too much at stake. And it was no longer just our lives, in a manner of speaking, that we had responsibility for. And so I moved a bit faster until I was side by side with Ricky, and then just slightly beyond. All it took was my foot held out and, *boom*, down he fell, seemingly in slow motion. Then again, him being a zombie and all, it really was in slow motion.

"Sorry, Ricky," I said, staring down at his writhing, groaning figure.

"Yeah, sorry," said Dara as she slowly sunk to her knees, handing me the satchel along the way. She then reluctantly, it looked like, and rightly so, grabbed Ricky's jaw and pried it open. "Phew," she added a moment later. "Someone's been skipping their brushing. Smells like a locker room that's been pelted by eggs and doused with milk, then left to sit for a few hundred years."

I loosened the satchel. "Gross."

"Understatement."

She held him as still as possible while I positioned the satchel above his now-gaping maw. Without the funnel, I'd have to be exact as possible, not even a few grains to be allowed to miss his throat. "See you on the other side, Ricky," I managed to say, my very soul filled with dread.

I then helped Dara back to her feet as the two of us waited and watched, necks craned downward as Ricky's writhing eventually slowed.

He coughed, once, twice, his eyes blinking shut before they slowly opened. Again he coughed. "Ricky?" Dara said. "You in there?"

Another blink, another cough, then the inevitable inevitablizing—and good like finding a grammartician for that one. See, there were bonuses to being in a post-apocalyptic world: Webster was long dead and we could proceed how we liked. In any case, right about then the only words we were hearing were, "What . . . what's happening?"

"Um." And that was about all I had. I mean, it's not easy to recap the past few hundred years in one sentence, let alone figuring out what to tell someone who, by all accounts, just rose from the dead. Mostly.

"Do you remember anything?" asked Dara.

Again his eyes blinked a couple of times, another cough tossed into his repertoire. "Just a bad nightmare."

She shook her head. "Yeah, about that. See, that wasn't a nightmare, sugar."

"I . . . I don't understand," Ricky rasped out. "Who . . . who are you. Where . . . am I?" And it was then that he noticed all the walking and groaning undead on all sides of us. "And what the hell are they?" Terror managed its way through his barely-moveable features.

"Don't worry. They don't attack their own kind," I informed. "Our brains aren't appetizing enough, I suppose."

"Flesh is kind of nasty, too," added Dara. "Dry. Like jerky."

"Moisturizing helps a bit," I tossed in.

"And sunblock, for sure. Plus a dust bath every so often."

He shut his eyes good and tight. "Please, you're giving me a headache."

"Doubtful," I retorted.

He opened his eyes again. "Fine. You're right. Now could you, uh, help me up? I seem to be . . ." He appeared to be searching for just the right word. "Stuck." And that, indeed, was just the right word for it: stuck. Not living, not dead, but in a sort of stasis.

I grabbed one arm, Dara the other, and the two of us yanked until three stuck zombies were standing, surrounded by a whole slew of unthinking, unfeeling, uncaring, uneverything undead.

"Thanks," he said.

"Don't mention it," I replied. As in seriously don't mention it. Because now he was my responsibility too, and, trust me, I already had way too many of those to contend with as it was.

Way, *way* too many.

CHAPTER 7
RICKY SHEA

With our hands still gripping his arms, we managed our way through the throng and off to a vacant alleyway. There we had breathing room. Stinky breathing room, yes, but at least we weren't playing zombie pinball anymore.

"I'm . . . I'm dead, right?" asked Ricky, right off the bat.

"Kind of, sort of, though technically—"

"Dead," he interrupted me.

"Yeah. Dead. But with benefits," I replied.

He sighed. Though it came out more wheezy rasp than anything else. "And you're . . ."

Dara nodded. "Zombies."

"Zombie drag queens," I quickly corrected.

His lip quivered. "You're joking."

I poked Dara in the ribs. "Look, it's a long story."

"*Really* long," Dara tossed in.

"Right. And we don't have much time. Our friends are picking us up early tomorrow morning. Down by the water. Beyond . . ." I pointed to the undead masses out ahead. "Them."

He blinked. "And these friends. They're all zombie drag queens, too?"

I couldn't help but grin. "Drag queens, yes. Zombies, no. In fact, we might be the only two zombie drag queens left."

Dara pointed her bony finger my way. "Creature here is the queen of the zombies, in fact. Has a whole herd of minions waiting for her back in Utah."

Again Ricky blinked. "Utah. Sure, that would be the place for them, right?"

I patted his back. "I know it sounds, um, *weird*, but you sort of have to take it all with a grain of salt."

"Or a satchel of it," Dara muttered.

"What was that?" Ricky asked.

"Never mind," I replied, throwing my love a warning glare. "In any case, you're sort of the key to a puzzle of ours, perhaps for all humanity, what little of it remains."

"Me?" he asked. "And what's different about me?" Now it was his turn to point to the ambling throng out ahead. "Compared to, well . . . *them*." He grimaced. Or at least grimaced more than he was already grimacing. Truth be told, in the zombie repertoire of top ten facial expressions, grimacing comprises numbers one through seven.

"Look, Ricky," started Dara.

"Lester," Ricky informed.

I laughed. It was hard not to. "Told you so," I said to her.

"I'll never remember that," she replied, looking his way. "Ricky is way easier."

"Than Lester?"

She nodded. "Hey, when you're a zombie, even one extra letter can be difficult. Besides, you look like a Ricky."

If at all possible, his grimace sunk even further south. "Doubtful, but, be that as it may, why am I talking and thinking and standing still, and they're not?" His hand was still pointing outside the alleyway. "And why and or how am I the key to your puzzle? You don't even know me, as far as I can recall."

I snapped my fingers, if only in my head. "Recall," I replied. "That's why you're the key, you see."

"No," he said. "I don't see. All I see are zombies, even if a couple of them are a bit prettier than the others."

I blushed. Again, if only in my head. "You think we're pretty?"

Poor Ricky. He wasn't looking at all happy about any of this. Oh well. "Please just answer the question. Any of them. Even just one," he pleaded, and I paused and Dara paused as well. "Anytime you're ready. Now would be good, though."

Dara spoke up. "Creature here, well, like I said, she's the queen of the zombies. They all listen to her. At least, um, they all used to. You, however, wouldn't. When you were . . ."

Again he blinked. "One of them." And still he pointed.

"Right," I said. "One of them. See, for whatever reason, which we're still trying to figure out, there's probably another queen or king out there, someone else the zombies obey. And this queen or king is trying to kill my friends, the ones that are picking us up tomorrow morning, and they're just about the last of all humankind."

"Apart from your minions in Utah," he chimed in with.

I nodded. "See, now you're getting it."

He shook his head. "Not even close, but do continue, please."

"Right," I said, soldiering on. "Anyway, you obey this other queen or king, seeing as you don't obey me. So, we figured, maybe you could—"

"Lead you to this queen or king." Now his head was nodding, as best it could, considering that it'd been locked in place, until recently, for more than three hundred years. "And then what?"

"Then what what?" asked Dara.

"Then what happens to me?" he asked.

Ah, the million dollar question. Have I already said go figure? Because it's worth repeating. I mean, go figure he'd ask that question almost immediately. "We're . . . um . . . not sure."

"You turned me," he said. "That much I know. I was like *them* and now I'm like *you*." Again his lip quivered. "Well, mostly like you. In any case, if you turned me then you can keep me, uh, turned, right?"

I looked at Dara and she looked at me, and we both knew what our answer had to be. Because, if the situation was reversed, we would've tried anything to make sure that we didn't turn back. So, I replied, "Yes, we can keep you like . . . like us." Give or take.

"We even have extra wigs and gowns and makeup back on the island."

He coughed. "Um, pass. But I will help. If I can. And you keep me, well, *me*."

"But can you help us?" Dara asked. "Do you remember someone else like Creature here, someone who issued commands to you?"

Ricky scrunched his eyes closed, which wasn't at all easy to do, let me tell you. Clearly, he was trying to remember something, anything that could help us. When he opened his eyes again, he was still frowning, but not nearly as much. "Ugh."

I nodded. "Yeah, we get a lot of that. Comes with the zombie territory. But, exactly, *ugh* what?"

"Ugh," he replied, "I think I might have helped to kill, killed or witnessed some killings recently. I don't know. It's just flashes across my mind, blips on the radar, there one second and gone the next."

"Humans?" I asked. "Were these people humans that were killed?"

He nodded. "I believe so. They look, in my mind, pink and not gray, so, yeah, must've been humans."

"With lots of makeup and fabulous clothes?" asked Dara.

Ricky nodded. "I . . . I think so. Like I said, it's just fleeting images, like I'm watching a movie that keeps blacking out."

"But why were you there? How did you get there? Who commanded you to go?" I tried, reeling off the questions as fast as my mind could think of them.

Again his eyes squinted shut. I stared at him. He was a nice-looking man. Or at least had been at one time. He was six feet tall or so, thick, black, wavy hair, with the remnants of what must've been green eyes, nice features, all locked in place if not a bit more gaunt and grayed, but there just the same, if you looked beyond the death mask we all wore. When he again opened his eyes, he replied, "I see a woman."

"A zombie woman?" I asked. "A man dressed as a woman? Or a real woman?"

He shrugged. "Not like I saw her uterus or anything, so it's hard to tell, but I do see a woman in my head. She gathered us, I think, loaded us onto a boat. I can feel the waves, smell the ocean. She told us to kill. I can hear the words. Then I see the killings, see the blood, taste it, hear the screams."

"And yet you're still, for lack of a better word, alive," Dara commented.

"The humans fought back. I must've got pushed in reverse. Eventually, I could smell the ocean again, feel the waves again. After that, I went back to roaming the streets. I don't remember seeing the woman after that, don't know if there were more zombie survivors. It's all black." He pointed to his head. "Up here." He shrugged. "I think I followed her command and that was the end of it. Until you two found me, that is."

I looked at Dara. "So maybe he's the only crumb. Maybe that's why he was all we could find."

"Crumb?" he asked.

"Sorry, the only zombie that can lead us back to this woman you saw. If we find her, then perhaps we can stop any future killings."

And still he shrugged. Or perhaps he got locked like that. Hard to tell. Zombies lock a lot, after all. "What's the point, though? Why keep the remaining humans alive? Why not just eat them and be done with it?"

"To quote you, *ugh*," I replied. "Besides, it's a symbiotic relationship. We need them to keep us, uh, *turned*, to help us manage our day to day routines, to lift us up and down stairs and do our hair and makeup, to dress us and give us dust bathes. On the flip side, we in turn protect them. In other words: no humans, no us, and vice-versa."

Dara nodded. "Besides, though it sometimes hurts to see them, that they remind us of what we've lost, at least we have them as a reminder, that we still have a connection to what we once were, a bridge to our pasts."

His shrug remained. It was definitely a lock. I'd have to help him with that. "Okay, fine, I'll have to take your words for it, seeing as I've only been back for less than ten minutes, but now what? How do we find this mystery person?"

"Well," I replied. "If you are, as we say, a crumb, maybe you didn't fall off the loaf too far from the bakery."

He looked at Dara. "Does she always talk like this?"

Dara shook her head. "This bakery kick is a new thing of hers. You're lucky, though. For a hundred years or so she was doing nothing but talking in country music lyrics." She paused and frowned. "With a twang."

Then he paused. I think we were confusing him. Par for the course, I suppose. "In any case, what Creature here is getting at, I think, is that this king or queen might still be somewhat near the place where I was found. If we return back there, perhaps he or she, most probably it, might be there. Right?"

"If you say so," said Dara. "Pronouns were never much my thing."

I nodded and patted his back. "Sorry, Ricky. Yes, that's correct. But can you find the spot?"

"Can you stop calling me Ricky?"

I shook my head. "Sorry, sugar. The name's already stuck. Besides, it could be worse."

"How, exactly?"

I didn't have the heart (literally) to tell him that his name could be Lester. So, instead, I changed the subject. "Look, the sooner we find the spot, the sooner we get out of here. And where we're going there are no zombies." I pointed once more to the milling, groaning, stinking throng.

"Apart from us," interjected Dara, pointing at the two of us.

"Right. Apart from us," said I. "And with our makeup know-how, it's almost impossible to tell that we're even zombies to begin with."

He sighed. Sort of. "Uh huh." Then he pointed outward and slightly up. "There."

I squinted into the distance. "Bitch can fly?"

His sigh turned groan and he looked at me skeptically. "Really?"

"Sorry," I apologized. "It's been a long day."

Dara nodded. "Tacked onto a few hundred years."

And I nodded. "Seriously."

But still he pointed up. "See that clock tower?"

Again I squinted. "Yes. And?"

"When this person who commanded me spoke, it was like a light had been flicked on, dim though it was. And though I still didn't have free will, didn't have any real consciousness, I could, suddenly, I don't know, somewhat feel, could hear and see and smell for the first time in ages and be aware of those sensations."

Which meant that at last we had some hope, dim, as he put it, though it was. "And what you *saw* was that clock tower?"

The sigh made its third and final appearance—for the time being. "Took you long enough."

"Don't be fresh," I cautioned. "I might not control you, but I still control *all* of them." Again I pointed outward.

He stared down at his withered, cracked, purple hands. "Trust me. Fresh I ain't. And sorry. In any case, yes, when this person commanded me, I saw the clock tower, locked at three, both then and now."

Dara stared at me. I stared at her. Ricky stared at the both of us. And we then in turn stared out at the sea of undead. What if we did find this person now? What if he, she or it had an entire army at their disposal? Would I start a war? Could I start a war? Was I even dressed for war? More importantly, should I wait for the humans in the morning, for reinforcements?

"Well?" asked Ricky.

"Yeah," said Dara. "Well?"

I gulped, or at least made a concerted effort to. "I suppose a little recognizance couldn't hurt. Much." And so I led the charge, though shuffle was more like it. Still, I wasn't taking any chances. In other words, we needed guards. "Everyone who can hear me," I shouted once we reached the beginning of the alleyway, "surround us as soon as we enter the street!"

All in all, it sounded really swell on paper, though not so much in real, um, life. "*Oomph*," grunted Dara a moment later. "Too close! Too close!"

"Nonchalantly surround us!" I quickly amended with. Which was about like telling a sheep to go and shear itself. In other words, nuh uh, wasn't going to happen, not without a whole lot of bruises and scrapes. Because a nonchalant zombie brought us back to the whole pinball analogy, like undead bumper cars without the much-needed bumpers.

"That didn't help!" Ricky shouted above the groaning din as the horde both surrounded us and simultaneously knocked into us. "Try something else!"

I nodded and bellowed, "Surround us, but keep a couple of feet away!"

Phew. Well, that pretty much did it. And then, at last, we started walking toward the clock tower. The zombies followed on all sides, creating a human(ish) shield. Yes it looked odd, to say the least, but it was protection, just in case.

That is, had the enemy attacked from where we were expecting them to attack from.

***

It was slow going to the tower. Three zombies were sluggish, at best, but a gaggle of zombies—a new phrase for me, and one I didn't necessarily delight in—was more like a caravan of snails, replete with slime trails. So by the time we made it to our destination, it was already getting dark out. And darkness was not our friend, seeing as the buildings were fairly tall and all we'd soon have to light our way with was moonlight, which would be fairly blocked by said tall buildings.

"This is not as fun as I imagined," admitted Ricky.

"You thought this would be fun?" Dara asked, shuffling all the while.

He pointed on all sides. "Better than the alternative." He stopped pointing. "If just barely."

The clock tower stood looking out over a small square, long forgotten stores and cafés on all sides, a massive groaning throng dead center to it all. I stared up, the sky a darkening blue, all traces of lovely gay pink obliterated. It should've been an omen of things to come, but, sadly, we weren't thinking that many steps ahead.

Though, we were quick to discover, someone else apparently was.

Cue the doom and gloom music.

"Um," said Ricky, "what's that? Looks like a light."

He was staring up, so I stared up. Like he said, there was now a light in one of the tower windows, not white, but a strange flickering orange. A sense of foreboding came over me, something I'd not felt in centuries. "Fire," I whispered, still unsure if I was actually seeing what I was seeing.

"No," said Dara. "Can't be."

But it was. And it wasn't alone. Soon enough, more lights came on, shining in windows all around the square, both high and low, but all from above. "That explains it," I said.

"Explains what?" asked Ricky.

I tried to move in reverse, but the throng was too thick. "Explains why you were the only crumb we found." I turned his way. "We were looking in the wrong place." I pointed all around. "Should've been looking up, not down."

Just then, one of the lights came hurtling our way, a flaming torch landing with a dull thud to our left, lighting a long desiccated zombie, then two, three, like so much kindling. *Poof!* they went.

"It's a trap!" shouted Dara, hysteria in her voice. Which meant that yes indeed someone was watching out for us. Watching and waiting, that is to say.

"All zombies HALT!" I shouted, my lungs burning.

Those zombies on our sides immediately halted, but still the fires kept coming and coming, raining down as if all hell had broken loose, which probably wasn't all that far off the mark. Still, at least with the zombies halted, we could run, to a certain degree, between them.

Had we been able to see.

Had it not been dark out.

Had the burning, blazing, fiery zombies around us not darkened the square with fine white ash and thick black smoke in about two seconds flat.

"Dara!" I shouted.

"Creature!" she shouted back, somewhere off to my side, though where I hadn't a clue.

The flames kept whizzing by, smacking into the ground, more zombies immediately engulfed, their groans at once extinguished. By then, I could barely see a foot in front of me and all I could hear were the belching flames as they took to the sky. I had to get out of the square; that much I knew. Had to find cover, escape the flying torches, escape certain, to use the word loosely, death.

Just then, the zombies under my control had started moving again, pushing me, bumping me, turning me this way and that. I could still make out the tower high above, so at least I was moving in the right direction, almost to safety.

"Everyone head where I'm heading," I managed to cough out.

Thankfully, that's just what the nearby throng did. As one, we made it to the edge of the square, the flames no longer reaching us, though the area we'd just come from was completely swallowed up in a sea of fiery red and sooty black, piles of mangled, scorched corpses everywhere.

"Dara!" I hollered. I waited, but there was no reply. "DARA!" I knew my heart was no longer beating, but I could feel the phantom pound just the same, lub-dubbing in double-time.

Somehow, Ricky was still by my side, separated by a mere few intact zombies. "I don't see her," he said. "Don't hear her."

I could barely make him out in the darkness. "She's there. I know it." And I felt it, too. After three hundred years, we had a connection of sorts, as if we were wired into the same circuitry. Perhaps, since I'd turned her, she and I were one, far greater than the sum or our parts.

"But can we afford to wait here for her?" he whispered as he pushed ever closer, until we were again side by side. "If the square was a trap, then what if this is as well? What if we're being cornered now? Could we even see the enemy approaching?"

I knew that what he was saying made sense, but I couldn't leave without her. I couldn't. But where was she? Still in the square? That was the one place we couldn't go, the torches still firing down upon it, the clattering of wood still evident. Up was also not an option, the memory of our all-too-recent slow-going stair adventure still fresh in my head. Plus, up was where the enemy was.

"I can't leave her," I cried out, turning his way. "I won't."

He put his hand on my shoulder. "You have to. You won't do anyone any good if you're captured. Or worse."

Oh, to still have tears, I thought. But he was right. If she was captured, injured, in need of me, I had to make sure that I was safe, had to make sure that I could be there for her, and in one piece. Though every moment I stood along the sidelines was another chance of getting caught, especially if this too was part of the enemy's plans. After all, someone had years to work it all out, perhaps decades, centuries. I, suffice it to say, barely had minutes.

I looked from the blazing inferno up ahead before turning back his way. "Fine, but close by, not so exposed. That way we can keep an eye out for her at the very least."

He nodded, and into the shadows we moved.

Eventually, we stopped hearing the clattering of torches in the square. The onslaught, it appeared, had ended. Did the enemy think we were dead? Impossible to say. Though, to be certain, dozens and dozens of zombies were now no more than ashes to ashes, dust to dust. But was that Dara's fate? I prayed not.

"She's out there," I whispered to Ricky as we hunkered within a tattered felled awning, the torn gaps allowing us to see the moonlit street in front of us, the zombies once again milling in all directions, oblivious to the recent massacre.

"How do you know she's out there?" he whispered in return.

I put my hand to my chest. "Trust me, I know."

We stood that way, crouched to a degree, backs bent, for what seemed like forever but couldn't have been more than ten minutes, fifteen at most. I could hear the wind as it whipped by, could hear the groans of the passing zombies and, all too soon, could also hear voices echoing in the distance.

I leaned my face closer to Ricky's. "They're coming," I whispered, terror now gripping me. I couldn't get captured now, not when she needed me, and so I simply I stood, motionless, my eye peeking through a gap.

"Find her!" I heard, the voice chilling my already frigid body to the bone. Oddly, it sounded vaguely familiar, almost long-forgotten. Almost. *My mind is playing tricks on me*, I thought. Fear, I knew, could do that to a person, even a long-dead person such as myself.

And then I saw the moonlit zombies pushing through, toppling the others like so many dominos. These weren't unthinking undead; these were beings such as myself, brought back and clearly taking orders.

In their hands they held torches, which they used to light the street around us, to incinerate any zombies that got in their way, all while they searched, presumably for yours truly. Ricky grabbed my hand when we both noticed the next group that followed, their steely grips keeping their lone prisoner in place: Dara. *NO!* I shouted, if only in my head. But at the very least she was still alive, for lack of a better word.

"Find her!" I heard yet again, the apparent leader the last to arrive, following the others, which were perhaps twenty in total.

And it was then that I knew whose voice it was I was hearing. Yes, it had been centuries since last I heard it, but it was hers, no doubt about it. Especially when she came into view, her face twisted by death, but hers nonetheless.

My very soul clenched at the sight of her, at the sound of her.
Blondella.

Not dead, not buried back on Liberty Island. But how? And, more importantly, why was she looking for me?

CHAPTER 8
BACK FROM THE DEAD

Despite their best efforts, the one place the bad guys failed to look was beneath a torn and weather-beaten awning. Score one for my hide and seek abilities. Or at least hide. Onward they went, the first group, then the second, with Dara as their prisoner, and, lastly, Blondella, until the street in front of us was littered with newly-dead undead, not even a groan to be heard among the scattered corpses.

When we were certain they were out of earshot, Ricky whispered, "That was who turned me. I remember now. Do you know her?"

I moaned. Even the thought pained me. "She . . . she's my friend. Or at least was. A long, long, *seriously long* time ago."

"Friends don't try and kill friends. Friend's don't capture friends. Not unless this is some sort of zombie ritual." He turned my way, both of us still beneath the awning. "Is it? Some sort of ritual, I mean?"

"Zombies don't have rituals. In fact, up until a few moments ago, as far as I knew, me and Dara, plus barely a few dozen others back in Utah, and, of course, you, were the only conscious zombies on the entire planet. Also, in fact, up until a few moments ago, Blondella was dead and buried, worshipped by the remaining humans who live around the Statue of Liberty, all of them, including the statue itself, drag queens. To add another *in fact*, Blondella, in fact, besides being my friend, however long ago, was one of three humans who turned me into the queen you see crouching before you right now. So why she'd now want me dead and/or captured, and why she did in fact capture my centuries-old partner and why she, apparently, attacked the drag queens back in the middle of the harbor, are all mysteries, each of these added to a growing list of them."

He seemed to be soaking all this in before eventually replying,

"I'm not even going to say that I'm lost. That would be like saying that I'm dead, both clearly foregone conclusions. All I know is that I was a New York dermatologist and the last time I checked, the Statue of Liberty was most definitely not a drag queen." He held up his hand and shook his head. "Please don't fill in the gaps; I have a strong suspicion that it won't do any good."

I sighed. Or at least tried to. "I guess it doesn't matter anyway. All you need to know is that I'm the good guy, dressed like a girl though I may be, and Blondella's the bad guy, dressed like a girl though she may be, and Dara is my husband, dressed like a wife though she may be, and we need to rescue her: Dara, my zombie drag queen wifely husband."

Again he shook his head. "You're really not helping, Creature."

At last I moved outside the awning, the moonlight now washing over me. Ricky was quick(ish) to follow. "The question is not, am I helping you? The question is, will you help me? Because I can't trust anyone back on the island, not anymore, not after what I just saw. They, after all, think of Blondella as a goddess, someone to be revered. For all I know, they're in cahoots."

He chuckled. "This sounds like a bad Scooby Doo movie."

"There was a good Scooby Doo movie?"

His chuckling promptly ceased. "Be that as it may, do I have a choice?"

I shook my head. "No. Sad to say, but without me administering iodized salt to you and without you administering iodized salt to me, both of us will be . . ." I pointed to the newly arrived zombies, the groaning once again starting up all around us. "Just like them." I dropped my hand and turned his way. "I love her. She is my life, which is really saying something these days. Out of all humanity, out of every zombie on this God-forsaken planet, billions and billions of them, she's the one I brought back. And, though you don't have a choice to at least stick with me, I'd like it if you wanted to stick with me, that you wanted to help."

He sighed, a real honest to goodness sigh, which, as it's been said, doesn't come at all easy to our kind. "What sort of music did you lip-synch to back in the day, Creature?"

I grinned. "Mostly Britney Spears."

The sigh repeated. "You're not making it easy on me, are you?"

"Sometimes Cher."

And then he grinned. "Better. And, yes, I want to help you. I just haven't a clue how. I mean, there's two of us and, at the very least, a couple of dozen of them."

"Judging by the number of fire torches that rained down on us, way more than that."

He shook his head. "You're not very good at instilling confidence, are you, Creature?"

"Sorry."

He patted my shoulder. "That's okay. It's been a trying day."

"A trying few centuries, actually." I stared down the street that Blondella had disappeared into. "And I wonder what she's been doing that whole time? Not to mention how she went from being human to zombie, which, as far as I'm aware, is technically impossible."

"Why's that?" he asked.

"All the zombies became zombies, you and me included, when the sun went haywire, a giant solar flare wiping out every living thing that wasn't miraculously behind a great deal of metal at the time. The ensuing radiation kick-started all the dead humans into what you see today, all of us operating on radiation power alone. Blondella, plus my friends, Destiny and Kit, they were in a converted meat locker at the time of the blast, and so they survived."

"Meaning, she was human the last time you saw her?"

I nodded. "And humans don't turn zombie, which she clearly is now. Mainly because only zombies can live three hundred plus years."

"And look that God-awful."

I shrugged and pursed my lips. "Well, she was never all that pretty to begin with." I looked from the street and back to him. "In any case, there's some sort of cover-up back on the island. There has to be. Someone then or now, or both, knew that Blondella wasn't killed in a zombie attack three centuries ago, despite the pretense that she was, despite being worshipped for being a martyr during said attack."

Strangely, he was smiling. Or at least seemed like he was. With zombies, it's awfully hard to tell. "All of which adds to that growing list of mysteries you mentioned."

"None of which we're any closer to finding the answers to."

Surprisingly, he lifted his bony index finger into he air. "Ah, maybe *one* we're closer to finding the answer to."

"Really?" I asked, eyes suddenly a tad wider. "Which one."

"I think I know why I followed her and why I didn't follow you. Why I'm this crumb you guys—um, *girls*—spoke of."

"Really?" I repeated.

"Really," he replied. "You ever work on a farm, Creature."

Those wide eyes of mine turned squint. "*Really*, Ricky?"

"Just checking," he said. "Anyway, my parents had a small farm, a second home when we were growing up. Just some chickens and goats, a handful of geese in the pond, a vegetable garden we all tended to."

"And?"

"And the geese, the chickens, even the goats, I remember how when they were born they always followed their mother, always knew the sound of their mother's voice apart from all the many and various other sounds surrounding them."

A spark lit within me, spreading just the slightest bit of warmth through my otherwise frigid body. "Imprinting. Of course." I slapped his back. "Brilliant!"

He blushed. Though that was probably my stellar imagination playing tricks on me. "Thanks."

"Just instilling confidence, Ricky."

"Touché," he volleyed back.

"Anyway," I said. "That explains why the zombies have always followed me. Among all the beings on this planet, I alone was unique. I was the first zombie brought back, making me the mother goose, as it were. The zombies follow me like a baby follows its mother and continue to do so even if commanded by another zombie. All the other zombies that have been turned have either been turned by me or after me. Those other zombies aren't unique, not mothers."

"All save one."

I grimaced. "Blondella." Damn, it sure would've been nice to be able to snap at a moment like that.

"Blondella, yes. When she spoke to me, commanded me, it was like I was a baby hearing its mother for the first time. Something in me snapped, latched onto her, followed her. Imprinting, just like you said." He looked my way. "And she's as unique as you are, Creature, a second mother in the roost. After all, she was human and then became zombie, and did so after the sun went all fucked-up on everyone."

"Mother fucker, more than second mother, but yes, that makes sense." That spark of mine promptly flickered. "Though none of that explains how she became a zombie or why she's attacking the humans."

"No?" his smile seemed to remain.

"Um, no," I replied. "Am I missing something here?"

"You ever hear of two hens ruling the roost? Two *queens* running the empire?"

It took a while for all the tumblers to fall into place, what with a severe oil shortage in my noggin, but eventually everything lined up. *Ding! Ding! Ding!* "Fuck," I cursed. "It's all been a trap. She couldn't come and get me, but she could sure as hell get me to come here by attacking the humans, all of whom knew of me, knew exactly where to find me."

"And if she kills you, she becomes the lone queen."

"And another mystery is solved."

"Little good it does us," he griped.

"Well," I countered, "it's more than we knew before. And at least we know what she's up to and why: kill me and the rule the planet." I couldn't help but grin at the thought. "Yep, sounds like a drag queen."

"Takes one to know one, huh?"

My grin widened. "Takes one *to beat* one."

***

We hightailed it out of there a minute later. After all, we couldn't let them get too far ahead. The only reason we found her this time was because she wanted us to; next time I knew wasn't going to be as easy, especially if we lost sight of her.

And next time, I promised myself, she wasn't going to get the better of us.

"There," said Ricky, pointing to a side street about thirty minutes into our trek. "There they are."

Their group being so large, they proceeded more slowly. Plus, even in the near darkness they were easy to spot, seeing as they moved as one and didn't simply mill about like the rest of the zombies all around us did.

"Let's keep our distance, though," I said to him. "We can see them and they can't see us. We have to make sure it stays that way."

"Agreed," he agreed. "Stick to the sidewalk. Should they happen to turn around and spot us, it will simply look like we're being forced to walk in a straight line, the buildings keeping us on the same path as them." And then he put the icing on the cake. Or, more accurately, pulled it off. "And better lose the wig and fedora because, trust me, you stick out like a platinum-blonde sore thumb in those things." He then had the gall to point downward. "And off with the heels."

I put manicured hand to non-beating chest. "Next you're going to tell me to wipe off the makeup."

He chuckled. "Actually, the makeup I can, um, *live* with."

"Bitch."

He shrugged. "I can live with that, too. Just so long as we both live or, more accurately, survive. And without the wig and heels, we blend in with everyone else."

My grimace returned. "Yeah, because that's just what a drag queen wants to do: blend in with everyone else."

Still, he had a point. And Blondella had Dara. So the wig and the heels were lost and, just to be safe, I smudged the makeup, making yours truly the best-looking raccoon-face on the block. After that, they led, while we followed and groaned just like all the other zombies.

Sadly, though, none of that mattered.

See, they knew where they were going; that sadly part was when we finally found out just where that was. I mean, I should've realized that Blondella hadn't been spending the past three hundred plus years roaming the streets. Street corners, fine; that was more her style. And so was an inner city nightclub that was practically the length of an entire block.

"Every queen needs a castle," I lamented as we watched her and her zombie entourage, plus my beloved Dara, disappear inside, the guards outside, a half-dozen of them, unflinching, unmoving, more like statues than anything remotely human, moonlight illuminating their pale, emotionless faces.

"Ten to one, they don't take bribes," said Ricky.

"Not unless you have some spare fresh brains on you, which the zombies love above all other organs."

He felt around his pockets. "Too bad."

"So sad."

"And now what?"

I looked up the block and down the block. It was obvious that the guards were standing outside the only entrance. Still, at least we had the cover of darkness on our side. "We need a diversion, but not one that's obvious. We can't let her think that we somehow found her, that she was followed, that we're nearby."

He grunted. "Gee, is that all?"

"Sarcasm will get you nowhere, sweetie." And, yes, even I found that statement laughable.

The grunt repeated. "Please forgive me. You see, returning from the dead after a few centuries takes the cheerfulness out of a person. I mean, everyone and everything I ever loved is gone, so I'm finding it awfully difficult to be all sunshine and roses."

I patted his shoulder. "I'm . . . I'm sorry. You're right. Were you, um, were you married, kids?"

He nodded. "Seven years plus some change. No kids."

"What was her name?"

He stared up at the moon, probably one of the only things that had remained unchanged in all this time, a constant. He squinted into the light. "Lola."

I grinned. "Was she a showgirl?" I knew as soon as I said it that it was in bad taste, but old habits, like old drag queens, die hard. "My bad."

He grinned. "Ironically, she was a showgirl. On Broadway. The Shubert Theatre. In fact, Barry Manilow sang her the song on her birthday last . . ."

Again I patted his shoulder. "Sorry, *Lester.*"

His grin quivered. "Lester is dead, Creature. Long dead. Just like Lola, just like Barry. So you might as well keep calling me Ricky. If anything, it helps me forget that I have a past."

I didn't have the heart to tell him that we never forget, that we can't forget, that our brain cells stay locked and loaded. And then a lightbulb shown brightly above my head, brighter than the moon even. "I, um, I don't want to get your hopes up, Ricky, but—"

"My hopes, Creature," he interrupted, "are lower than the Mariana Trench right about now. So, well, *up* is the only way they can head." He lowered his face and locked eyes with me. "She's out there, though, right? Like me, like *us*?"

"A zombie, yes," I replied. "More than likely. And the sun went berserk during the day in the middle of the week. The zombies you see now are the ones who were outside when the flare hit. The rest, most of everyone in North America, were and still are locked inside. Without consciousness, a doorknob, a handle, they mean nothing to a zombie. So your wife, Lola—"

His face amped up a few hundred watts. "Is more than likely still at work."

"Talk about your overtime."

His frown, however, abruptly reappeared. "But we're across the East River now, not to mention miles away from lower Manhattan, not to mention on rickety feet, without any form of transportation." He sighed, loudly, and pointed skyward. "For all its worth, we might as well be on that moon up there."

"What are the odds that Lola had a dream to be on Broadway and then actually made it to Broadway?"

"She had better odds of winning the lottery."

I nodded my head. "And yet she made it there just the same."

His sigh repeated. "It's not the same, Creature. Nothing is the same."

I too pointed heavenward. "Some things stayed the same. The moon, for instance." I then pointed to the building in front of us, to where I knew Dara was being held. "Love," I added.

He didn't say anything, not for many seconds; he eyed me instead. "You made it from Utah to New York."

"On an ancient plane flown by a drag queen," I told him. "So anything is possible."

"Lola had to have been at work. If I'm here in Queens, then I was at work, probably just on a break at the time of the flare. And Lola never, ever took a break."

"Which is how she made it to Broadway. And we'll make it there as well."

"And then you can change her."

Normally, I hated doing just that. But there was nothing normal about this, about any of this. And I changed Dara for love, so why not Lola? "Did your wife wear yellow feathers in her hair?"

His smile returned. "Only on Halloween."

"Good enough," I told him. "And, yes, I'll turn her."

He rubbed his parched, cracked, gray hands together. "Then let's rescue Dara and get the hell out of here."

"And the diversion?"

His hand stopped rubbing. "Leave that to me."

***

"Why are we here?" I asked him about twenty minutes later. "Looks like a school of some sorts." It was a big, imposing building with thick columns, all of which had stood the test of time.

"Med school, actually."

"Um, I know you said you were a dermatologist, but brushing up on your skin diseases now isn't going to help the likes of us." I pointed to the milling zombies on all sides. "Or them. Heck, a truckload of Clearasil wouldn't clear up those complexions."

"What happened to 'sarcasm will get you nowhere'?"

I shrugged off the comment. "Do as I say, not as I do?"

"Nice try," he replied. "In any case, we're here to get the one thing that will lead those guards away without anyone thinking you had anything to do with it. Because you can't command them, as we well know, and having a zombie posse suddenly attack will be a dead giveaway, pun intended, that you're somewhere nearby."

"But nothing will lead them away. If she commanded them to stay and guard, then stay and guard is what they'll do."

"Wanna make a bet on that?"

I reached inside my dusty dress pockets. "Does this casino take lint?"

He grinned. "Never mind. Just follow. And don't worry because there's one human vice which almost always trumps all the others."

"Vanity, dear Ricky, is not a vice. It's simply a way of life. Or death. Take your pick."

He climbed the stairs, however slowly and wobbly, then pushed open the front door before turning my way and replying, "No, Creature, not vanity. Gluttony."

I shrugged. For a change I decided to follow instead of lead. After three hundred years, I figured I could use a break. "Did you go to school here?" I asked as we trudged through the layers of dust and debris, the windows barely letting in much moonlight, but just enough to illuminate our way.

"I taught here some years back." His frown returned. "Well, that is to say, a few hundred plus some years back."

I felt bad for the guy. None of this could be easy on him. Me, I had centuries to get used to the idea of what I was and what had happened; he had less than a day. Still, all things considered, he was doing remarkably well. Including the fact that we found what we were looking for in less than an hour, with minimal contact with any students, most of whom seemed to be locked inside of the various classrooms.

"Unbelievable," I said when he held the jar out for me, its lone content sloshing around in some sort of preservative.

"Well, you asked for fresh brains." He smiled. "Not exactly fresh, but I'd think, or at least hope, they'd do in a pinch. And they are human." He pointed around the room we'd found ourselves in, the zombies held back by my command. "Gross anatomy class."

I cringed. "Emphasis on the gross. But considering how many humans are left and ergo how many brains, beggars, as they say, can't be choosers."

"My thoughts exactly. And if it's instinctual for the undead to feast on human flesh, brains in particular, than instinct will trump obedience any day." He squinted into the darkness. "Or night."

"So the guards will simply walk away, with no indication that we were behind it."

"In theory."

"Way to be positive."

He smirked. "All things considered . . ."

I took the jar of brains and headed us out of the room. "Got it."

He walked by my side, trying his best, it seemed, to ignore the other zombies, the ones held by my orders and the ones scraping the doors and the walls, out of sight, though sadly not out of mind. "Shouldn't we let them out?"

"What would be the point?" I replied. "Hell is still hell, whether you're in the fire or out of it."

"Do you think they know that?"

"Did you?" I countered with.

He paused before replying. "I suppose not."

I knew what he was feeling. I'd felt it myself countless times. "Morality, Doc, is only pertinent when dealing with a thinking, feeling *other*. These others have neither thoughts nor feelings. They simply are. Like a blade of grass is. And you wouldn't free a blade of grass from the front lawn, would you?"

He chuckled. "Are all drag queens this deep?"

Me and the brain headed outside, a cool breeze suddenly whipping over us. "An onion looks simple from the surface of things, but look how many layers it's got."

"Plus, they taste good on a sandwich."

"Well, it's got me beat in that regard, but still." We slowly made our way down the steps before I again turned his way. "Have you ever met a drag queen before, Ricky?"

I could see his smile in the near darkness. "Nope, you're my first, Creature," he replied. "You ever met a dermatologist before?"

My smile matched his. "If I ever had a zit, it was covered by pounds (seriously, pounds) of makeup, so what would've been the point? Besides, show me a drag queen with adequate health insurance and I'll show you one with a rich husband who has way more than one kink in his coil, if you get my drift."

"Not a clue."

"Give it another hundred years or so then."

"God that sounds weird."

And it was about to get a whole hell of a lot weirder.

***

We walked back the way we'd came, Ricky by my side, the bait still sloshing about within the large jug. Thankfully, it was well-sealed, otherwise, no doubt, we'd be awash in zombies. Ricky stared from side to side now. I think he'd grown accustomed to the milling, groaning undead.

"How, um, how long before we revert back to *that?*" He was pointing to a herd to our left side.

"I reverted back once, centuries ago. The salt cure seems to last about a week. Then the radiation pulses through again, clouds our brains, our thoughts, until we're—"

"*That.*" And still he kept pointing. "And when's the last time you had any?"

"Just before we left the island. And you took all we had on hand. Which means that you and I have roughly five days before—"

"*That.*"

It was neither a pretty picture nor a pretty thought. Still, it wasn't like we weren't always near the cure. All it took was a well-stocked restaurant or corner store. "Don't worry. We'll find some more soon enough."

He nodded, but didn't reply. I knew he was worried, despite my telling him not to be. I suppose he had good reason to be, not only for himself but also for Lola now, for Dara. Heck, for all humanity, if that in fact was what Blondella was after.

When we neared the nightclub-turned-fortress, I halted all the zombies we passed. Because if I didn't, I knew we'd be overrun once the jar's lid was removed. In fact, that was still a possibility, given what Ricky had said, that instinct trumps obedience.

"We have to make sure that the brains are eaten, the evidence destroyed," I told him. "Otherwise, hundreds and hundreds of zombies will descend once the aroma hits them. And that we have to make sure doesn't happen. It'll tip her off for certain. Plus, the guards have to come back before she realizes they're missing. And we have to sneak in while they're gone."

He nodded. "Right."

"And what if the brains don't work? What if they really do need to be fresh?"

"Backup plan?"

I looked his way. "Which is?"

He looked my way. "Beats me. I just barely came up with the one we came up with." He looked ahead, to the nightclub cast in moonglow, to the guards who were nothing more than ominous shadows now. "In any case, we at least have to try."

Fifty feet became forty, forty to thirty, frozen zombies on all sides, milling ones at the periphery, perhaps a hundred or so that we could make out in the darkness. Which meant that there was plenty of room for the guards to move in, to dine and to return to their posts, all without anyone being the wiser. It would work. It *had* to work.

Sensing my worry, Ricky turned and smiled. "Set the jar down, Creature. Then lift the lid and start moving as quickly as you can toward the entrance. And don't worry. We'll be inside before you know it."

I nodded and did as he said. The lid was sealed, but zombies, though restricted in terms of flexibility, still have terrific strength, especially since we don't feel pain and can keep twisting and pulling to our nonbeating heart's content. And so, a minute or so later, the lid came undone, the aroma of brains and formaldehyde permeating the night air.

Oh how those zombies groaned then, moaned and groaned and grunted up a veritable storm, the frozen ones fairly trembling, trying to break from my commands, the peripheral zombies heading in, slowly and surely. I pointed dead, as it were, ahead. "Look," I managed to say.

Ricky clapped. Or at least tried to. "They're coming this way. The guards. All of them."

He started moving in their direction, fast as his legs would allow. I did the same, both of us hurtling our bodies toward the building. The guards passed us midway, their moans as loud as the others, all of them streaming toward their first meal in centuries, more than likely.

I turned as we reached the entrance, a crush of zombies now standing where we'd come from, a black mass of them, the moans louder from the epicenter.

"Yum," I croaked out.

"Ditto," said he. "Now, inside we go.

And inside we went.

Inside the belly of the beast, that is.

CHAPTER 9
BELLY OF THE BEAST

Inside was nothing like outside. That is to say, while the inside was certainly filled with zombies, hundreds and hundreds of them, absolutely nothing else was even remotely similar between the two. Mainly because the club, unlike the streets we'd come from, was brilliantly lit, ancient disco lights turning and churning and swiveling, beaming a rainbow of colors across every square inch of space as they bounced against one of the largest disco balls I'd ever seen. The music blared, Donna Summer's voice instantly filling my head as a soft moan escaped from between my lips.

"Home," I instinctively rasped.

"Circa 1978."

"It's beautiful," I whispered, reverently. Now, suffice it say, I'd been trapped in a salt factory in Utah for the past few hundred years, so even a swatch of something other than concrete-beige or steely-gray would've set my soul on fire, but this, well now, this was truly magical—apart from the milling undead, of course, the sound of them, the stench of them, rising above the music like a layer of fog.

I then gazed around. Everything was solar-powered, it looked like, judging from the skylights you could peek up through. But as to the whereabouts of the queen bee, that still remained to be seen.

"It's, um, different," Ricky said, amending my statement.

I turned to him. "Trust me, different is next to near impossible these days. Better revel in it while you can."

Further inside the belly of the beast we walked. The zombies here were like the zombies outside. That is to say, they were unthinking, unfeeling, simply shuffling to and fro, all of them clearly under Blondella's spell. This I surmised because none of them paid heed to my commands. Stupid zombies.

"It looks like she's amassing an army in here, Creature," Ricky said, just above the din.

I nodded. "But I wonder what's taken her so long? She could've done this ages and ages ago."

"No, *you* could've done this ages and ages ago. The jury is still out on her," he retorted.

I moved to the center of the disco floor, the lights drenching us in color, turning our standard shades of gray and muted purple to brilliant orange and red and yellow. I shuffled my feet, dancing(ish) for the first time in centuries. It felt, surprisingly, well, fanfuckingtastic. "You lost me," I eventually replied, finally taking in what he'd said.

He shuffled next to me. I grinned. After all, I was pretty sure that I'd never danced with a straight guy before, let alone a straight undead one. First time for everything, I supposed. And then he explained, "The order you went in was human, solar flare, dead, undead. The order she went in was human, solar flare, *living*, dead, undead. So perhaps her talents are not like yours. Perhaps whatever caused her transformation impaired her ability to act. Until now."

I smiled, despite the dire circumstances we were in, namely Dara's capture and our being trapped inside, the guards probably having already returned. "Yeah, her talents were few and far between when she was alive, so Lord only knows what they're like now. Still, we know she can command zombies, just like I can. And we know she's a zombie, seeing as she still, um, *is*. So what differences can there be?"

He shrugged and did a little knee dip: cute if not dangerous, all things considered, because a zombie who falls generally stays felled. "Hard to say what the differences are. But it is curious, as you noted, that she's doing whatever she's doing now and not years ago."

"Unless she just got bored being a local bitch and decided to move it on to a grander scale," I countered with.

"She that bad?"

I stopped shuffling and swaying. In truth, we had been friends. Like I'd said, she turned me, protected me, laughed with me, cried with me. She was a bitch, fine, but so were we all when it came down to it. It made for better tips, stronger drinks, bigger laughs. It made us larger than life. Ironically, that's what we all now were: larger than life, beyond life, kicking sand in the face of life. *Suck it, life!*

"No," I eventually replied. "Well, not the best lip-syncher, no, and not the best stylist, no, and certainly not the prettiest drag queen you've ever seen, but, no, she's not that bad. Or at least wasn't. A long, *long* time ago."

"Time changes people, Creature," he said, now also standing still.

I stared down at my mottled skin and bony fingers. "Tell me about it." Then I stared up at him. "Come on, let's just go find Dara and get out of here." I looked around at the wall of zombies and forced a sigh. "One good thing you can say about time: it's the great equalizer."

He nodded. "Yep, we certainly do blend in."

I cringed. Not what a drag queen likes to hear. "Please don't repeat that." Then I looked around again, hoping to spot where Dara had been taken to. "You're right, though. At least no one can tell us apart from all the others. Unless Blondella—"

"KILL THEM!" her voice bellowed from a catwalk high above.

I gulped and finished the sentence. "Spots us."

Donna gave way to KC & The Sunshine Band. Boogie Man indeed. "Now what?" Ricky asked, eyes wide as saucers as the entire club instantly turned on us.

"Do you trust me?" I asked.

"Do I have a choice?"

I shook my head. "Not really, but trust me anyway," I reiterated. "Fall forward, onto your hands. Then start crawling to the door."

"They'll catch us in seconds," he hollered above the moaning din.

I fell forward. "They can't bend down this far. And if they fall, they can't get up. And zombies, apart from the likes of us, don't crawl." I turned my head and looked up at him. "Fall, damn it! Now!"

He fell and landed next to me, while the crush of zombies, well, *crushed*, knocking into one another and not getting very far.

"KILL THEM!" shouted Blondella yet again, her voice insistent, full of menace.

"I thought we were friends!" I hollered in return, now crawling, knocking as many zombies over as I could, which I knew would make a barricade against the others that followed.

"Silence!" she shouted, her voice echoing above KC's. "Do not question the queen!"

Ricky tapped my shoulder as we continued our crawl, the zombies trying and, thankfully, failing to bend far enough down to reach us, most of them toppling over as they tried. "I think she's lost it," he said.

I nodded. "Well, she didn't have far to go in that regards."

And still we crawled, zombies writhing on all sides of us now, the music at last silenced, the colors no longer swirling. "Not to rain on your parade, Creature, but, um, falling was one thing. How about getting back up again?"

I paused. Clearly I'd forgotten that I no longer had my human minions around. In any case, right about then, that was the least of our worries. "We have your partner!" she yelled down at me, the words stabbing like daggers into my very soul. "Stop or I'll kill her!"

"Technically—" I started to say.

"I'll lop off her pretty, little head!"

I stopped crawling. Ricky stopped crawling. I turned to him and frowned. "Um, that would do it, alright." Then I added, loudly, "Let's call it a trade then: take me and let the other two go!"

"No," grunted Ricky.

"It's the only way," I replied.

"How about: run away and live to fight another day."

"She already has us," I countered with. "How far can we get like this before she stops sending zombies and simply rains fire down on us once again?"

His grunt repeated. "I'll come back for you."

If I could've cried, I would've. "Don't. Too dangerous. You and Dara go find your wife, go back to Utah, or stay on Liberty Island. In any case, just leave me. Perhaps she can be reasoned with." Even as I said it, I knew that wasn't going to happen. In life she was unreasonable; in death, she was obviously a few french fries short of a Happy Meal.

He reached across the gap that divided us, grabbed my arm and gave it a squeeze. "We can't turn my wife without you. Besides, that's not why I'm coming back for you."

"You don't even know me, Ricky."

He smiled. "And, yet, you're all I have."

I smiled. "Poor you."

He shrugged as Blondella's guards at last made it our way. They were no mere zombies. They were like us: thinking, feeling. After all, Blondella knew about the salt, so it wasn't too difficult to turn one of them. "Yeah, poor me. But it could be worse." Barely, but true.

"Just be careful then. And don't trust anyone but Dara."

He nodded as the guards kicked the fallen zombies out of their way before reaching us. Though stiff, like us, they could think and reason and plan. Meaning, eventually they managed to right us, holding us in place until Blondella had time to make her way down to the dance floor.

The minutes ticked by ever so slowly, the waiting interminable. Still, she was standing in front of me a while later. My friend. Undead. And wickedly grinning my way, all cat finding the canary like.

"Long time no see," she said, bloodshot eye to bloodshot eye.

"I could've waited a bit longer," I quipped, then added, "I thought you were dead."

"The news of my death has been greatly exaggerated, Creature."

"They worship you, you know. The humans. What few remain." Flattery, I hoped, would get me somewhere.

Her grin went maniacal. Not pretty. No sir, no how. "Smart humans. Too bad they have so little time left." She poked me in the chest. "Too bad you have even less."

I shot her a grimace. "But we've only just found each other. Don't you want to celebrate the grand reunion?"

She twirled her bony finger in the air and whooped. "There. Celebration over. Now you die, officially, and I'm left to rule the planet, to rule all of zombiekind, forever!" She chuckled, the sound evil, twisted, mad. Though, to be fair, she sort of sounded that way a few hundred years earlier, if memory served. Which it did, of course.

"Why bother?" I asked. "It's like ruling bowling pins, Twinkies, trees."

"None of those things heed me, though. And with you gone, with the humans gone, with those few who obeyed you soon to follow, the world will be eternally mine."

I nodded. There was no point in arguing with her. Then again, there never was. Poor thing. Her wig had always been one notch too tight. "But why now? What have you been doing all this time? You knew where I was, where the humans were. It's been over three hundred years since your, uh, *death*."

Her frown sagged further on her overly-made up face, her fake hair askew, dress dusty and tattered. This was both Blondella and not Blondella, a funhouse mirror image of the drag queen I'd known so long ago. "This thing we have, that we are, it's an infection, a virus, spreading through us, *changing* us."

I shook my head. "It's the radiation that does that."

Again she poked me, hard. Thankfully, I had little to no feeling left in me. "No," she hissed. "The radiation maintains what we are, keeps us in stasis, but ultimately death is the infection, snuffing all else out."

It hit me what she was saying. "It infected you, you mean."

She nodded, the scorn spreading like wildfire across her ghastly face. "Between the time we found you, me and the other girls, and the time we parted ways, we encountered so many of these retched beasts, fought so many of them, rekilled so many. At some point, an errant scratch must've occurred, a tiny prick . . ."

And, yes, my lips cracked open of their own accord, ready to make a joke at her expense. Old habits, like I'd said, had indeed died hard. Ironically, dying hard seemed to be in my near future as well.

In any case, she knew me all too well, the final poke of her bony finger nearly tearing through leathery flesh. "Don't even think about it." Too late. I nearly smiled, but caught myself. After all, she really was the queen bee, and tiny prick or not, she could still sting with a hell of a lot of force. "In any case, the infection spread by the time we made it to Liberty Island, and with the radiation levels still high enough in the atmosphere, in the ground, in the very water that surrounded us, the virus was able to survive, to slowly replicate."

"Slowly," Ricky repeated. That, after all, was the key word here.

I frowned. I knew the sad implication. "You've been dying this whole time, cell by cell, year by year by year. That's why you had to wait to attack; you weren't strong enough."

Her grin was terrifying. "Until now."

I felt for her, I really did, despite what she was planning. After all, it must've been like Chinese water torture, the drips replaced by decades, turning her into the maniac standing before me. And then a new question popped into my head. "The zombie attack centuries ago, your graves, your clothes, did any of that really happen?" And then I remembered what I'd discovered back on the island. "But that wasn't your grave I saw, of course, which is why the combined plot was so narrow. And those weren't your clothes in the case, just like I thought."

She nodded. I was now being pushed forward, Ricky as well,

parting the sea of undead as we moved away from the dance floor. "All made up. A story to tell the kids before they went to bed, and one that went from generation to generation, until it was believed to be true. Kit and Destiny and me, they saw something in us, to be certain, something worth emulating, a joy, a strength, a beauty."

"*Inner* beauty, you mean," I countered, clearly unable to control myself.

She pushed me harder, until we were in a private office that she'd unlocked with a swipe of a card. Once inside, we found Dara tethered to a chair. A smile burst free upon my face, hers as well. The guards retreated, leaving the three of us and our captor alone. "How did you end up here then?" asked Ricky.

"Years after we remaining humans found one another, after the island started taking shape, they knew something was wrong with me, the fact that I wasn't aging, that my skin grew grayer. They worried that it could be contagious, that I'd brought something to the island, that *we'd* brought something, me and Kit and Destiny."

I groaned. "Oh no."

She suddenly looked angrier, her eyes steely, seething. "You say they worship me and the other girls. I know nothing of this. The emulation started in our lifetimes, yes, that much I saw. The rest, whatever the bedtime story became, that I never heard." She paused, looked away, a pool of hatred obviously boiling up inside. She then turned and finished her story. "The zombies came one night. The islanders must've lured them over, taken the ferry when everyone was asleep. The girls were the first to be slaughtered, but the zombies never attacked me. After all, they never attack their own kind, as you well know."

"Minus you attacking me," I couldn't help but say.

She shrugged. "We are not the same kind. You need the salt; I do not. The infection changed me, but my humanity, what remained of it, is also still there. So I am as different from you as you are from them. That is why they follow you, the zombies. That is why they follow me as well. We are unique."

"Imprinting," spat Ricky.

Her shrugged repeated. "Call it what you will. Doesn't change anything. They follow her and they follow me. Soon only the latter will be true."

"You didn't answer the question," added Ricky.

She sighed. "How I got here?" The shrug stopped, her shoulders in mid-bunch. "The zombies, like I said, didn't kill me and the humans didn't have the stomach to do it either. Instead, they sent me adrift, knowing, or at least thinking, that would do it, that I'd be powerless against them, that I'd eventually turn zombie like all the rest and they'd be rid of me."

"They made martyrs out of you," I made note. "Out of all three of you."

She nodded. "I suppose so. I've, of course, seen them over the years, the humans, seen them when they make their excursions to the mainland. I've followed them, kept up with their activities. Know thine enemy, it's said. That's what I've done. So, yes, I know that they eventually became like me and Kit and Destiny, came to look like this, like some sort of hero worship on their parts. So what? What good did it do me, dying by inches out here, utterly alone? Worship is meaningless if you never hear the praises."

Now *that* sounded like the Blondella I knew. Once a drag queen always a drag queen. "But I'm here now. You're not alone. Why not just come back with me? Start a new, um, *life*?"

Her face was suddenly an inch away from my own. Too bad zombies didn't use mouthwash, I thought to myself; a little Scope would've gone a long way. "You're here because I brought you here. I knew they'd look for you, that they knew where to find you. If I was a martyr, if the girls were, then I assumed that you too were venerated. And if the legend of your powers persisted over the centuries, they had little choice but to bring you back to the island, to counter whatever it was that had attacked them."

"A trap," I lamented.

"Says the fly to the spider," she hissed. "You're here and your humans in Utah, the descendants of those we left you with, are defenseless, while mine are marching even as we speak. Your friends, in other words, will be just as dead as you will be before long. The humans on Liberty Island will be next, finally getting what's coming to them. And I, at long last, will be the lone queen standing."

"Teetering you mean," I hissed back.

"Bitch," she spat.

"Takes one to know one." And it was then that I realized what she'd said. "Lone queen? But we made a deal. You said you'd let Dara go, Ricky here as well."

She nodded. "I did and I will, after the salt in them runs out. Then they can go wherever they please."

I turned and looked at my beloved. A mixture of fear and hatred washed over her face. Same for Ricky. "You'll return them back to their hells?"

"So what? Not like they'll even realize it. Like you said, they're no different than bowling pins, than Twinkies, trees."

I pointed to my heart's desire. "She's not a tree. She thinks and feels and loves. You loved once, too. Johnny was his name, right?"

Just for the briefest of moments, her face softened. "Don't," she whispered.

"You loved him. Like she loves me and I love her, like my friend here loves his wife, the women who I'm going to help him find."

The scowl returned almost as quickly as it had disappeared. If my one-time friend really was both human and undead, as she'd said, it was clear which part was stronger. "Johnny is dead. They're all dead, Creature. It just takes some people longer to realize that."

I gave up. There was no point in arguing with her anymore. She wasn't the queen I'd known, just a close facsimile. In any case, seconds later, she was gone, the door locked behind her, the grains of sand in my hourglass quickly running out.

"Well," said Dara, "she's even lovelier in person."

I moved to the chair and tried to untie her, but my hands being what they are, or, that is, what they weren't, it was pointless. I looked around for scissors, but the room was devoid of anything but furniture and a few yellowed sheets of paper and some odds and ends in the drawers, nothing sharp, nothing that could free her or us from our prison.

Or so it seemed.

"Look," said Ricky, his skeletal index finger aimed at the open drawer. Inside his hand went, outside it emerged, a book of matches revealed, the logo of the club on the cover. "Sanctuary," he read. "An apt name."

"You're going to burn the bindings?" I asked.

He nodded. "To start with." He righted himself and opened the book of matches. There were but two. "First, and just checking, but are we zombies, um, water-proofed? Or, like the Wicked Witch of the West, do we simply melt when wet?" He pointed to the ceiling, to the smoke detector.

"You think that thing still works?" I asked.

He scrunched his face. "Not a clue. But there is power in this place, so perhaps. Now what about that melting thing? I mean, there's something sizzling inside me. I hear it, feel it."

And then I nodded. "That's the radiation. But our skin, our flesh, it's too leathery now, no longer water-permeable. To a point, I mean."

"But the sprinkler would still be a good diversion, even if it didn't melt them all," said Dara. "Worth a shot anyway."

"Except we'll still be locked in here," I countered with. "Trapped and wet." Then I laughed. I couldn't help myself. Because, finally, centuries after working in a club, my experience would at last prove useful. "Wait," I said. "Wet, yes, trapped, maybe not." I pointed to the door. "It locked behind her, automatically. But should the alarm go off, if this club met its fire safety codes, then every automatic lock will unlock. That way, anyone trapped will be untrapped and the firemen don't have to break in anywhere."

Dara grinned. "Oh goody, big, brawny firemen."

"Wrong century," said Ricky.

"Way to rain on my parade," she retorted, pouting all the while.

Ricky gripped the matches and pointed to the ceiling. "If all goes as planned, yes." He smiled. "The rain part, anyway."

I grabbed a sheet of paper and held it near the matchbook. Wasn't easy, but Ricky managed to light a match, the paper going up a second later. I then leaned over and set the rope between Dara's hands on fire. "Yank," I told her. The age-old rope burned quickly, so that when Dara pulled her hands apart, her bindings quickly split in two, the fire then squelched between my clapping hands. "Yippy for deadened nerves," I said, staring down at my sooty digits.

"My hero," Dara cooed, slowly rising from the chair.

"Plural," said I, tilting my head Ricky's way. "Now all we have to do is set the alarm off, start a rain shower, escape, and hope they're too disoriented to notice our escape or the fact that we're suddenly missing." Dara frowned. Ricky frowned. "Um, yeah. I realize how unlikely that all sounds, but you gotta have faith, right?" I pointed to the ceiling. "In an ancient sprinkler system." Then I grinned. "On a bright note, at least I got to dance to Donna Summer again."

Dara's frown deepened. "While I was being held prisoner?"

I shrugged. "To be fair, I was worried the entire time I was dancing."

"Uh huh," she grunted. "To be fair."

I quickly changed the subject. "Light the match, Ricky. And then let's get the hell out of here."

He nodded, gripped the book, yanked the last match out, and struck it against the strip. Sadly, he struck too hard, the red tip grating against the back of the book before breaking apart and crumbling to the floor. "Uh, oh fuck," he cursed, locking eyes with me.

"Times a hundred," said I, looking inside the drawer again, then the one beneath it, but the book of matches we had was the only one. "Oh fuck."

Dara sighed. "Yeah, been there, done that, now what?"

Ricky rubbed his temples and squinted his eyes shut. "Now what? Now what? Now what?" he repeated, clearly trying to come up with yet another plan. He then opened up his eyes and again looked my way. "How exactly does the radiation inside of us work, Creature?"

An odd question, but I played along. "It powers us somehow, bridges the gap between our brains and our bodies, allows what should by all accounts not work to work."

"So we control it in a way?" he then asked.

I paused. After all, I'd never really given it much thought. I was dead, then I wasn't, and I knew that I had the radiation to thank for it all. Guess I took it for granted. "I suppose, in a way, we do. I mean, one of the reasons we're so slow, apart from death's stronghold on us, is because I need to think of an action and the radiation needs to make that action take place, to power it. It's like adding an extra step to everything. Why, do you think I can also direct the radiation to make the door unlock? Seems unlikely."

"Seems impossible," said Dara.

Ricky nodded. "It is impossible. The radiation only works inside of us: our own personal nuclear reactors. But . . ."

I took up where he left off. "But if you can control a nuclear power plant, you then control quite a bit of power."

He nodded and attempted to touch fingertip to nose. It landed on his cheek. So much for that control. Then again, he had been dead, like really dead, for centuries now, while I had plenty of time to sort of, kind of, almost master my bodily operations.

Just to make sure, I too touched fingertip to nose. "Bull's-eye," I said, proudly.

"Bravo?" said/asked Dara, seemingly unsure what either of us was talking about.

"Now the true test," said Ricky. "Concentrate and stare at the paper." He lifted a sheet off the desk and held it a foot from my face. "Just a little. Don't want to blow up the entire place, not with us still inside."

"Amen," said Dara. That, it appeared, she was clear on.

To say that directing a beam of radiation from my eyes was weird was putting it mildly. In fact, though it seemed that my brain did direct the radiation to help me crook a finger or bend a knee— neither of which I did all that well, mind you—it was still a subconscious exercise; this was anything but. Plus, I hadn't a clue what the end result would be, besides perhaps burning my eyes clear off my face. And, yes, *ouch*.

"Well, here goes . . . everything," I murmured, eyes locked to the paper, brain focusing, the rest of the world fading to the periphery. I felt the push, too, felt the energy rising, my eyes taking it all in, absorbing it before . . . before . . . *WHOOOSH!* "Well fuck me."

Dara coughed. "Again, been there, done that, but *that* never happened before."

The *that* in question was the hole in the paper, the edges of which were still on fire and spreading to the four corners. "I'm friggin' Superman," I coughed out, stunned, amazed and, yes, so sue me, just a little pompous.

Dara snickered. "Catty Woman is more like it, but fine, we'll go with it. Just don't go aiming those beams my way next time I accidentally ignore you and piss you off."

"Accidentally."

She touched fingertip to nose. It landed on her upper lip. "That is difficult, huh?"

Ricky sighed. "Can you please lift the paper to the alarm now? *Before* it stops burning, I mean."

I nodded and quickly(ish) lifted the paper. Then I waited. Then waited some more. Until the paper reached its fiery crescendo. And then, *WAA, WAA, WAA,* went the alarm and down, down, down came the rain and *click* went the door.

"Well fuck me," I said, yet again.

"Last time, been there, done that," said Dara. "Now run!"

Which we did. Ish.

CHAPTER 10
LOST AND FOUND

Back to the disco floor we went. The startling red emergency lights had flicked on, all other lights doused. From every corner the sprinklers sprinkled, soaking the zombies, who, as per usual, remained oblivious, even as they skidded and fell and tripped and writhed. Still, they were ordered to kill us, even though it had been a while since that particular nefarious order had been given, and so kill us is what they tried to do, the entire discoful of them aimed our way as one by one they noticed our attempted escape.

"KILL THEM!" we heard, yet again.

"You sound like a broken record!" I hollered, though I hadn't a clue where that crazy bitch was hollering from this time around. I'd say she had eyes in the back of her head, but her wig was so friggin' huge that it would be next to near impossible to see through it.

Dara then tapped me on the shoulder. "There's too many of them, Creature."

Ricky tapped me on the other shoulder. "And falling and crawling, in all this water, might not work to our advantage this time."

"Thoughts?" added Dara, her eyes scanning back and forth and back again, looking for a way out of this mess.

"We should've stayed in Utah." Yes, that was my immediate thought. Which might have been the only time in all of history that anyone anywhere *ever* said such a thing.

"New thought?" amended Dara as the crush of zombies began to surround us on all sides.

I nodded. Surprisingly, I did have an idea. "Zombie skin is too leathery for water to penetrate. At least with this kind of soft downpour."

Dara nodded. "Uh huh, and?"

I grinned. "Leather can be cut, though."

They both paused, clearly picturing what I was getting at. "Think you can do it?" asked Ricky.

"Worked wonders on that sheet of paper," I replied.

"Which was a foot in front of your face and considerably thinner," said Dara.

I shrugged. "Any other ideas?" Not surprisingly, there was no response. "Thought so." And then, once again, I concentrated, constricting the radiation into a sort of internal beam, building it up, Up, UP. And then, when I could no longer hold it in, out it shot, through my pupils, two invisible rays that lanced everything in front of it, slicing through long-dead skin like the sharpest of knives.

You could smell it before you saw it, the stench of searing flesh, worse as the water seeped inside and mixed with the radiated tissue within. Then came the steam, the groans notching up, the zombies crashing to the floor as I shifted my head this way and that, taking them down one by one by one. Heck, Wyatt Earp had nothing on this old queen.

"Can I say it?" asked Dara, finally smiling.

"Be my guest."

"Well fuck me."

"Has a nice ring to it," I retorted, grabbing their hands as we pushed through the crashing throng.

"KILL THEM!" we heard yet again, though she was smart not to come down and try it herself. I'll give her credit for that much.

"Better luck next time, bitch!" I hollered in return as we sidestepped the zombies, who were now falling on all sides of us, creating one obstacle after the next, trapping Blondella and her minions inside as we in turn headed for the emergency exit toward the rear of the club.

Minutes later, we were outside, the sun yawning its way to life, turning the streets a warm golden hue. The door slammed behind us, the sound of the alarm suddenly muffled.

"My hero," cooed Dara before planting a kiss on my cheek and a pat on my ass.

"Heroine," I corrected her, then flicked my wrist her way. "And poppycock."

"I used to know a drag king by that name."

"Huh?" huhed Ricky.

Dara grinned. "Papi Cock. Fierce he-dyke."

Ricky looked my way. "Is she serious?"

I shrugged. "I can never tell." Then I pointed down the street. "In any case, I say we put some major distance between us and this place, because once they dry out, my beams won't have the same effect, the radiation having nothing to mix with." I grinned as I said it: *my beams*. I mean, that's pretty fucked up that I had these super powers all along and didn't even know about them.

Made a guy/girl wonder what else he/she could do by putting his/her mind to it.

***

Twenty minutes later, we were far enough away to be able to breathe a little easier, if only in our heads.

"So now what?" asked Dara as we stood in the middle of a mostly-deserted street, the silence around us all-enveloping, like a crypt or a tomb. Oh, what I would have given to hear a horn beep or a bird coo or a bum ask for a quarter at that very moment. Heck, Miley Cyrus could've sung right then and I would've cried like a friggin' baby.

"You mean," said I, "do we head back to Liberty Island, where we don't even know who we can trust anymore, or do we stay here and fight? Because Blondella is a lot of things—seriously, a lot—but a quitter ain't one of them. And if she came after the humans before, she'll do it again." It was then that a pit ricocheted around my belly. "Humans," I repeated. "She sent an army after ours back in Utah. We have to go home and save them."

Dara snickered. "You called it home. You've never done that before, not in that way. Not in three hundred years"

I paused and scratched my chin, if only for effect, because, like those horns and birds and bums and Miley, itching was also something I sorely missed. "Well, I suppose it's the closest thing we've got."

Ricky sighed. "Which is more than I can say." The sigh repeated. "In any case, it'll take weeks and weeks before those zombies make it from here to Utah, if ever. Which gives us enough time to, um, well . . ."

"Yeah," said I. "To well what? To kill Blondella? To find out who if any of the humans are on her side? To save Liberty Island from certain destruction? Or just save our own asses?"

"I do so like my ass," quipped Dara.

"Ditto," I readily agreed.

Ricky shrugged. "I plead the fifth."

"Wise move," said I, patting his shoulder. "So, do we take a vote then?" I lifted up my hand. "I say we stay and fight. Those queens on the island, more than likely, can't be trusted. And if we go back there, they might try and do to us what Blondella just tried. And, with their bendy limbs, they might have better luck at it."

Dara lifted her hand next. "I agree. Those queens came and got us. Perhaps it was for protection or perhaps it was out of loyalty to Blondella, who they clearly worship. In any case, regardless of who did what or who knew what, it was still a trap."

Ricky was the third and final vote. He pointed to the few zombies that trudged this way and that. "At least here we have a dedicated army at our disposal." He looked my way. "Or at least you do."

Which was true, but if I amassed fifty, a hundred, two hundred zombies, Blondella could do the same. And what would that get us but a mess of even deader zombies. No, we needed to infiltrate the enemy and take that ancient tramp down, then make sure the islanders knew she was in fact down, then have them fly us home before the zombies reached my minions. Easy peasy.

"I think I have a plan to kill two birds with one stone," I offered.

Dara frowned. "No birds. And good luck tossing a stone these days."

"Figure of speech," said I. "In any case, it involves dressing up."

Dara clapped—well, as best she could. "Goody!"

And now Ricky frowned. "Dressing up? In dresses? *All* of us?"

Poor guy. It was like Sleeping Beauty being kissed awake by RuPaul. "No, Ricky. Just me." Again Dara frowned. "Sorry, you can dress up, too. But only I have to actually be seen."

"You lost me," said Dara.

Ricky raised his hand. "I've been lost this entire time."

I grinned. "Then it's time to be found, sweeties. Time to be found."

***

We had hours to make it back to the pier where we'd originally been dropped off, according to the watch still strapped to my arm. It would be cutting it close, but we had time, pardon the expression, to kill. The marina was a nice one, so there were ample shops to visit, shops that, we hoped and prayed, would contain what we needed in order to pull off the start of yet another plan.

"Does it get any easier?" asked Ricky, about halfway there, the sun a bit higher in the sky now, the silence no less annoying.

"Walking?" I replied.

He shook his head. "All of it. The unendingness of it. The tedium, years and years of it, with no sleep to break it up with."

I turned and looked at him. "You picked up on all that in less than a day?"

He looked my way and patted his chest. "I feel it."

"The radiation?"

His head kept shaking. "Eternity, like this, the way we are. Unchanging."

That was a hard one to answer. In fact, they were all hard to answer. And so instead I looked to Dara, who simply smiled in return. She knew the answer as well as I did. "We'll find your wife, Ricky," I told him. "That will help."

He looked back to the street again and kept trudging forward. "And if we don't?"

Dara sidled in closer to him. "Then you have us. And if anyone can break up tedium, it's Creature and me."

He chuckled. It was a nice sound to hear. Not Donna Summer, no, but nice just the same. "Trust me, I've seen you two break up tedium. In a word: scary."

He meant it well, and that's how I took it. Still, I let it drop. Because even with Dara by my side, the tedium, the unendingness, as he put it, always threatened to smother you, to trample you until you begged for the end. This was the way of the world now, the way of our kind. Like a Yoko Ono album, it wasn't pretty, but, like I said before, it sure as hell beat the alternative.

In any case, a couple of hours later, we saw the bay and the empty pier. Soon enough, the queens would arrive. What would happen next was anyone's guess, but at least we were now hedging our bets.

A high-end women's clothing shop was first on our list. The shop was unlocked, the zombie sales woman finally smelling fresh air for the first time in centuries. We let her out, if only to make ourselves feel better. Besides, not like she was going to be recommending styles and colors or the latest trend, seeing as the latest trend was sun-drenched and dusty duds.

Once inside, Dara and I had ourselves a look around, while Ricky stood outside and stared at the lifeless bay.

"Is he alright?" whispered Dara.

I shrugged. "Haven't a clue, but at least he's still up and running, so to speak."

Eventually, we found the perfect dress, silver, sequined and so tight that if I still had a pulse it would've been strangled to death. The store also had shoes. If I could've drooled, I would have. I mean, the closest I ever got to a pair of Jimmy Choos were the knock-offs you bought from a guy on the street, the kind where the glue holding on the heel melted away if the temperature shot above ninety. Good that I lived, past tense, in San Francisco, where ninety was the cost for lunch and not something the thermometer ever reached.

"Can you manage in them?" asked Dara. "I mean, the heels are kind of high."

"Can I manage in them? Can I manage in them?" I looked at her with ridicule.

"Well, can you?"

I froze. "Not a clue, but I'll give it the old college try."

"You didn't go to college, dearest."

"School of hard-knocks doesn't count?"

She helped me lift up my feet before sliding the shoes on. "Well?" she asked, staring up at me.

"Like butta."

"Yeah, but you can't walk in *butta* eitha."

Still, like the song went, I put one foot in front of the other and soon I was hobbling out the door. Because, yes, drag queens wobble, but they don't fall down. Or so it's been said. And probably by a drag queen.

Next shop was two doors over. This one was a hair salon. We couldn't free the seated patrons, but we managed to scoot out the workers. More karma points for us. Though, to be fair, they and the store both needed some heavy airing out.

This time we required Ricky's help, though. Because getting in a dress and shoes were one thing, and difficult things at that, but putting on makeup was a job for three. Heck, if we had six zombies it still wouldn't have been enough, but three was all we had and so three would have to do.

"You're joking," he balked, upon entering the salon.

"Not without tips," said Dara. She grinned. "God that felt good to say." Yes, it had indeed been too long since we heard it. "In any case, the tubes are too small, the brushes too delicate, and if we all don't work as a team, Creature's gonna look like one hot mess. Or Tammy Faye Bakker."

"What's the difference?" I asked.

"Point taken," she answered.

Ricky held up his hand in submission. "Never mind. I'll help."

Straight men: so easily pussy-whipped. Even when the pussy is created by one good tuck. Which is also why drag queens don't fall down, by the way. Because tucking plus falling equals massive, massive pain. And yes, even in death, dick and ball crushing hurts, though maybe that was only in my head. Both of them.

Anyway, took longer to do the makeup than the dress, but eventually I looked as close to the real deal as I could get. But the pièce de résistance was the wig. Now that had to be perfect. If the eyes are the windows to the soul—and the jury was still out whether I even had one of those left—then the wig is the curtains. Luckily, the salon had the perfect window treatments.

Dara helped me crown my head. "Big and platinum and teased to hell," she said.

"But do I look like her?" I asked.

She nodded, grinning all the while. "Blondella's own mother wouldn't be able to tell you two apart."

I'd met said mother before. The apple didn't fall too far from the tree in that regard: both of them were overly ripe and withered around the edges. Still, I'd take it. After all, that was what we were going for. Plus, we had distance on our side. And distance is a girl's best friend. Though a few drinks often helps. And some dim lighting. Or, in Blondella's case, all three.

The marina was fenced in. Apart from the ferry landing, you needed a key to get through a gate to be able to get to your slip, to your boat. All we had to do was find the key. Luckily, that part wasn't as difficult as it sounded.

"Whoever has a key to the gate," I shouted, "come to the gate, now!"

There weren't that many zombies milling about behind the gate. Most of them were trapped on their boats, but there were a few grizzled-looking workers walking from dock to dock, one or two ramming against the fence over and over again, like a bird who encounters a window and keeps trying to fly on through. Also, the docks had raised trims, so for centuries they could never simply walk into the water and out of their living hells.

"There!" said Ricky, pointing far up the plank and down the length of the fence.

Lo and behold, a man was now lumbering our way, dressed in a blue jumpsuit and a cap, keys swinging from his side, the sound of them the only one besides the water lapping against the boats and the wind whipping the sails.

"That's our man," said Dara.

"Or one hell of a fashion victim," added I.

In any case, a few minutes later, he was standing on the opposite side of the gate, groaning as he stared into the oblivion. I, in turn, stared at the keys. I then reached through the gate and unlatched the metal wad from his belt loop. They jingled and jangled in my hand as I yanked them back through, gleaming in the early morning sunlight.

"Thanks," I said to the dock worker zombie. "Now go back whence you came." And, yes, talking to zombies required a little bit of theatrics and a smidge of talking down to. Same for children. And squirrels. And, um, Republicans.

One key led to two, two to four. The fifth one grabbed hold of the lock and turned, the gate in desperate need of some oil but giving way just the same. The zombie had already backed away, and so we entered, quickly making our way to the first rickety, rusty vessel after we locked the gate behind us. Then Ricky and Dara helped me down into the boat, while Dara hid as best she could and Ricky stood off to the side. After all, they hadn't a clue who he was.

And so the stage was set.

And a drag queen just adores a stage, even a floating one. Heck, this one even had a bar, so, naturally, I felt right at home.

Not ten minutes or so later, we saw the Liberty Island ferry approaching from out in the middle of the bay, chug, chug, chugging its way toward us. The horn blew to alert its arrival. I assumed that was for my benefit.

"Show time," I proclaimed, butterflies (or perhaps bats would be more apt) taking wing inside my belly.

I watched the ferry pull in to dock, the plank slide in to place and, lastly, the queens, one by one, emerge into the sunlight. They chatted cattily as they moved briskly toward the long-forgotten marina, their voices echoing all around me.

That us, until, also one by one, said voices died away.

I watched them as they in turn stared, gaped and gawked at me. This is what we'd been planning on, to see their reactions, to see what they would do next.

Ginger whimpered first and immediately prostrated herself, Aflo quick to follow. Or, well, quickish. I mean, with her rotundity, quick wasn't exactly her forté. VaVa and Topaz looked to the other two and then at each other. It was brief, perhaps the barest of split seconds, but some sort of message went from one set of eyes to the other before these two also prostrated themselves, their tight dresses barely allowing for such a maneuver.

I turned to Ricky. He turned to me. We'd both seen it. They were surprised to see me, but not in the same way the other two girls were.

"Goddess," wailed Ginger. "You've returned!"

"Speak to us, Goddess!" loudly moaned Kit.

Luckily, Blondella's cigarette-infused, boozy she-voice wasn't all that difficult to mimic. Besides, with no other sounds to drown me out, I didn't need to speak all that loudly. "Traitors," was all I said, that and no more. *Plant the seed of doubt*, I thought to myself. *Plant it and watch it grow.*

After that, the zombies started pouring in on all sides, from behind the gate and in front, from east to west, the aroma of human, of breakfast, carried on the wind. The queens had little choice but to retreat back to the ferry, to remove the attaching plank and to wait for me, the real me, not the gussied up me, to return to the ship, all while the zombies kept on coming. Soon, the entire pier was teeming with them. But it wasn't to the undead that the queens stared. Nope, it was to me: the star attraction—and about damned time.

But did I lip-synch to a non-existent soundtrack? Did I bow and curtsey to the likes of them? Did I even deem to acknowledge their presence? No, no and no, I did not. I already gave them their sighting, their message. Now it was their turn to act as they saw fit. Besides, Dara and Ricky and I already had our answer: Blondella was not doing this alone.

Morning gave way to afternoon, afternoon to early evening, and still I stood and still Ricky stood and still Dara hid. By then, the marina was crammed with an army of zombies, every square inch of space filled to the brim with them. After that, all we had left to do was wait the queens out. And zombies are good at that. Not a lot else we do well, but standing around doing nothing, yep, that we can most certainly do.

It was only then, when it was fairly obvious that I wasn't returning, that it would've been next to near impossible for me to even work my way through the throng, with Dara in tow, that the ferry at last pulled into the harbor and headed back to Liberty Island, the queens staring at me until, I was sure, I was barely a blip on their radar.

"That was interesting," said Ricky, once we were alone again.

"That was *long*," added Dara as she emerged from her hiding place.

"But worth the effort," I said. "At least now we know who we can trust and who we can't."

Dara nodded. "VaVa and Topaz, the priestess, born of the House of Blondella. I suppose that makes sense then. They worship her above all others, would, it seem, follow her to the ends of the Earth."

"The ends of their lives is more like it," said Ricky, now helping me off the swaying ship I'd been on. "So what do we do about it? You said we stay and fight. Is that still the plan?"

That I had to think over. Stay and fight? With what and to what end? "Just before they came and got us from Utah, there was a zombie attack on the island," I said. "To pull that off, to drive the ferry boat, to dock it and undock it, to lower and raise the connecting plank, all that took human help to pull off."

Ricky nodded. "Zombies, even conscious zombies, wouldn't have been able to do all that, no way. Heck it took three of us just to get your mascara on."

Dara chuckled. "And just barely, by the looks of it."

"Thanks," I said, with a grimace. "Is it that bad?"

She shrugged. "Blondella was no prized catch to begin with, so we didn't have to do such a great job anyway."

My grimace sagged further. "So, yes, that bad. In any case, to do all that, and successfully I might add, they had to be in communication, the bad queens and Blondella."

"And?" said Dara.

"*And*," said I, "With the recent sighting of the fake Blondella, the accomplices are sure to be confused, are sure to get in contact, to see what's going on, to see what *traitor* meant, to see why she showed herself. Right?"

Dara nodded and then promptly shook her head. "And?"

Okay, she had me on that last one. "Not a clue. But if we can be there when contact is made, maybe we'll somehow be able to turn the tables on them. Maybe if the good queens find out about the bad queens, if we can prove all this to them, then we'll have an army to back us up with. Because, as things stand right now, no way are the good guys going to attack someone they see as a goddess simply by our word. Plus, if we accuse Topaz or VaVa of anything without said proof, the queens might just leave us out here to rot, forever."

"Forever," said Ricky, a sadness to his voice I'd yet to hear. "Really? Forever? Like this?"

I dreaded answering him. I kept forgetting that, as far he could recall, he'd been human just a short while ago, while Dara and I had centuries to grow accustomed to the idea of who and what we were, what we'd always be. "It's, um, impossible to say, Ricky. Decades, centuries, millennia. Who knows?"

His grimace stamped mine into the dirt. "Maybe it is best to stay zombie then, ignorance equating to bliss."

I pointed to the sea of zombies on the other side of the fence, all of them still clamoring for the long departed ferry. "That look *blissful* to you, sweetie?"

He looked from them to me. He didn't reply. He didn't have to. Perhaps there were no winners in all of this. But, just in case, I was hedging my bets that it was going to be us.

"So what do we do next?" he asked

"Be there when they make contact, I suppose," I replied.

"But what if contact is made mechanically, by radio or the like?" he thought to ask.

"That would make the most sense," agreed Dara. "Doubtful that the queens make contact in person, not with all these zombies around. Too dangerous."

"But we didn't see any communication device in the disco," I countered.

"There are certainly more rooms inside," counter-countered Ricky. "And we know they have electricity, as do the islanders, I'm assuming." Dara and I nodded. "So that means—"

My last and final grimace would've made a hound dog seem like it was smiling in comparison. "Back inside the belly of the beast we go."

"Fuck," said Dara.

"Yep," said I.

"And not the good kind of fuck either," she reiterated.

"Got it," I added, pointing back to the marina, to the shops we'd come from. "But storm cloud meet silver lining."

"Shopping," she fairly cooed.

Ricky, of course, knew what we were getting at. After all, despite being with us for only such a short amount of time, a short amount of time was in fact all he needed. "Fuck," he repeated. "As in no *fuck*ing way."

CHAPTER 11
TABLE FOR ONE

We didn't have much time to do what needed to be done. Then again, we really didn't know when or if the queens would or could contact Blondella. Still, better safe than sorry, so we rushed. Which wasn't saying all that much. Especially since we had to sidestep a few hundred zombies in order to reach our destination.

"Thoughts?" asked Ricky once we were finally back inside the boutique.

I shrugged. "We just can't look or smell like we did the first time they found us."

"Smell?" asked Dara.

My shrug remained. "No telling if the zombies can recognize us by our scents as well as by our looks." I lifted up a dust covered bottle of perfume and turned it over. "Best money can buy." I gave it a shpritz and then promptly coughed my friggin' head off. "Let me rephrase that: best money *could* buy."

Dara crinkled her nose. "Guess it expired."

Ricky nodded, covering his face as he did so. "A couple of hundred years ago." He then squinted his eyes my way. "And, to repeat myself, in case you weren't listening the first time: no fucking way am I wearing any of the clothes in here."

I grinned and walked over to one of the racks. I lifted up a frilly and oh-so-ridiculously priced blouse. "This would look darling on you."

Dara lifted up a complementary skirt. "Ooh, and with this you'll be the belle of the ball." And before he could object, she added, "Ironically, I used to know a drag queen by that name."

Ricky grunted. "Bella la Ball?"

"No way," she said, clearly stunned. "You knew her, too?"

118

The grunt repeated. "No, but I'm quickly getting to know *you*. In any case, should the time come, you're never going to say that you knew a drag queen named Ricky Shea, either."

I put the blouse back on the rack. Dara did the same with the skirt. "Spoilsport," she said, now pouting. If she could've folded her arms across her chest, she would have, if only for effect.

"Speaking of sport, I'm going two store downs to the golf shop. You mentioned that I can't look like myself anymore," he said, already opening the door. "Don't take this the wrong way, but I don't have to look like the two of you either."

"Is there a right way to take that?" I asked.

He paused and grinned. "If I can't look as pretty as the two of you, then why bother?" He then turned and headed down the sidewalk. He tried to whistle. *Good luck with that*, I thought.

Dara watched him go. "He makes a valid point."

"He was just trying to appease us."

She went back to shopping. "I can live with that." She seemed to reconsider her choice of words. "Well, you know what I mean."

Indeed I did. All too well, in fact. Be that as it may, when given the choice to either shop or ponder my rather lengthy demise, I think it's obvious which one I chose. And since I couldn't look like Blondella and I couldn't look like myself, I went hooker-chic instead, topping it off with a flaming red wig.

Dara smirked when she got a good look at me. "Luckily, you don't have to breathe in that get-up."

I nodded. "Even if I could, it'd be dangerous. In any case, Creature would never be caught, pardon the expression, *dead* in an outfit like this, so no way is anyone or anything going to recognize me now."

"Heck, you could've walked right by me and I wouldn't have even recognized you." She took a whiff. "Plus, with three hundred years of dust on those clothes, you also smell very unCreature-like." Because, yes, I might've been dead, but that didn't mean that I generally neglected my grooming habits.

A few minutes later, we had Dara dressed in a sleek boating outfit, skirt and blouse silky and light, her new blonde wig topped by a sailor's hat, silver anchor-shaped earrings hanging from her grayish lobes. "How do I look?" she asked, giving me a twirl.

"Fishy." I meant it as a compliment, and that's how she took it.

And then Ricky walked in, plaid from head to toe, from his pom-pom-topped tam right on down to his golf shoes. "Well?" he asked.

"Hole in one," I commented.

"What's that smell, though?" Dara asked, nose scrunched up.

Ricky held up a bottle of Windex and then sprayed himself with it before tucking it into the back of his pants. "Nice vintage."

I nodded. "And it makes your elbows shine."

"Yep, win/win," he quipped. "Now let's get a move-on. No telling when the call will come in. Because, if they're in some sort of partnership, like we're pretty certain they are, then they certainly need to somehow communicate."

I nodded my agreement. "Think we can make it back to the disco before the queens make it off the ferry?"

Ricky was smiling. I think. Hard to tell with a zombie. He then pointed outside. "Your carriage awaits, Madame."

I followed his point with my eyes. They landed on a golf cart. "Marina Security," I read aloud. "No way can that thing still work after all this time."

"*You* still work after all this time," he pointed out.

"Barely," whispered Dara out of the corner of her mouth.

"Hey!" shouted I.

"In any case," interjected Ricky, "I already checked. Sucker is solar powered. Yippy for the green movement."

I couldn't help but smirk. "Ironic, huh? They thought that the sun would save them and, in the end, it was the sun that did them in." I looked his way. "But will it still run?"

He shrugged. "Only one way to find out."

Again I stared at the ancient, rust-covered cart. "What if it simply explodes instead?"

He winked and walked outside. "We'll go with ironic again, seeing as the one thing that can save us will, in the end, do us in."

"Funny," I groaned.

"I wasn't trying to be," he replied.

"And she was being sarcastic," Dara informed, the three of us doing our best to board the cart. "It's what we drag queens do. It's like breathing for us."

Ricky was now sitting, sort of, in the front seat. The key was still in the ignition. "But you don't, in fact, still breathe."

He turned the key. Nothing happened. I tapped his shoulder from the passenger seat. "Lucky for you, though, I can still remember how to drive." I pointed to the pedals. "Your foot is on the gas, Doc. Try the brake."

He blushed, if only in my head. "My bad." He tried again. The cart wheezed and buckled and chugged and died—it and me both, I realized. He tried again. At last, the motor revved, the sound glorious to my ears. Plus, it semi drowned out the constant zombie groaning.

Out of the marina we then drove, golf-cart slow, but certainly faster than had we been on foot. "Miracle," I reverently whispered.

"That this thing is moving?" Ricky asked, turning my way, bloodshot eyes twinkling just the same.

I shook my head. "That I flew in a plane, drove in a golf cart and danced to Donna Summer, all in the same week. In Utah, we have fun by tipping zombies."

"The cows are all dead," informed Dara, just in case he'd missed that part.

Anyway, seeing as, like I'd said before, our brain cells stay locked and loaded at all times, we knew exactly which way to travel. And, since we were now motorized, it didn't take us all that long to make it back to the disco and park nearby.

"Guards," noted Dara from the back seat, pointing, *gulp*, dead ahead.

I looked over at Ricky. "By chance did you bring the Windex?"

He nodded. "Yeah, why?"

I pushed and pushed and soon toppled out of the cart. "Bring it and follow me."

The following me was easier said that done and, considering there were a half-dozen glassy-eyed zombies locking in on us all of sudden, it wasn't even all that easily said. Still, the guards weren't approaching us, so at least, I figured, they also didn't recognize our little group, seeing as Blondella's orders, as I remembered it, were to kill us. Or, that is to say, re-kill us. Unkill us? I don't know, with zombies the verbiage is never all that simple.

Dara soon appeared by my right side, Ricky by my left, the three of us ambling their way. The six of them then left their posts and lumbered our way. Suddenly, it looked like the showdown at the Not-So-Okay Corral.

"I hope you have a plan," whispered Dara out of the side of her mouth.

I nodded. "Hell to the yeah," I whispered in reply. Then I gazed upon the guards. "Suck it, bitches!" As Ricky sprayed them with Windex, my gaze, suffice it to say, promptly turned lethal. *Zap* popped my radiation beams, *slaaash* went their desiccated belly flesh and, lastly, *ugh* they all grunted, the Windex sizzling through as it mixed with their internal radiation. It was like Chernobyl on a smaller, stinkier scale: nuclear zombie meltdown.

"Good aim," I said to Ricky as we walked around the pile of fetid, steaming corpses.

"Aw shucks," he twanged. "T'weren't nothin', ma'am."

Dara leaned in and said in my ear, "Is it weird that that turned me on?"

I chuckled. "It would be weird if it didn't, dearest. After all, it's been several hundred years since I've been that butch."

And then she chuckled. "Says the man in the size two dress."

"Bitch."

"Which is why you love me."

Ricky, who could obviously hear us the entire time, merely shook his head. And then, two minutes later, we were walking up the stairs to the club. "Go in, split up and look for some sort of communication device," he said. "And act nonchalantly."

My chuckle returned. "Zombies do blasé quite well, sweetie, so no worries there."

He opened the door for us, um, *ladies*, and we were in like Flynn. Though Flynn, I'm guessing, had never tried to infiltrate a disco filled with mindless zombies before. Lucky Flynn. The jury was still out if we would be so fortunate.

In any case, Ricky went left, Dara went right and I went straight— um, directionally forward, that is to say, seeing as the only thing straight about me was the jacket (of the straight variety) I now so richly deserved for putting us smack-dab into the belly of the beast once again.

The floor was still wet and a great deal of the zombies were still writhing about, so it wasn't necessarily easy going, but going, nevertheless, is what I did. And then I recalled our first encounter with Blondella, when she'd screamed for her minions to kill us. The sound, I remembered, had come from above. I craned my neck up, my eyes landing on the catwalk. It was dark up there. Still, I assumed there must be rooms nearby, a reason for Blondella to hang there instead of nearer to the dance floor.

I turned. Ricky and Dara had already disappeared from my line of sight. I looked back up, then turned my head from side to side, searching for a stairwell, anything that would get me from here to there. I moved away from the dance floor, my feet sloshing through the puddles that remained, sidestepping the downed zombies as I went.

Eventually, I found a kitchen, a small number, meant, I was certain, to be used for catered events. And there, thank goodness, is where I found the elevator. I say thank goodness because the idea of finding a stairwell and then walking up it was fairly terrifying, especially so soon after our recent stairway debacle. I mean, you could fall down a flight of stairs easily enough, but gravity had a lot to say about doing such a thing in reverse.

And so into the elevator I stepped. It was small and silver and claustrophobic, not to mention horribly lit by fluorescent lights that made my skin look gray—well, okay, gray*er*—but it did work well enough, slowly taking me to the upper floor.

Had my heart still worked, I'm sure it would've been beating furiously from within my padded chest. Instead, I felt the phantom pounding, like when your hand is lopped off and you can still feel your fingers as they clutch the silk of your dress. I stared down. My fingers were clutching the silk of my dress. Go figure. And then the elevator went *ding* and out I stepped.

There were few zombies up there, which wasn't at all surprising. Zombies, after all, are ground dwellers. Which is also not surprising, considering that's where we're meant to be: in the ground. Me, I preferred being six feet above it rather than six feet below, in heels whenever possible. Anyway, these zombies were cognizant, minions, just like the ones I had back home. Thankfully, they also didn't seem to recognize me. Proof of this was the fact that they were neither chasing me nor tossing my nearly lifeless body over the side of the catwalk. *Phew.* In fact, they were doing nothing but milling about, probably waiting for Blondella's evil commands.

"Where are they?!" I heard, seconds later, her voice bellowing behind a door.

The they in question was obviously us, and the where part was also obvious, at least to me. The only thing not obvious was where the device was that allowed Blondella to communicate with the treacherous island drag queens. "There has to be one," I whispered to myself. "It's the only way they can safely communicate without being found out by the others."

I kept walking. There were two more rooms up there. One, I quickly found, was a long-unused storage closet. The other . . . "Bing-fucking-o."

The bitch was using some sort of CB radio device. It was one of those big, bulky numbers with a hand-held transmitter. I picked it up and whispered, "Breaker one-nine, breaker one-nine." Which was about all I learned from watching numerous trucker movies on Lifetime. In any case, all I got in return was a bunch of static, meaning the ferry and the queens aboard hadn't made it back home yet or at least weren't on their end of the line. In other words, the two camps hadn't communicated yet. "Thank goodness."

Except, of course, seeing as our luck as of late was on the rather shoddy side, my 'thank goodness' was a bit premature.

"Drop it," I suddenly heard, my hand frozen (more so than usual) to the transmitter.

Slowly (again, more so than usual), I turned. Blondella was standing in the doorway. And that, of course, would've been bad enough except that on either side of her were her goons, which also would've been bad enough except that they were holding my struggling compatriots in their death grips. Which meant that in order to shoot my radiation beams at them, I had to go through Ricky and Dara. Plus, there was no water around now, so even if I tore through the bad guys, it would do little good except to make them even nastier-looking than they already were.

"Checkmate," said Blondella, with a self-satisfied smile (sort of) on her rather twisted-looking face.

"If memory serves, dear one, you don't know how to play chess." I sneered her way. "Or balance your checkbook, or correctly work a cell phone, or set the clock on your TV, or—"

"Enough!" she interrupted—which was something, at the very least, that she still did quite well. Bitch never did like sharing the stage, after all.

"Let them go," I said, trying, and failing, to keep my voice even, especially as my eyes locked with Dara's.

"Sure," she replied.

"Sure?"

She nodded, repeating as she had the first time we were in this damned-similar predicament, "After you're dead and after their salt runs out, then sure, no problem." The bitch sure as hell had a one-track mind.

"I'm already dead," I retorted, anger now rising, boiling up.

She shrugged. "Semantics."

Things weren't going well, I knew. But I also knew that I had to do something. And, since I obviously couldn't rescue my friends, at least not at that very moment, I still had one chance to throw a monkey-wrench into her sinister plans. And so I charged up my batteries and widened my eyes. "You asked for it," I spat.

"You can't," she barked. "You'll slice your friends open."

I released my beams. "Not what I was going for." And out they shot, slamming into the CB radio instead, which instantly began to sizzle and spark and belch black smoke. "Whoopsie," I then added, once I was sure that the two enemy groups were now permanently incommunicado.

"You bitch!" she hollered.

And now it was my turn to shrug. "Takes one to know—"

"Silence!"

"You know," I said, ignoring the command, "you've become quite the drama queen in your old, old, seriously *old* age." I again focused my beams. "And if you don't let my friends go, that pretty, *ugh*, face of yours is going to have more holes in it than your head. Which I believe is really saying something."

Immediately, she lunged behind the guards. "You'll never escape," she said. "I turned the water off to the building. That trick of yours won't work again."

"Apart from wrecking your, *ugh*, beauty."

"Guards!" she then hollered. "Seize her!"

Now then, the guards, not caring about their, *ugh*, beauty as much as Blondella did, started moving toward me. Though with their captives, who were still struggling, held tight, their moving, which was sluggish at best, was no walk in the park. In other words, I had a moment to think. And to act.

Again I turned, again charging my beams, only this time I fired at the window behind me. It shattered and split a moment later, glass raining down two stories below. I moved a few feet over and stared down. We were in the rear of the building so rather than staring into the street, I was staring into a dumpster, ages old garbage still piled high within.

"Ta ta," I then said, leaning in and over before I too rained down two stories below. Because those who fight and run away live—oh the irony—to fight another day. And fight was what I had to do, to rescue them, to rescue my Dara.

I landed on my back, staring up at the blue sky above. And then I was staring at Blondella, whose head was now poking out the window. I slashed her face with a concentrated beam even before she knew what hit her.

"BITCH!" she bellowed.

I grinned, despite the awful circumstances I was in, and despite the garbage I was in, and despite the fact that I was flat on my back with a dumpster beneath me and not a minion in sight. "Yeah, I think we covered that already," I replied. "Next time it's your heart. Oh, wait, you seemed to have lost that a few hundred years ago."

Her face was no longer poking out, but I still heard her loud and clear. "Just like you lost your friends here, forever, and, soon enough, all the remaining humans as well. And then I'll be sending an army for you, to tear you limb from fucking limb."

And with that she was gone.

Though certainly not forgotten.

Try as I might.

I forced a sigh. "Creature Comfort, table for one," I lamented.

I then recapped my predicament to myself: I was in a dumpster; Dara, my life, my love, had been drag-napped (again!); my lone minion had been taken prisoner and would soon revert back to zombiehood; and the one group of possible help was full of traitors who would rather see me dead(er) than victorious over a stark-raving-mad drag queen from hell.

"Yep, that about covers it," I said as I teetered back and forth and back and forth until, miracle of miracles, I was able to roll over onto my face and into a bag of garbage that had been sitting out in the sun and rain for centuries. "Gross," I coughed, then pushed myself up and managed to grab on to the edge of the dumpster. A moment later, after again falling, albeit from a much lesser height this time, I found myself face down on the ground. "Not a good day," I groaned, but at least I was safe and, uh, sound. Though my new dress had certainly seen better days.

Still, I had little time to revel, because, knowing Blondella, I was sure she and her henchmen were on their way down to capture me at that very moment. I turned my head to the side and spotted the rear door to the building, the one I was certain they'd be pouring out of at any moment. If that happened, all hope, which I now had very little to spare, would be gone. Again I groaned and then mustered all the energy to shout, "Any zombie within the sound of my voice, run this way!"

Run being such a subjective word, they still managed to trudge and totter and traipse and trod my way, dozens upon dozens of them, all heeding, thank goodness, my command. When the front of the pack was a mere ten feet away, I added, "Block the door to the building! Put your bodies into it!"

And that's just what they did, all of them, at least a hundred walking corpses slamming themselves into the rear of the building, blocking the exit completely, their collective grunts and groans a wretched cacophony which, all things considered, was music to my ears. Especially once I heard the banging coming from within the disco. "Take that, assholes!" I hollered as I put one hand in front of the other and slowly—seriously, slowly—crawled away on my belly.

Not a pretty picture, but at least I was safe.

Just me. All alone now. *Ugh*, one final time.

CHAPTER 12
HER NAME WAS LOLA

I managed to right myself by using the stairs to a nearby building, then teetered as fast as my rickety legs could carry me back to the golf cart. Thankfully, if such a word was even still possible by that point, neither Blondella nor any of her henchzombies had made it there yet, and so I was home-free. Minus the home. And the only thing I was free of was my one true love and my one true friend. And all because I had the bright idea of returning to the scene of the crime, which, even after seeing countless episodes of *CSI*, I should've known better than to attempt.

In any case, with a torrential flood of sadness gushing through me, I drove away from the disco. I didn't have a plan for rescuing Dara and Ricky, nor one for defeating Blondella and saving the Libetians and my minions back in Utah. My only plan, in fact, was to come up with a plan, and, to be quite honest, I sort of always relied on Dara for that sort of thing. Two heads, in fact, were better than one, especially when one of those heads was mine.

I stopped the golf cart once I was far enough away. I sat there praying for an idea, but nothing was coming to me. All I had was love to keep me going, Dara's voice inside my head, the image of her bolstering my ever-dwindling confidence. She was, in fact, what kept me sane these past few hundred years. Without her, I was lost. Everything, in fact, was lost: all of humanity, what little of it remained.

And then, at last, I had an idea, knew what would win the day.

"Love," I said, again with my foot on the gas.

As mushy as it sounded, love was, as I'd told Ricky when we first met, the one true constant in a world where quite literally everything had changed. What I found with Dara was that connection. With love, anything could happen. I smiled as I zoomed (at ten miles per hour) down the block, "Multiply love by two, and who knows what could happen."

Now then, I'd been to New York before and had a rudimentary understanding of the layout: where the landmarks where, where north and south and east and west was, and what major arteries got you to where you needed to be. For the time being, I was still in Queens. I knew that if I took the Long Island Expressway, I'd end up in Midtown Manhattan. Then it was a straight shot to Broadway. To love. To Lola.

And if anything could save the day, it was two humans, even long dead ones, trying to save their mates. Good over evil. Brains over, well, Blondella. And she had said that she wouldn't kill them, just let the salt run out, which, to be quite honest, was a fate worse than death. But would she stay true to her word on that? Of course, I hadn't a clue. All bets were off when it came to the likes of her. Still, without help, I didn't even have a chance.

So, yes, I began my search for Lola. I had, after all, promised just that to Ricky; I was simply doing it a tad earlier than expected. And if I couldn't find her? Well, you don't get anything in life, or death for that matter, without at least trying.

***

Ten minutes later, I'd found the exit for the expressway. It was then that the golf cart proved invaluable. Mainly because, a few hundred years earlier, all traffic, everywhere, had come to a complete standstill, and the only way for me to drive was to veer between the long-dead cars. The long-dead drivers were, of course, still in them, staring dead, as it were, ahead. Sad, I know, but I'd long ago come to grips with how the world was now.

I gazed forward, never looking directly left or right, waiting for the New York skyline to poke its formidable head up. Lord knew how long it took, what with me going at the cart's full power, which, like my own, was meager at best, but eventually the skyscrapers appeared, growing taller and taller as I puttered steadily along, deathly silence everywhere save for the sound of the tires on the road and the voice in my head telling me to keep going.

Strangely, or maybe not, said voice was Dara's.

The expressway ended and Midtown began. Here, unfortunately, I was in trouble. See, the expressway had been wide enough for me to maneuver through, but thousands upon thousands of cars all stalled in the city, well now, there was just no way for me to drive between them.

I groaned as I gazed into the maze of traffic, though not nearly as loudly, of course, as the throng of undead on all sides, milling everywhere, also blocking my path. I looked left and right and up and down seeking a solution. I managed the slightest of grins as I repeated the process, my head frozen in the up position, because though I was in a golf cart, yes, it was a security golf cart. In other words, there was a motorized speaker system welded to the top of the vehicle.

My grin widened as I took the transmitter into my hand and pressed the button on the side. "Um, any requests?" I asked. "Some Barbra might be nice, yes?" Now, wouldn't you know it, but my voice boomed out in all directions and every last zombie in the reach of it promptly froze, still and lifeless as mannequins. It was the effect I'd always had on them, ever since the beginning of all this, except magnified now by the speaker and magnified even further than that by the steel and concrete buildings that bounced my voice hither and yon. "Move off the sidewalk!" I bellowed. "Now, bitches!" I gazed down at the metal in my hand. There was a repeat switch near the top. I hit it. *Move off the sidewalk! Now, bitches!* It played and replayed, over and over again.

In other words, I now had free reign on the sidewalk, me and my lowly, weather-beaten, marina security golf cart chugging along, nothing in our path now, the undead lifelessly staring my way from the sidelines as I rode by. I gave them all a queenly wave as I made my way toward my destination, hand held up high, flicking right and left.

In a few minutes, I was on 42nd Street, zooming (ish, as usual) past Grand Central Station, the building just as it had been several hundred years earlier, still central, though far less grand, seeing as the trains and buses were way (seriously way) late. Next on my city tour was the New York Public Library. I frowned as I stared up at the great expanse of it, all wasted now, seeing as reading was no longer fundamental. In fact, the only thing fundamental was finding a woman I'd never met before for a man I'd only met just recently to save a drag queen who was my whole reason for being.

Bryant Park came and went, the grass and the trees severely overgrown, wild, jungle-like. And then, soon enough, there I was: Times Square. I pictured Mary Tyler Moore throwing her hat up into the air. Would *I* make it after all? In any case, everywhere I looked, the lights were off, the usual sound of cars and horns and people, save for my speaker on repeat, long vanished, the joy, the spectacle of it all, gone as well. It was a ghost town, except that the dead people all around me, everywhere, had failed to give up said ghosts.

I didn't hang around there except to take one final, long look at it, trying to remember what it had felt like so many years earlier to stand there in that spot. I smiled because, of course, like everything else in my head, the memory was easily accessible. The last time I'd been there was with the girls, just before a show, Blondella included. And then my smile promptly vanished. "Stupid bitch," I muttered, revving the golf cart yet again.

I turned up 7th Avenue, the zombies parting in my wake, then over to 44th Street, the Shubert Theater just ahead now. It had taken many hours to drive barely fifteen miles, but at last I was there.

"Please, Lola," I said, just beneath my breath. "Please be here." I managed to make the sign of the cross over my chest, then a Jewish star as well, barely missing a couple of the end points. I wasn't sure what the signs for Buddha and Allah were, so I merely ended my praying with hands clasped and held heavenward.

I then pulled the cart in front of the building. Apart from the dusty, cracked sidewalk, it looked as it had the last time I'd been there, aged but no worse the wear. The cities had fared well over the centuries, the buildings meant to last. In the towns outside of my salt factory, the wooden homes hadn't weathered as well, most of them rotted out, gaping with holes or crashed-in altogether, taken over by the grasses and trees that returned around the same time that the rains had. But here, here in the city, especially if you were looking up, it seemed that no time had gone by.

I stood in front of the theater, the posters out front so sun-bleached that it was impossible to make out what they had once said. Even the sign on the marquee was gone, beaten into submission by time. I squinted up. "I know just how you feel," I said to the nonexistent sign, because I too had very nearly been beaten into submission.

I paused as my hand reached for the front door. This was it. All or nothing. If she wasn't there, if she couldn't help me, then Dara and Ricky would more than likely turn back to their zombie forms and be released from their discotheque prison into yet another prison, with no chance of a parole.

I pushed the door open, then breathed a forced sigh of relief as it gave. I stepped inside the lobby. The only light was that which filtered through the filthy windows, plus a few cracked ones. I hadn't counted on the darkness. My salt factory, the disco, they had power. I'd rarely stepped into any place else since the sun went all solar-screwy on us. The darkness, the stillness, was creepy, eerie, bleak.

Squinting into the dim light, I spotted a mere few milling zombies. Still, there was noise, and lots of it, coming from behind the doors to the inner-theater. I knew what that meant. There must've been a matinee going on when everyone was turned. Which meant that hundreds and hundreds of undead lay beyond, all trapped in their seats or shuffling around in the pitch-blackness.

Just then, a zombie walked by. Like many of the midday theater goers, this one was old when he undied, a man with a walking stick still gripped in his hand.

"Stop," I said to him. He froze in mid-shuffle. "Drop the cane." He tried, he really did, but his hand had been locked like that for too long. In other words, he needed some help. From, *yuck*, me. "Sorry," I said as I wrenched each finger loose from the wood, the sound of popping knuckles and cracking bones almost too much to bear. Still, eventually, the cane went from his hand to my own. "Um, thanks much." He didn't reply, just stared into the oblivion. "Guess your intermission went on a bit longer than expected, huh?" I got a groan for my troubles. Hard to tell if it was for my dark sense of humor or not. I was going with the latter.

In any case, after that, I found some loose rags behind a nearby bar. I stared longingly at the vast array of dusty gin and vodka and tequila bottles before wrapping the rags around the end of the cane. Had I been able to drink, without the consequence of promptly exploding from within, I would've gladly glugged every last bottle. Because three hundred years of forced sobriety was, to be quite honest, cruel and unusual punishment.

After that, I dribbled some vodka on the rags, fired up my ocular beams, and, voila, instant torch. The fire felt warm against my cold flesh, though even that was muted by the death that constantly enveloped me. I paused, then moved to the theater doors. This wasn't going to be nice. No way, no how. I mean, outside was one thing, and one bad thing at that, but a room chock-full of zombies, thousands of them, confined, was sure to be nasty. No, wait. *NASTY*. That's more like it.

And, yes, I wasn't disappointed. Or, better yet, yes I was. Big time.

I swung the door open and was very nearly overcome by the stench of them, by the sound of them, by the utter darkness that filled the huge void within, stretching far beyond the light of my makeshift torch.

"Silence!" I shouted, my voice echoing out in all directions, the acoustics in the theater, not surprisingly, first-rate.

The moans and groans abruptly stopped. Too bad the heady aroma of death and decay kept coming. And coming. Until my nose felt like it was fairly melting off of me. "If anyone has some Binaca, now would be a good time to use it." I waited. "No? A Tic Tac? Altoid? Anything?" Still nothing. Oh well. At least they were an attentive lot. And a drag queen simply adores a rapt audience.

I looked at my flame. It was already starting to flicker and die. This was my chance. No way was I going any further into the cavernous crypt if I didn't absolutely need to, and so, with face tilted up, I bellowed, "If your name is Lola, um, *groan*, please." In an instant, I heard it coming from the stage, one deep, rumbling growl that made my very bones shake. "Lola," I whispered. "Thank God." I stared ceilingward. "Sorry it's been so long. Guess I've had little to be thankful for as of late."

Still, the groan had come from the stage. Me, I was barely inside the theater. And no way could she see, let alone climb down any steps to get to me. If there was a back door, it was sure to be locked, so that wasn't an option either. Which meant that I had to go and get her, in a densely-packed theater full of stinking zombies, and, in mere minutes, in the pitch black, unless I lit and relit the torch until we were both back outside. And Lord, thanked or not, knew how long that would take.

"What to do, what to do," I lamented. And then, in a burst of inspiration, I thought of another option. This was, after all, a theater. Not a music theater, mostly, at least not the sort that played my kind of music, but the concept was the same. Meaning, this could work: "Everyone that still can, stand up. Those in the front of the theater, move to the edge of the stage."

Now then, if the sound of one old man's hands popping and creaking and crunching was almost too much to take, imagine if you will the sound of hundreds upon hundreds of long-unused legs and laps and knees straightening as one. Satan himself would've cringed at what followed.

"Everyone in the audience, lift your hands up!" I hollered next, my voice echoing out in all directions, before I added, "Now, Lola, walk to the front of the stage and fall backward." I couldn't see if she'd done what I said, but I assumed her rigid body was now prone, lifted high above the undead audience in a truly gruesome sort of mosh pit. "Okay, everyone who comes in contact with a zombie above your heads, pass her to the back of the theater." I grinned. "And no gropie-hands. The lady, after all, is married."

And so I waited there, as my torch dimmed and flickered and sputtered, whistling a happy tune, if only in my head. Then, fifteen minutes later, after lighting and relighting my flame, using a jacket I found in a nearby empty seat to replace the rags, there she was. Or, at least, there her back was. "Set her down," I instructed. "Gently."

Which was like telling an elephant to walk quietly. In other words, down the zombie hands went and down she fell, landing in a dull *thud* at my feet. I bent down, not easily, mind you, and helped her up, which was very nearly impossible, especially with one hand, seeing as my other hand was still carefully holding the torch. Because if I'd started a fire in there, it was impossible to tell which would make it to the front of the building first: it or me.

In any case, eventually, there she stood. "Lola," I whispered, the fire dancing across her face. Miraculously, she looked amazing. That is to say, without decades upon decades of wilting sunshine and other various elements forever beating down upon her, she looked much like she had, I assumed, at the time that death took a front row seat. Oh, sure, she was a bit gray and certainly dusty, but, even given all that, she was, to be quite honest, rather lovely. For a long-dead zombie, I mean. "A pleasure to make your acquaintance, Madame." I bowed, or at least tried my best to.

For her part, and par for the fucking course, she stared into the nothingness and groaned. And so I took her hand in mine and led her from the theater and into the lobby, returning forthwith to the bar. Luckily, there was a full canister of iodized salt still sitting there, unopened, pure as the day it'd been packaged.

I snuffed the fire out in the sink, grabbed the salt and led us outside onto the sidewalk. The sun was fading by that point, her face lit up in the pink and red of a promising sunset. In three hundred years, I hadn't seen a zombie such as her, preserved as she was by utter darkness, very nearly human in appearance, or at least as close as any of us was ever going to get. Had my breath not be taken from me so long ago, it would've been knocked out as I stood there gazing upon her.

"Ricky is a very lucky man," I said, hoping beyond hope that I could still use the word *is* and not have to change it to *was* in the very near future.

After that, I led her back to the golf cart and tried my darndest to get us both seated, or at least inside enough without the risk of being flung to the pavement. I then looked for a spot that was relatively zombie-free. I found it in a small nearby park, behind a fence. Like everywhere else where the grass and the trees managed to come back to life, after the drought that occurred post-solar-flare, this place was overgrown, a forest nestled in front of a bleak steel and concrete backdrop.

I walked us to a slight clearing in between two ancient oaks. The zombies in the distance could still be heard, but at least muffled now, like the hum of a great machine buried deep within a factory. Again I looked at her, her face cast in shadow, the sky turning a brilliant purple and pink. "Tilt your head back, Lola," I commanded. "Mouth open as wide as you can get it."

She was shorter than me by far, so I wouldn't have needed the funnel my minions usually used on us. She simply tilted and I simply poured, the salt cascading down her gullet until I was certain she had the proper dosage. I then did my best to dump a good bit down my own throat, just to be on the safe side.

"Mouth closed, Lola," I told her. "Head facing me." Again she did as I asked. And then I waited, eyes wide, watching intently, waiting for the inevitable. "Lola, can you hear me? Lola?" My body was abuzz as I stood there. Even though I hated doing this, hated bringing someone back, with her it somehow felt different, promising in fact. "Lola?" I said, yet again, softer this time.

At last she blinked, coughed, blinked again. A cloud of salt particles puffed through the air, glittering in the soft light of dusk like tiny floating diamonds. "What . . . what happened?" she croaked out.

I nodded and smiled, even if it was only for her sake. "You're okay, Lola. Everything is okay." Which was about as far from the truth as you could get. Like quoting the *National Enquirer.* Or Fox News.

Again she blinked. She clearly knew that everything was not okay. She had a memory, that much I knew from experience, even if it came to her in fits and starts, more like a dream than anything else. "Who . . . who are you?"

"Creature," I replied.

"Who," she repeated. "Not what."

Ouch. "No, that's my name. Creature Comfort. I'm friends with your husband, Ricky . . . er, um, *Lester,* I mean."

Again she blinked. "Lester." She suddenly looked panicked, as if she was remembering what had happened to her. Though, really, what could she know, trapped for centuries in the dark of a theater? "Is he . . ."

Dead? Alive? Was there really a difference for us? She couldn't put a word to what we were. After all, it was a hard concept to digest. And so I chose for her. "Cognizant? Yes. But still dead, like us." I nodded, ruefully. "I'm sorry, Lola. The whole world, or just about the whole world, is dead(ish). Except, you and me, Lester even, for now, we're, like I said, cognizant." I lifted the salt canister up for her to see. "Thanks to this."

She ignored the cure I was holding. "For now?"

Figures she would latch on to that. "Well, um, yeah, you see, there's an evil zombie bitch holding him captive in a disco in Queens," I replied so sheepishly that I almost said *baa* at that end of it all.

Again she blinked. "That's . . . a lot . . . to take in." The blink repeated again as she stared around at the jungle that surrounded us. "All of it." She then looked back my way. "And you're here to—"

I interrupted her. "To find you."

"Took you long enough."

I grinned. "I only recently found out about you. In fact, up until a couple of days ago, I didn't even know Lester. In fact, up until a few days earlier than that, me and my husband, Dara Licked, who's also captured in the same disco, were living, pardon the word, in a salt factory in Utah, before an island of drag queens reached out to us to help them defeat the evil bitch in said disco holding said husbands captive."

She didn't reply. I guessed she was trying to process it all. Good luck with that, I figured. "Your *husband*, Dara?"

I nodded. "You do seem to sink your hooks into the oddest parts of what I'm saying."

"It's all odd, though."

My nodding amped up a notch. "True, but, to be fair, the whole world is odd now." I pointed to the forest around us. "Case in point: this used to be a park."

Her nod suddenly echoed mine. "And I used to take coffee breaks here." Again she looked around. "And the sound, the hum at the periphery?"

My nodding and my grin promptly ceased. "Zombies. Millions of them. Everywhere. But at least they only eat humans, not other zombies, and they all heed my commands, except for the ones that heed the commands of the evil bitch, Blondella."

"Uh huh," she replied. "At least." She tilted her head. "Blondella? Does everyone have strange names now?"

"Long story," I replied, the grin quivering again. "Your husband, in fact, well, we call him Ricky."

"Ricky?"

My nod made a triumphant reappearance. "Ricky Shea."

She snorted. "My husband, the doctor, is going by the name *Ricky Shea*?" The snort repeated. "Happily?"

And now I shrugged. "More like resignedly, but still."

She sighed. It was probably the last bit of air still in her lungs. I envied her that. "So, if we don't rescue my husband, *Ricky*, and your husband, Dara?"

I pointed past the trees. "Without the salt, they'll turn back. And she'll release them. And, more than likely, we'll never see them again." I returned my hand to my side. "And then Blondella will kill all the remaining humans and be the queen of the zombies for all eternity, or at least until the radiation that keeps us animated runs out."

"I'd say I was dreaming, but I have a feeling that that's no longer possible, right?"

"Sorry."

This time the sigh was forced, as it would be from here on out, for the rest of her, well, *life*. "So why do you need me then? Why not just command an army of zombies to go rescue them? Why not find all the salt in New York City, bring a thousand people back and take my husband and your husband from her? Wouldn't a thousand thinking, uh, *people* find that easy enough to accomplish?"

I held her hand and moved us out of the clearing. In a minute, we stood behind the fence, watching the parade of zombies as they trudged past, hundred and hundreds in every direction, the constant groan instantly jarring. "You listed two points, Lola. If I did the first one, if I commanded an army to attack, then she would just do the same, until the streets were littered with bodies and we'd be no closer to rescuing our husbands." I pointed to the throngs. "These *things* are slow, unthinking, unfeeling. If we started a war, it would take days to reach a conclusion. By then, Blondella would more than likely be long gone."

"And the second point?" she asked. "Bringing back a thousand zombies to, well, to this state we find ourselves in? Wouldn't you at least have an army, perhaps to help find our husbands should they be released?"

I squeezed her hand tighter in my own and frowned. "If I don't give you more salt in about a week's time, you'll revert back, Lola. I've given you, for lack of a better word, *life*. How could I forgive myself if you didn't get the salt? How could I send you back to . . ." Again I pointed to the undead all around us. "To *that*." I looked back her way. "You're my responsibility now, Lola. As is Lester. As is Dara. As are the few minions I have with me in Utah. All of them. All of you. Forever."

She nodded her head, slowly. She understood. "So what do we have to do?"

I grinned and scrunched my shoulders up. "Beats the hell out of me."

"You're joking."

I grinned. I couldn't help myself. "Not without tips. In any case, you're my Plan A and my Plan B. In truth, it's fairly miraculous that I thought to come and get you in the first place *and* that I found you."

I looked her way and winked. "So, tag, you're it."

She rubbed her temples. "You're giving me a headache."

My smile spread. "Yeah, I get that a lot. Even if it is technically impossible."

"Tell that to my head, Creature," she retorted. "Because it doesn't seem to have gotten the memo."

CHAPTER 13
THE PLAN

The moon was high in the nighttime sky by the time we made it back on to the expressway. During our drive, I filled her in on what the world was like now, plus my world in particular, seeing as my world pretty much encompassed all that was left. She remained fairly silent throughout the retelling. Probably from shock, I assumed. After all, this shit was fairly shocking, even for me, and I'd lived (sort of) through it.

"So, not only do we need to rescue our husbands," she said, once my recounting had fully recounted, "but also we have to vanquish this drag queen bitch of yours."

"Vanquish?" I said, with a chuckle. "Good word for it. Very theatrical."

"Comes with the territory. Me being in the theater, and all. Trapped in it, really. For three hundred years." She groaned, and not the typical zombie groan either. This one came from a much deeper place.

"Again, sorry, Lola."

She nodded. "I know." She then turned my way as I slowly wove between the cars. "Is this *life* we have now any better, though."

I pointed at all the zombies trapped in all their various long-dead cars. "Probably."

She also chuckled. "Oh goodie. I always did so like a definite maybe."

I patted her back. "Want to know the bright side?"

"Really? There is one?"

I shrugged. "Dim, but sure."

She turned and looked my way. "Shoot."

I quickly glanced her way. "You're easily the prettiest corpse on the entire planet."

She coughed as she laughed. "Thanks, I needed that."

My shrug remained. I forced it to uncinch. "No, seriously. You barely look dead at all. You're sort, of, well, locked in place. Take away the gray and a few purple veins and you could pass for a human."

"Gee, Creature," she replied. "That's the . . . *oddest* thing anyone's ever said to me." She then slapped her hands on the dashboard. "That's it!"

I stopped the cart. It came to a screeching halt. "What's it?"

"The plan," she replied.

"We don't have a plan, Lola."

Again she slapped the dashboard, then my arm. "No, we *didn't* have a plan. Now we do."

"You lost me," I freely admitted. "What does your being a pretty corpse have to do with anything?"

"This Blondella, she sounds like the bitch of all bitches, vain, egotistical, narcissistic."

"Yes, yes, and yes," I agreed. "Narcissus, in fact, would seem modest standing next to Blondella. Narcissus would cower at her Manolo Blahniks."

"Exactly."

I grunted. "Still lost. Sorry."

She patted my hand. "We need to get in her good graces, trick her into thinking we can help her, then get her alone and lop off her head or something alone those lines. And if I'm pretty, even in death, what if we can promise her the exact same thing?"

"But we can't," I reminded her. "You're like this by nothing more than a shear fluke."

"But she doesn't know that."

"Huh," I huhed, the proverbial lightbulb at last flickering above my not so proverbial noggin.

"Yeah, huh," she huhed back. "It's like those miracle cures they sell—um, sold—on television: too good to be true, but something you'd fork over $49.99 for, in two easy installments, just in case."

I smiled at her ingenuity. "Melt belly fat with one pill a day, erase wrinkles with a laser wand, go from bald to bushy without expensive and painful surgery—"

"And return to your former human glory, all in the comfort of your own, uh, *disco*."

"Genius!" I shouted.

"To be fair, I sort of did two infomercials in between gigs once, but, yeah, I'll take it just the same. I might not have the best motor skills or much of a central nervous system anymore, but at least I can still put two and two together."

I counted in my head. "Four, right?"

Again she patted my hand. "Good, Creature." She then pointed, pardon the expression, *dead ahead*. "Now step on it! Our husbands aren't rescuing themselves!"

***

And so I stepped on it. Though, at ten miles per hour, it felt more like a tap. Still, we arrived, in the cover of darkness, back where I'd started. Or at least a block away, so that we weren't spotted. In fact, we stopped in front of a Walgreens.

We exited the golf cart. She zigged, while I zagged. "Why are you going in there?" she whisper-shouted. "I thought we were here to save our men."

I nodded and waved her back my way. "Just hedging our bets."

She followed me inside. The place was pitch black, but, luckily, the makeup counter was right at the front of the store. And so I grabbed a small metal basket, dumped a bunch of items I could barely see by the moonlight that managed its way through the windows, and we hightailed out of there. I then found a swatch of sidewalk where the moon wasn't blocked out by the buildings that surrounded us. It wasn't ideal, but it'd do.

"Um, not to sound unkind, Creature," she said, which was a sure-fire bet that unkindness was quick to follow, "but maybe do my makeup like you do your makeup, but, uh, by *half*." She squinted at my overly-shellacked pores. "Or maybe make that a quarter."

In other words, I'd been wrong before when I said that people didn't read anymore. Mainly because I'd just been read, big time.

I frowned as I nodded. "Less drag, more . . . *natural*?"

"You said it, not me."

"But you implied it."

She matched my nod with a placating smile. "Just go with a lighter touch, is all." She stared at my cache. "Just one or two of those. Not the whole kit and caboodle."

I laughed despite the sugarcoated put-down. "I used to know a drag queen by that name."

She tilted her head at me quizzically. "My turn, Creature: you lost me."

Again I laughed. "Kitten Caboodle. Did a whole routine with hand puppets and sparklers."

"An odd combination."

I shrugged and pointed at the two of us. "Sometimes, an odd combination is just what's needed."

She grinned as I started in on her Revlon makeover: light on the foundation, even lighter on the lipstick and blush, and heavy on the eyeliner. Because, come on, a little drama goes a long way. Plus, it brought out the blue in her eyes. At least that's what it looked like in the moonlight anyway.

"How do I look?" she asked, once I was through.

I gave her the once over, twice. "Like a living doll."

She giggled. "Emphasis on the living."

I giggled as well, but on me it sounded more like a steamroller grinding over gravel. Oh well. "She'll fall for it, hook, line and stinker."

"*Sinker*, you mean."

I shook my head. "Did you get a good whiff of that theater you were in?"

She groaned, clearly remembering said theater. "Got it. And, luckily, a sucker is born every minute. Or, in Blondella's case, dies."

"Exactly," I said, touching fingertip to nose. Or at least trying to. "Let's just hope that she's the only thing that dies around here. Or, um, re-dies. Unlives?"

See, stupid zombie verbiage.

***

Okay, so now that we had a plan, we needed a plan to help enact the plan. So, while I've said it before that the undead don't get headaches, I was beginning to second guess myself. Because this one was a doozie.

"I think I've got it," Lola said, the moon now on the other side of the sky, the promise of a new day already on the horizon.

I stared up at her. "Do we get to do some shopping?" She shook her head no, while I frowned, nodding resignedly just the same. "Okay, I'm listening anyway."

"Way to instill confidence, Creature."

I lifted my hands up into the air and whooped, "I'm listening!"

"Better," she said. "In any case, you're able to command the zombies because of imprinting, like you're the mother zombie goose and they're the baby zombie gooselings."

"Nice imagery."

"I try," she said, with a smile. "In any case, Blondella is able to do the same thing. Both of you are unique, both shining like beacons to the undead, like mothers to them."

"Mother fuckers is more like it," I grumbled. "At least in Blondella's case."

"Off the point," she chastised.

"Sorry," I apologized. "Please, do continue."

Her smile returned. "Right, so, what if there was a third leader, another person, if you will, that the zombies follow."

"You?"

She nodded "Me."

"But they don't," I told her. "They don't follow you. You're unique, but not in the same way that Blondella and I are."

"But she doesn't know that."

I scratched my head for effect. "But she will when the zombies don't obey you."

"Except that they will, if *you* tell them to."

That lightbulb of mine again sputtered to life, just as the sun on the horizon was doing the exact same thing. "Okay, I see your point now. Sort of," I said. "That would, in fact, draw her attention to you. Then what? She goes after you, tries to kill you too, and then I rescue the husbands?"

She slapped my arm. "No, Creature. No one is going to try and kill and/or rekill me."

"Unkill? Dekill?"

"Missing the point, Creature."

I shrugged. "Wouldn't be the first time."

She sighed or at least tried to. It took some practice, really. Three hundred years usually did the trick. "Remember, she's vain, and I have something she doesn't have, namely *natural* beauty. I can also lead the zombies, so I'm powerful. Now, what if I can promise her the former and, with the latter, we can lead together. Wouldn't she go for that?"

I nodded. "Yes." Then I shook my head. "No."

"Which is it?"

My shrug was still there from before, so it didn't have far to go. "She'd join with you only to try and trick you, to get your beauty secrets and then, to use your word, vanquish you."

"But not before we tricked her first, got on her good side, got inside the disco, rescued the husbands and killed her before she killed us."

"Sounds risky."

This time her sigh sounded right on the mark. Guess she didn't need all that much practice after all. Guess a few hours alone with me was tantamount to three hundred years, give or take. "Do you have a better idea?"

Heck, I didn't even have a worse idea. "Nope. But I do need a disguise first."

She pointed to the JoS. A. Bank store across the street from where we were standing. "And there you go."

"No way," I said, arms folded (at least halfway) over padded chest. That's a *men's* clothing store."

She gave me a what-the-fuck look. "And *you're* a man."

"Semantics."

"Which also has the word *man* in it. Which you are."

I shot her a no-fucking-way look in return. "No fucking way, Lola. Besides, what does *JoS* mean anyway? Sounds satanic, if you ask me." I pointed to the Betsey Johnson store next to it. "I vote for that."

Again she sighed. Damn, she was getting awfully good at that. "JoS. is short for Joseph, Creature."

I squinted her way and then at the store. "Pretty cheap, if you ask me. Three letters, just to save a few inches on their signage." Again I pointed to the store next to it. "Betsey Johnson was eighty trying to look twenty. It's a perfect disguise."

She put her hand on my shoulder. "No, a perfect disguise is dressing like a man. She'll never expect it."

This time my own sigh came easier. "Or recognize me."

She gave my shoulder a squeeze. "Ta da!"

Her face lit up. Mine sunk in on itself. In three hundred years, I hadn't worn guy drag. Life—what there was of it—was drab enough. Still, she had a point. In fact, she was pointing to the store, her squeezing hand pushing me toward it. "You don't have to shove."

She chuckled. "Don't I?"

Stupid theater folk, I thought; bitch knew her gay men all too well. And so in I trudged, shooing off the two undead store clerks before we perused the musty, dusty, beige and navy and gray men's clothes. "*Blech*," I wretched.

"It's not that bad," she cooed, her hands pushing through the racks of clothes when I no longer had the heart (figuratively speaking) to. "How about this outfit?" she asked a short while later, slacks and a button down and loafers held out for me.

"The heels are less than a half an inch high!" I protested.

"You're not helping, Creature."

In truth, I wasn't trying to. Still, Dara and Ricky needed me, and quickly, so I stopped my belly-aching (again, figuratively speaking) and got dressed. She had to help me, which was even more embarrassing, and then had to peel and pry and scrub and buff the makeup off my face, but eventually I was, *sob*, dressed like a boy.

"Did I already say *blech*?" I asked, both of us staring at my refection in the dusty mirror.

She nodded. "Yep."

"Can I say it again?"

Her hand was again squeezing my shoulder. "Pretend in your head that you're made up like Marlene Dietrich, like a girl dressing like a boy."

She was now pushing me through the front door. "Genius," I allowed.

"Yes, we've already covered that," she said, once we were again heading to the disco. "Now, amass the troops."

Standing in the middle of the street, with zombies trudging this way and that, I lifted my hands up to the sky and shouted, "If you can hear my voice, surround us!"

Suddenly, I knew what the cowboys felt like when the Indians were circling the wagons. Except that the Indians knew to keep a certain distance. "Too close," panted Lola, her fingers pinching her nose.

"Too close!" I shouted. "Everyone keep a foot or so between

146

each other and three from us."

It took a while for them to figure that one out, mathematics not being a zombie's strong point, but eventually we had a ring of about fifty or so of them around us, like an undead fortress wall.

"Now tell them to obey me," Lola said.

I nodded. "Whatever she says goes!" I looked her way and smiled. "Care to take a crack at it?"

Her smile mirrored mine as she glanced round and round. "Stop groaning!" she commanded.

And, wouldn't you know it, that's just what they did, a welcome silence enveloping the area around us. "Good job, Queen Lola." And a queen knows another queen when she sees one.

"But how long will my *powers* last?" she asked, squelching my smile in an instant.

"Hard to say," I replied.

"Try."

I squinted my eyes and thought of the last time I'd commanded zombies to do something, and ones that weren't the ones back home. "If I don't give them a booster shot of some sort, I'd say you have a good hour or so, give or take ten minutes. Then they'll simply wander off until I command them again. Moving forward, they'll only ever listen to me, which is how imprinting sort of works, I believe."

She grabbed my hand. "Then we better hurry."

And so, en masse, we hobbled toward the disco. Once we arrived, a swarming circle of us, we found that the building was now surrounded by guards, way more of them than before. Blondella, it appeared, wasn't taking any chances. Not this time.

"Tell your queen that she has company!" shouted Lola, at the dead (seriously dead) center of our group.

The largest guard, the one blocking the front door, who was, in fact, almost as large as the front door itself, moved an inch forward. "And who the fuck are you?" He was scary to behold (seriously, scary).

Lola put her hand to her chest and turned her face in profile. "I?" she projected. "I Am Lola Fontaine. *The* Lola Fontaine."

He eyed her, clearly unsure of how to respond. I was quite certain that his only job was to guard the door, presumably from me. But here was Lola, who, by all accounts, looked human. Had he even seen a human since his death/undeath? Doubtful, not unless he was used by Blondella on Liberty Island. And I doubted any of the traitors came to Blondella because you'd have to be one hell of a crazy-ass human to surround yourself with brain-hungry zombies. Heck, they even gave me the heebie-jeebies, and I'm one of them, give or take.

"Up the ante," I whispered her way. "Give him no choice but to go get her."

She nodded and again turned his way. "Tell Blondella that I know that she has accomplices on Liberty Island."

His eyes grew wider. This had to be secret numero uno, secret prime. "Wait here," he barked. "I'll see if the mistress is available."

I snickered as I stood there, scowling. "The mistress. Please, Mary. Give me a fucking break. Bitch is from Sacramento. Bitch shopped for her clothes on Amazon. Even her wigs were hand-me-downs." A head shake joined my snicker. "Mistress my stunningly perky ass."

"Calm down, Creature," Lola whispered back my way. "She can call herself the Queen of Sheba, just so long as she comes out here." She saw me seething and patted my arm. "Breathe and count to ten, sweetie." She realized the error in that and edited it down some. "Or just count to ten."

As it turned out, I only needed to make it to eight because Blondella appeared a moment later. "No!" she yapped, standing fifteen feet away.

"No?" Lola replied, looking utterly confused.

"I mean, no, it can't be," rephrased Blondella as she pushed her way through the crush of guards. "Lola Fontaine! *The* Lola Fontaine!"

I locked eyes with my newfound friend. "Do you really deserve that *the*?" I whispered.

She nodded. "Two-time Tony winner, Creature." She grinned. "Didn't you know?"

Blondella was suddenly barreling down upon us, or at least teetering at a relatively unsafe clip. "Not a clue," I whispered. "Congrats." I leaned in a little closer. "And play it up. Blondella's a total show queen."

She grinned, very mischievously. "Mhm, I know the type well."

And then Blondella was pushing and shoving our zombies aside until she was face to face with Lola. Me she didn't even notice. Then again, she'd so rarely ever even saw me out of drag that, in the clothes I was now in and with my face without makeup, let alone the ghastly shade of gray that it now was, it was beyond the realm of possibility that she could possibly recognize me. Of course, none of that mattered, really; her eyes were glued, locked, stapled and frozen to Lola.

"I can't believe you're here," she cooed. She then eyed Lola suspiciously, the bitch inside of her wrestling with and then promptly pinning the fan inside of her. "But what exactly *are* you?"

Lola held out her hand. "Lola Fontaine, star of stage, screen and numerous Lifetime movies, albeit in severely underrated roles."

Blondella nodded and shook the proffered appendage. "Severely, yes." She then smoothed out her too-tight dress and primped her too-high platinum wig. "And not *who* are you, but *what*?"

Lola's smile was bewitching. "Ah, what indeed. What do you *think* I am?"

Blondella craned in closer, eyes marveling at the stunning star in front of her, nose twitching, sniffing. "You're a zombie," she uttered. "But how?"

"You know the how," came the reply.

"No," said Blondella. "I mean, how do you look like you look? How are you cognizant? How do you control these . . ." She deigned to look at us bit players. "These *things*?"

I neglected to retort that it took one to know one. In fact, I neglected to even make eye contact with her. We were, after all, pushing our luck as it was with me just being so close to her. Because if she recognized me then all hope was lost. For everything and everyone.

Lola smoothed her hair back and nodded. "You're cognizant," she replied, then pointed at the guards behind her. "And you clearly control these *things*, so is it not entirely probable that there are others out there like you?"

Blondella squinted her eyes, clearly mulling the question over. "Fine, I'll give you that. The world is, or at least was, a large place. And if there's one of me, then it stands to reason there are more." She again closed the gap between them, the squint even squintier. "But what doesn't stand to reason is a zombie who looks human. Dead, after all, is dead."

Lola flipped her hand over and ran the back of her fingers against her smooth skin, smiling as she did so. Gave you goose bumps to see her, really. Or maybe dead-duck bumps, but still. "The Fountain of

Youth is closer than you can possibly imagine," she replied, ever so cryptically. She held out her dainty hand. "You know my name, by the way, but . . ."

My old and dear *friend* turned back to admiring fan. "Blondella," she informed, grabbing the proffered hand. "Blondella Bombshell."

Lola grinned, catlike. "Befitting. *Blondella.* I like it." The smile grew wider. "And I like you, too."

I could see Blondella fairly melt at the admission. "And I *love* you."

"How sweet of you to say," Lola practically purred. "So perhaps we can join forces, you and I." Before Blondella could protest or simply kill her outright, Lola added, "And I can then show you to this Fountain of Youth of mine, make you appear human again, as beautiful as you clearly were in life."

I forced back a snicker. Even in bar light and under twenty pounds of makeup, Blondella could barely boast statuesque let alone beautiful. Still, flattery, even in this zombie age of ours, could continue to get you everywhere. "Would you like to see my home, Miss Fontaine?" she asked in reply.

Lola nodded ever so slightly. "Please, call me Lola. All my friends call me that."

I grimaced. Ironically, or perhaps sadly, I was her only friend now, her husband's only friend as well, Dara's too. It was a lot of responsibility, all of it resting heavily on my iron-stiff shoulders. Still, there was little time to ponder this, what with Blondella suddenly leading us up to the building she now called home.

CHAPTER 14
SUPERQUEEN

"Welcome," said Blondella as she opened the door to the club, a ferocious beat instantly greeting our ears.

Up the steps we hobbled and inside we went, the water from my previous visit cleaned up, the overhead lights back on, swirling and gyrating as before. As for the music, it was very nearly intoxicating, especially considering the fact that what lay beneath was a constant groaning drone. Even Lola seemed impressed, but, then again, she'd already witnessed the alternatives.

Further inside we were led, pushing our way between the barely-animated bodies, not one of them appreciating the fine music that washed over them. Me, I ached to dance again or, better still, knock the head bitch down and go searching for my comrades. Neither, however, was an option at that very moment, at least not yet. And so I merely went with the flow. And the flow was quickly heading toward the kitchen, which meant to the elevator, which meant that we were now royally screwed.

"Darn," said Blondella, turning back our way with mock pity on her mock face. "There's only room for a couple of us in here. Your *friends* will have to stay down here and wait for you."

Lola, it seemed, forced her smile to stay put. "What's up there anyway?" she asked.

The elevator door opened. "My private quarters," she replied. "Only fully-aware zombies are allowed up there. Makes it, shall we say, homier."

Lola glanced my way, if only for the briefest of moments. I nodded at her, hoping that our hostess with the leastess hadn't noticed. Besides, as long as Lola kept her Fountain of Youth secret just that, a secret, I knew she was safe from harm. After all, the whole point of us being there was to lull the bitch into a false sense of security, the secret being what we were using to do the lulling. If that meant that the two of them needed to be alone together, so be it. Plus, with Blondella occupied, I could snoop, could potentially divide and conquer.

So, yeah, I nodded and, yeah, inside the elevator they went and, yeah, once again I was alone with a bunch of stinking—and I mean that quite literally—zombies. And, no, I was none too happy about it, despite all the plus-column items previously mentioned. Because two seconds alone with Blondella was two seconds too long, secret or no secret.

"But what choice do I have?" I said, aloud, nothing but groans reaching my ears in reply. "By any chance do you guys have a flip side to this album?" I waited for a reply that I knew would never come. "No? Okay then, guess I'll go check out the place instead, see if I missed something the previous times I was here." No surprises, they groaned in response. "Uh huh, same to you."

Outside the kitchen I went, emerging into the disco once again. Lady Gaga's voice filled the space, bouncing off the walls and inside my head. Surrounded by the beating pulse of it, I almost felt alive again, like my old self.

Fine, I knew I wasn't there to enjoy myself. I was there to find my husband and Lola's husband. And so I searched, but all I found beyond the enormous dance floor was the DJ booth, a couple of bars, a storage room that was filled with booze I could not drink and snacks I could not eat, the office Dara had been locked up in before, now empty, plus one locked room, the sign above telling me it was the coat check. Clearly, it seemed to me, Ricky and Dara were upstairs, which was the one place I couldn't go, not safely, not anymore.

Or so I thought.

As I leaned against a wall, staring out at the zombies that crisscrossed the floor, I spotted one I'd slashed during my earlier trip. Even I found it funny that hundreds of years had passed and, up until just recently, I hadn't a clue that I had Superqueen powers. Then again, I really hadn't a need for them before. I could, after all, control the zombies with the merest direct order; slashing and burning them seemed excessive, even to me—until the current circumstances deemed it necessary, that is.

And that put a new thought inside my addled brain: what else could I do with my radiation apart from cutting through leathery flesh?

"Can I fly?" Even if I could, right about then all I'd manage to do was slam my head into a ceiling, or worse, a spinning light array. I scratched my head, missing my wig all that much more all of a sudden. I turned. There was a huge speaker by my side. "Can I . . . *hmm* . . . can I lift heavy objects?" I placed my hands on either side of the speaker, made them rigid, vise-tight, then crouched, as much as physically possible, which wasn't much at all, then uncrouched. The speaker was right where it had been before, but I was certain that I'd done some serious damage to a few of my vertebrae. "Thank goodness for those dead nerve endings." Still, I was not to be deterred. "What else could Superman do?"

I flipped through the pages of the childhood comic books that resided inside my head, but, drag queen in training that I was back then, all I saw was Betty and Veronica up to no good. And the only super powers they had were to make Archie and Jughead pop boners—and then probably jack each other off, which was hot, but not getting me anywhere now.

That is until the comic books reached their last page or two, where the ads were placed that appealed to the nerdy kids who read them, like those Charles Atlas placements where the scrawny guy gets sand kicked in his face. And that's when it hit me, a super power I could in fact possibly, maybe, hopefully possess. Because those ads also promoted X-ray vision glasses, and what geeky kid wouldn't want those? Or what queen wouldn't? Or, better yet, what Superqueen? And what, exactly, where the X-rays made up of? Drum roll please . . . "Radiation." And radiation was something I had plenty of.

Again I turned to the speaker, the atoms somewhere deep inside of me bubbling up, that all too familiar snapping and crackling and popping rising, building, before . . . *POW! ZAP! ZAM!*

Now, I'm not sure what *ZAM!* is, but it slashed a nasty-looking gash right through the side of the speaker, the smell only minimally better than that of the company that surrounded me. "Too much *POW!* not enough *ZIP!*" I told myself as I started in on attempt number two. This time I willed the radiation to a lower level, the mental setting switched from ten to five. Again I felt the familiar sensation, but this time all I got for my troubles was a crackling noise, like static. Again, it was better than the sound the current company was making, but not what I was going for.

Attempt number three was a mixture of *POW!*, *ZAP!*, and *ZAM!*, but this go around I managed to modulate the three, forming, it felt like, a wave of some sort instead of a constant beam. I stared at the speaker, bombarding it with this new sort of ray that shot forth from my eyes.

"Whoa!" I yipped, with a grin. "Look at that!" Suffice it to say, the zombies around me ignored my outbreak, but me, I was looking. Boy howdy was I looking. In fact, I was looking at, in and through, could see every circuit and wire and nut and screw. "Superqueen has fucking X-ray vision!" Gaga was singing my praises overhead. It was a few hundred years too late, but I'd take what I could get.

I rubbed my hands together, happy as a, well, an undead clam as I walked to the door that I'd recently found locked. I probably could've blasted it with my max-ten ray, perhaps exploding the lock off altogether, but that would have, of course, called attention to myself. And so I went with option number two, my X-ray vision— take that Charles Atlas!—looking into the door rather than blasting through it. It took a few tries, but soon enough I could actually see inside, the contents of the room instantly revealed.

What I beheld were two sets of items. One side of the smallish room had stacks of boxes all filled with canisters of salt. That made sense. I mean, our enemy had minions, and they all needed salt to remain cognizant. As to the other side of the room, well, that gave me pause. I couldn't tell for certain I was seeing what I was seeing, basically because none of the boxes had markings, but, based on what was held inside them, which was some sort of powder, it looked like explosive devices.

"Is this what she has planned for Liberty Island?" I asked myself. "Is this what she was doing on the island before she was discovered, before her troops were annihilated?" That explained what she was doing there in the first place, apart from ensuring my inevitable arrival. I mean, it did seem to me like a fool's mission. And Blondella was lots of things (seriously, lots), but foolish wasn't one of them. Still, judging by what remained in the coat room, it appeared she hadn't finished with her mission before she'd been thwarted. Best guess, though, during the melee, the traitor Libetians managed to get a hold of some of this stuff, perhaps had even rigged the island with them already or perhaps had been rigging it all along, on the sly. "Not good," I lamented. "Not good at all."

I turned my head-beams off and looked back to the disco. Gaga had given way to Katy Perry—*yawn*—and my first foray, namely the coat room, had given way to my second, namely my search for Dara and Ricky. After all, I no longer required the elevator to take me to where I needed to be in order to look for them.

And so once again I shot my radioactive load, so to speak, this time up instead of out. It was difficult at first, because I had to adjust for distance and depth, to shoot through the ceiling and up to the next level, but with a few tries I was able to adequately see into the rooms above. The images weren't as clear as when I was looking a few feet ahead, but Superqueen being, well, *super*, I could still see what and, more importantly, who was in each of the rooms.

On the catwalk itself there were perhaps fifteen milling zombies, presumably cognizant minions, each waiting for their next command. I shifted my gaze. In one of the rooms, Blondella stood talking to Lola. Too bad I only had video and not audio, but beggars couldn't be choosers. And, at least, Lola appeared safe and in one piece.

I then shifted my head, the beam slicing through the wall and into the adjoining room, and there, thank God (really, THANK YOU, GOD!), were Dara and Ricky, both tied together and tethered to a table. They were alive—to use the word loosely—and apparently well. That is to say, their heads were still attached to their bodies and their mouths were moving in what seemed like a conversation.

I breathed—again, to use the word loosely—a sigh of relief. We weren't too late. Not yet. There was still a chance to rescue them, to thwart Blondella's plans, to return to Utah and save my minions. It was odd to think that, to desire to return to Utah, but we'll go with that whole beggars/choosers rationale again.

Sad to say, however, there was little time to celebrate my X-ray achievements. I saw their shadows a moment later as they reemerged onto the catwalk. Lola and Blondella were returning. And so I hotfooted it—rather coldly, of course—back to the elevator, staring blankly into space, waiting for their arrival.

Two minutes later, the elevator door parted and out they walked. "Follow me!" shouted Lola, our initial group springing to, um, *life*. She led and we followed, all of us pouring inside the DJ Booth,

Blondella, thankfully, not joining us.

"What gives?" I whispered, once we were again alone(ish).

"Welcome to our *sleeping* quarters," she whispered in reply. "We've been given sanctuary, at least for the time being."

I smirked. "You mean until she deems otherwise, right?"

"Presumably. But, for now, it seems we're in the blissful courting phase of our relationship."

"Mainly because she idolizes you," I couldn't help but say.

She shrugged, mostly. "Be that as it may, we're safe, for now."

My smirk turned smile. "As are our husbands."

She sucked in her breath, or at least made a valiant effort to. It came out, in fact, more like a grinding hiccup. "They're down here? You saw them? Did you speak to them? How's Lester?"

I patted her shoulder. "Calm down, sweetie," I told her. "They were in the room next to yours, not down here."

She tilted her head my way. "Um, huh?"

I turned my beams on, scanned her really quickly and replied, "Your dress is a size four, made in France and is dry clean only."

Her head tilted further. "Um, huh?"

"You said that already."

"Bears repeating."

I bowed, though about two inches was all I could muster. "Superqueen at your service, Madame."

"Not a clue what you're talking about," she admitted. "Plus, I'm a size two, Creature."

"Not what the tag on the back of your dress says."

It took her a minute to figure it out and, when she did, she covered up her boobs. "Stop that."

I grinned even wider. "Little good those hands do. I can see through walls now, ceilings even. Flesh ain't nothing to Superqueen." She dropped her hands. "Besides, they are rather lovely boobies." Her hands again flew up. "Are they real?"

She smacked me. "Next topic, please," she admonished. "And, yes, very, very *real.*"

"Fine," I told her, quickly filling her in on my newfound powers and the room full of explosives and Blondella's supposed ideas for world (what was left of it) domination. "As to that aforementioned next topic, any thoughts on our plan to trick the bitch and thwart said plan? I mean, we can't stay in her good graces forever, let alone this booth."

Her smile suddenly matched mine. "In fact, I have had thoughts on that matter and I've already shared them with said bitch."

"So quickly?" I asked, duly impressed. "How did you think of something in the scant few minutes you had?"

She winked. "You're the one who called me a genius. I was just driving the point home." She aimed her index finger at our cramped quarters. "Welcome home."

It was easy to see why Lola was a star. Even in death she radiated it, that hidden something that set her kind apart from the rest of the miserable world, from us lowly peons. Lucky Ricky, I realized, and even luckier me, now. "And this plan of yours?"

"The Fountain of Youth?"

I nodded. "Yeah, that."

She held her hands out in a *ta-da!* stance. "Sleep!"

I scratched my head. "To quote a genius I know, *um, huh?*"

"Tissue repair occurs only in sleep, Creature," she explained. "All living things require it. It allows cells to grow, to replenish themselves, to, as I said, repair."

I stared at her, lost as usual. "But we aren't *living things*. And, more importantly, we don't sleep." I pointed to my arm, to my tissue. "What you see is what you get. Forever."

"Really?" she asked, her smile quivering. "Forever?"

I shrugged. "No clue. But certainly a long, long, *really long* time. In any case, your secret, like Blondella's head, is full of holes."

"As you see it," she retorted.

"And how does she see it?" I asked.

"She sees it like I explained it to her, namely that I've found a way for us to sleep, to rejuvenate, to . . ." She ran her hands around her face. "To ultimately look like *this*."

"I'll say it again," I said again. "Genius." I paused before adding, "But that's the why, not the how. Because we really can't sleep, not anymore."

"And yet I look like this and, for all she knows, I did it by sleeping." Before I could question her further, she added, "Which I can train her to do, though it requires a great deal of practice, all of it alone, in peace and quiet. No groaning to distract her."

"Can I say it again?"

She snickered. "Genius, yeah. Yada, yada, yada. In any case, we can now get on her good side, trick her into thinking we're a team . . ."

"And get her alone, presumably away from the disco, away from her guards, and then kill and/or rekill and/or unkill the fuck out of her, pardon my French."

She snickered. "Right, so now we just need that first part, to get her alone."

"Before the salt runs out."

She paused. "*Whose* salt?"

"Ricky's," I repeated. "Dara's. Because if that happens in the meanwhile, and she releases them, and we're not there when she releases them, then all the fake sleep in the world isn't going to save them."

Her snicker turned like so much sour milk. "Any more monkey wrenches you feel like throwing our way?"

I mulled it over. "Nope," I replied. "That should just about do it."

"And how long do you think we have?" she asked. "Before said salt runs out?"

I shrugged. Kind of. Still, the point came across. "Couple of days, maybe three at most."

"Plenty of time."

My shrug remained. "In theory."

Her sour puss turned rancid. "You always this positive?"

"Sure, except when I'm stuck in a DJ Booth in the disco from hell," I quipped. "Otherwise, I'm all moonbeams and lollipops."

She stared out the window of the booth, zombies moving this way and that, Blondella nowhere in sight. "Yeah, I see you're point." She again glanced my way. "Two days then. That's what we'll shoot for. Two days to trick her, get her alone, and . . ." She made a slashing move across her pinkish gray throat. "Think we can do that?"

Since my shrug was now stuck in the up position, I replied. "Sure as hell gonna try."

She pointed out to the dance floor. "Well, we're in the right place for it," she grumbled. "*Hell*, that is."

I closed the gap between us and patted her shoulder. "You get used to it, you know."

She nodded, ever so slightly. "That's what I'm afraid of."

***

Then it was just a matter of formulating some strategy, which we did, just before Lola thought of something I had not. All things considered, that wasn't too surprising. All things considered, however, what she thought of was.

"So, let me get this, for lack of a better word, straight," she said. "You can use your radiation to cut through flesh."

"And speakers."

She grinned. "And speakers," she echoed. "And you can use your radiation like a sort of X-ray machine."

"Uh huh."

"And what else?"

"What else what?"

Her grin widened. "What else can you do? I mean, radiation, I'd imagine, is, or at least was, used for a lot of things, way back in the day."

"Such as?" I asked, curiosity strangle-holding my cat.

Her grin promptly flatlined. "I'm a Tony Award winning actress, Creature."

I squinted my eyes at her. "Yes, I believe we've covered that already. And?"

Her squint matched my own. "And I wasn't cast in the role of Madame Curie."

I chuckled. "Ah, so not so genius after all, huh?"

"Says the drag queen."

"Touché," I grunted in reply. "In any case, what you're getting at is that neither one of us has a master's degree in science, got it. But maybe it's simpler than that. Maybe it's something basic, something we can glean from our past."

Her squint went squintier. "Our past? Too bad I left my yearbook at home then."

"No need," I informed. "See, when you, well, um..."

She gulped. Or at least tried to. "*Died?*"

I nodded. "Yeah, that. When you did that, all the cells in your body, in your brain, sort of froze. In other words, all your memories are retrievable. In fact, it's pretty easy. Just try and think of a memory and, *poof*, it's there." I grinned. "And the poofter knows poof."

She managed a nod, her squint turning to eyes shut tight. "Huh, I can see it."

"What?"

She smiled now. "My wedding day. Clear as day." Her eyes popped open. "Neat."

"Now go back further. Sort of like scrolling through a Rolodex," I told her. "Stop on a card that might hold a clue as to what else I can possibly do with my radiation."

Again she closed her eyes. "Okay . . . going back . . . going back . . . no, no, not that . . . *hmm* . . ."

"*Hmm*, what?"

And again her eyes popped open. "Before I made it to Broadway, I used to work at a radio station, behind the scenes, but I did pick up a rudimentary understanding of how everything worked."

"Lucky you," I said. "Before I was a drag queen, I worked at The Cheesecake Factory. So I have a rudimentary background in how to make an oversized salad with a monumental fat content."

She didn't seem impressed. Oh well. "Right. In any case, radio waves are, if memory serves, some sort of electromagnetic radiation."

"*Ding, ding, ding,*" I chimed. Then I paused. Then I contemplated. "Lost me."

"Then why did you *ding?*"

"You said radiation," I replied. "After that came the lost thing."

She rubbed my cheek with her index finger. "Well, at least you're pretty."

"Really?"

She stopped rubbing. "In any case, back to the radio. What if you can transmit?"

"Nice deflect."

She grinned. "You're welcome. In any case, you already told me that you could modulate the radiation inside of you, which allowed you to go all Superqueen. What if you could modulate it again, create some sort of radio wave instead of an X-ray."

"Fine," I allowed. "Then what?"

"Then we talk to our husbands, fill them in our plan, let them know that we're out here trying to save them," she replied. "A little bit of hope goes a long way, you know."

She had me there. "Maybe I should practice first then."

She nodded. "Yes, but on a zombie, not me. Just in case you screw up and slice a hole in my money-maker." She ran her hand around her beautiful face as she said this.

"Good point." And so I pushed the radiation up from its core, the atoms bursting from some deep, hidden place. I looked at a zombie in the rear of the booth, adjusted the speed and strength, and then let go. *Lift you right arm*, I said inside my head, transmitting the thought. Sadly, he didn't budge. Groaned, yes, budged, no. I tried again. This time, I got some singed flesh and a nasty whiff of death for my efforts.

"Thank goodness this is only practice," said Lola.

"Well, you're welcome to try then," I told her.

She sighed. Or at least grunted, but still. "I have been. I've tried both your tricks, but I can neither slash through anything nor see through anything. I tried and tried, and nothing. It must be something about you, perhaps the fact that you've been cognizant for so long. Maybe you're in better control over your body as a result. Maybe in a few hundred years I'll be able to master it. But, for now, everything is resting on you."

My eyes went wide. "Gee, no pressure, Lola."

She pointed to the zombie. "Just keep trying."

Which is what I did, turning some inner unseen knob this way and that. Perhaps, just as Lola had said, it really did take a few hundred years to be able to do what I was doing. And also perhaps that's why I didn't know about my powers until now, or maybe, like I thought, I just didn't need to see through walls or make zombies lift their appendages before. In any case, eventually the zombie did indeed lift its right arm, apparently hearing my transmission.

"Amazing," said Lola. "But can you hear him in reverse?"

I shook my head. "The him in question doesn't think, doesn't transmit. So I'll, uh, have to practice on you next."

Again her eyes went squinty. I mean, here I was, a zombie she just barely knew, asking permission to access her head and, perhaps, screw up and radiate her into oblivion. "You sure about this?" she asked, hesitantly.

"Nope."

She cringed. "Can you get sure, please?"

Again I nodded. "Okay. I'll try. The setting seems to be locked in already. All I have to do is push." I forced a smile. "Ready?" Now it was her turn to nod. "Three, two, one . . ." I pushed and willed my thought her way. "Contact?" I asked, inside my head.

Her face lit up like the Fourth of July. "I can hear you," came the reply. "Can you hear me?" I gave her the thumbs up. "Good, now get the fuck out of my head and pardon my own damned French."

I laughed and flicked the power off, feeling the burbling deep within simmer before dropping down to normal—which was a strange use of the word, I admit. "Weird," I said.

"Tell me about it." She then pointed ceilingward. "Now to tell the husbands."

My smile, like my inner juice before it, flickered. "But what if my transmission is wider than we think? What if I aim it that way and Blondella picks up on it? Then not only are we back to square one, but also, and more than likely, gonna be buried beneath it. And we might've cheated death once as of late, but twice is highly unlikely. Fool death once, shame on you; fool it twice and it kicks your mother effin' ass.

"Good point," she allowed. "But I'm scheduled to meet with her shortly, to start our sleeping lessons. I'll make sure to keep some bit of distance between us and you and us and the husbands. Plus, if she hears anything, I'm sure I'll be able to tell. Mainly because she'll probably kill me in a, to use the word loosely, *heartbeat*."

I grinned, despite the implication. "Lola, you always this cool under pressure?"

And then she grinned. "A cucumber ain't got nothing on me, pal. Besides, what choice do I have?"

"Exactly," I allowed, none too happily. "So I guess we wait until the *mistress* calls upon you then."

She pointed through the glass and out to the dance floor. Blondella's platinum beehive was already weaving our way. "Show time," she murmured, just beneath her breath.

Suddenly, I prayed that those two Tony Awards were for acting and not set design.

CHAPTER 15
GONE, BUT NOT FORGOTTEN

Lola exited, stage right, and I was left to do my one-man show. I waited until I could no longer spot them, knowing that Lola had made sure to keep as much distance as possible between us and the queen bitch. I then hobbled out of the DJ booth and made my way to just below the catwalk and as close to the husbands as I could get. Meaning, I wasn't taking any chances when it came to my newfound and sketchy-at-best powers.

As soon as I was well-situated, I powered up my X-ray vision and sent it beaming. Again I found Dara, same spot, staring at the door and looking rather forlorn. I then modulated the radiation, as I'd done in the DJ booth, one wave instantly replacing another. "Earth to Dara," I transmitted. "Come in. Over."

I could no longer see her, now that I'd switched one power off to turn the other on, but I could, in fact, hear her. "Oh shit. Now I'm hearing things. They say that sanity is the first thing to go."

I chuckled. "As if you had much of that to begin with."

"Bitch," came the reply.

"And amen to that."

I heard her laugh inside my head. "Are you dead, my love? This some sort of spirit world trick?"

"I was already dead to begin with, Dara. So, no, no trick. Radiation leak is more like it," I replied. "I'm a Superqueen now."

The harmonious laughter returned. "And you're using your powers for good instead of evil? Now there's a switch. Did hell freeze over, oh wifely husband of mine?"

"Nope, just my heart," I retorted. "In any case, this thing you're hearing is sort of like a radio wave. Short distance."

"How short?"

"Hmm, maybe fifteen feet. Directly, give or take, below you."

She sucked in her breath, if only in her head. "Won't you be spotted?"

"And in boy drag," I amended with.

Again she laughed. "Will *I* even recognize you then?"

"To hear it told, I'm quite handsome this way."

"Says who?" she was all too quick to reply with.

"The wife of the man you're tethered to. One Miss Lola Fontaine."

"*The* Lola Fontaine? That's Ricky's wife? No fucking way." He paused, if only momentarily. "Wait, how did you know we're tethered together?"

"Long story, sweetie. In any case, we're here, we're queer, or at least one of us is, and we're coming for the both of you. Just try and keep the zombie inside of you at bay as long as possible."

She sighed, again if only in her head. "Easier said than done, hon," she replied. "I can feel it already. It's not too far off. It's like the sands in my hourglass are running out, just a handful of grains remaining. Ricky said it's the same for him, too. In other words—"

"Hurry, I know," I transmitted, quite literally finishing her train of thought.

Sadly, as to the hurry part, we had a limiting factor to contend with, and when it came to her, namely Blondella, hurrying was out of our control. In fact, we didn't even know if we could get her alone, let alone kill and/or unkill her once we did. Plus, I had no say in the matter. Heck, I truly had no say, period. Far as Blondella was concerned, I was nothing but an unthinking, unfeeling minion. Still, Lola had a plan, and between the star and the bitch, I was putting my money on the former.

In any case, the star herself reappeared an hour or so later. She found me where she'd left me, inside the booth, dancing alone in a dark corner. Yes, our loved ones were in peril, but if I was going to die and/or undie and/or redie, then at least I was going to get one last twerk in. Though, yes, my twerk needed some work.

"You okay?" she asked, upon seeing me. "Do zombies have seizures?"

I threw her a smirk as I worked on my twerk. "*That* was dancing."

"If you say so," she replied. "Any luck with the hubbies?"

I nodded. "They're in on the plan. Any luck with Blondzilla?"

She tilted her head. "Nes."

I tilted mine. "That a showbiz word?"

"Nes," she repeated. "No and yes."

"Which is it?"

Her head untilted, though it took a considerable amount of effort. "Yes, we practiced sleeping, out back, outside the disco—"

"Terrific!" I yipped, thereby interrupting her.

"But surrounded by armed guards."

"Oh," I ohed, clearly now deflated.

"Yeah, oh," she also ohed. "Bitch is none too trusting. Go figure."

"And the bigger problem?" I hazarded to ask.

"I thought that was the bigger problem."

"No," I said. "The sleep problem. How did you train someone to sleep when they can't, when you can't, when none of us can?"

Her oh turned ah. "Ah," she ahed. "The only thing bigger than that bitch's hair is that bitch's ego. So if I told her that I could sleep, then she was certain that she could as well. Heck, she even said that she drifted off for a minute or so."

"That sounds like her," I murmured. "So now what?"

"Now we wait, I suppose," she replied. "Try again and again, as long as it takes to get her alone."

"Before the husbands turn, which is going to happen way sooner than way later, according to Dara," I informed. "Plus, even if you can get her alone, I'll need to be there, right? To do the bitch in once and for all, if that's even possible. Unless you think you can do it, to kill what's already so very much dead."

"I did play the lead in Sweeney Todd, you know."

I grinned. As much as I liked Ricky, Lola was fast becoming my all-time favorite zombie. Albeit, the list to choose from was a rather short one. "No, no I didn't. But, be that as it may, killing someone, even a dead someone, even a dead bitch, isn't as easy as killing with a prop barber's razor. Trust me, I know." And all too well, in fact. "No, we need to lay a trap next time." I grinned as I stared out into the disco. Or better yet, above it. "And I think I know just the thing that should help."

***

We didn't see Blondella again that day or most of the day after. By then, we were getting worried that she was on to our plan, that she had figured out that Lola couldn't sleep and couldn't teach anyone else to, that she herself was being tricked and we were soon to be lambs for the slaughter. Worse still, as if that wasn't bad enough, the longer we waited, the shorter our better halves remained cognizant.

And, yet, wait we did. The music, which was preset to play, was our only diversion. Then, when we couldn't take much more, mainly because someone had programmed a Ke$ha medley, there she appeared, her ginormous wig cutting through the undead throng.

"You're on," I whispered to my cohort.

"Wish me well," she whispered back.

"Well."

And then Blondella was at the door of the DJ booth, motioning for Lola to follow.

I watched as the two left together and continued watching as Lola stopped Blondella in the aptly-named dead-center of the disco. This was the plan we'd hatched. I prayed that, in keeping with the theme, we hadn't laid an egg.

"Cut the music!" Lola shouted, making everyone jump, me especially.

I went all automaton-like and followed her command, the music going from ten to zero in a split second, Ke$ha snuffed out after three hundred years. Better late than never, I figured.

Blondella looked my way and then Lola's. "Why did you stop the music?" she barked, the disco suddenly filled with the sound of groans from all around now that the music was off. "Silence!" she added, her bloodshot eyes flaring, mouth in a snarl. After that, you could practically hear a pin drop, which was great for me because then I could hear the conversation as it continued. "Aren't we headed outside?" she asked. "To practice?"

I feigned a smile. It seemed Blondella was still in on the game, even though she was now pawn instead of queen. Lola smiled as well. "Yes, practice," she replied. "But not outside. The peripheral groans are a distraction, even the wind, but, more importantly, I believe the disco itself might hold a way for us to speed up the process."

Blondella looked at her quizzically. "You mean help me to sleep?"

Lola's grin widened. "Deeper, longer and harder," she replied.

Which was just as Blondella always liked it, if rumors were true.

"And how, pray tell, will the disco help? Because, truth to be told, I have been practicing, and, well, the results have been, shall we say, tepid at best."

"Yes," said Lola, sagely. "It certainly takes more than a day or two to master it." She then pointed all around. "But the lights in here, they're hypnotic, in a way. I believe they might let your mind go blank easier."

I forced back a chuckle. "Not too far to go on that one," I mumbled to myself, preparing for what was to come next. My nonexistent heartbeat was racing though a furlong right about then.

"Makes sense," said Blondella. "I used to always fall into a trance while dancing."

I covered my mouth. "Sure, we'll go with that," I muttered behind my rigid digits. "And not the six/seven cocktails and the occasional joint beforehand. Not to mention that too-tight wig cutting off the blood supply to your too-loose head."

"Exactly," said Lola. "Now, please lie down here and stare up at the lights as they swirl around you, concentrating on nothing but them, letting the rest of the world melt away, to fade into nothing."

I grinned. "It and you both, bitch." And then I watched with glee as her minions helped her descend to the disco floor, then cleared the area of the undead, until all that was left was Lola and Blondella and the silence and the swirling colors, the guards ringing it all, the lights now the only movement in the entire cavernous space.

"Okay," said Lola. "I'm going to count backwards from ten to one." Her voice was lower now, soothing. "Keep staring up. Let the lights cover you like a blanket. Let them warm you inside, cradle you. And with every number I utter, you'll start to get sleepier and sleepier, until I reach the end, and then you and sleep will be as one."

"In more ways than one," I said, no longer staring at my friend, my eyes fixed elsewhere all of a sudden, the radiation growing and growing inside of me as Lola started her countdown and slowly began to move in reverse, away from the prone queen, a few inches with each number called out.

When she reached five, the atoms inside of me were at their maximum frenzy, slamming and jamming into one another as they waited for their inevitable release. I held them back, listening intently for the final number to be spoken, for my signal, my turn at stardom, for Blondella to (at last) exit the stage.

"Four . . . three . . . two . . . one . . ."

The floodgates parted, the beam of radiation moving faster than lightning—and just as white-hot. It hit the metal chain, which glowed upon impact, a puff of smoke rising to the ceiling, seen only if you were off at a distance. Seen, that is to say, only by me. Of course, I was also the only one who saw it buckle and bubble and crack and quickly split into two.

And then the silence was shattered as that giant disco ball, the largest one I'd ever beheld, came crashing down.

It was the last thing she ever saw, not to mention the most beautiful thing I'd seen in decades.

I turned off my internal, infernal beam and stared across the floor. Lola was gazing down at the motionless corpse on the ground, Blondella's wig and fingertips all that remained outside the crash site. The guards, in the meanwhile, stared at one another in confusion. This, after all, was their meal ticket, even if said meal consisted of nothing but salt. They then turned to Lola for an explanation, something, anything. After all, they hadn't thought for themselves in ages and ages.

"Oh no," she sobbed, ever the glorious actress, falling to her knees to see if there was anything to be done. "She's dead," came the eventual conclusion.

"Um . . ." said one of the guards, clearly thinking the obvious.

Lola glanced up. "And gone. Forever." To which she added, "Now you'll have no one left to command you. What will you do?"

The realization hit the guard like a, well, ton of disco ball. "I hate this fucking music," he replied. "Hated it for years and years and years. Always on fucking repeat. Day in and day out."

"Amen," said another of the guards.

"Ditto," piped up another.

"I'm outta here," said the first. "Grab the salt."

"Ding dong the witch is dead," added the second.

Ten minutes later, the guards had departed, each with a box of salt over their heads, the disco again silent save for my footsteps as they approached the crime scene. I stared down at her. Though of course I was glad she was gone, a small part of me was sad to see her go. She was, after all, one of the last vestiges of my former world, of my former self, and at one time my friend.

"Are you okay?" asked Lola, staring at me as I in turn stared at the flattened body and the now motionless giant ball, a thousand lights shooting off of it, a fabulous send-off for a fabulous, if not entirely bitchy, queen.

"I wish you'd met her in her better days," I grieved.

"Would I have liked her?" she asked.

I chuckled. "Probably not. She wasn't everyone's cup of tea."

"I hate tea," she informed. "Hated, that is."

"See."

I helped her up off her knees. She put her hand on my shoulder. "Let's go get our husband's, Creature. Three hundred years is a long time to be apart."

I nodded. "Three days has been too long." I stared at her, at her face now bathed in swirling color. "I'm glad I finally got a chance to see you act, though."

"And?" She was smiling.

"If I had a third Tony, I'd give it to you. Gladly."

She patted my shoulder and pointed to the disco ball. "That's all the award I need, Creature," she said, slightly nodding her head. "Now let's go."

I followed her across the floor, never looking back. The past, after all, was just that. And, with Dara, I had the future to look forward to.

So to the kitchen we went, into the elevator and then up. The catwalk was now deserted, one door up there open, the other still closed. I looked to Lola as she looked at me. "Ready?"

Her smile was brighter than the beams shooting all around us. "Uh huh!"

I reached for the knob, my still nonexistent heart beating a still nonexistent rhythm in my very real, strangely unpadded chest. I smiled, trying to recall the last time Dara had seen me completely out of drag. I then turned the knob and flung the door open.

"Surprise!" I shouted, my grin quivering, quaking and promptly fading altogether.

"What the . . ." said Lola.

"Fuck," said I, finishing her sentence.

"Where are they?" she asked, panic now blanketing the joy that had just recently been there.

I willed the radiation up again, then turned the dials and released my X-ray beam, moving it left and right, sweeping it this way and that, covering the length and breadth and width of the entire disco, but all I saw were empty spaces and milling zombies. "They're gone," I barely managed to squeak out.

"Gone?" she fairly sobbed. "Reverted back to zombies and released?" Her eyes went wide, manic. "We have to go find them before it's too late."

I grabbed her wrist. "Wait!" I then bent down, which was easier said than done, and, with my free hand, retrieved a strange object off the dust-covered floor.

Lola stared at it as it sat nestled in my upturned gray palm. "A miniature Statue of Liberty? How did that get here?"

I looked from it to her. "Dara had it. She picked it up at the graves back on the island."

"And she dropped it before she . . ."

"No," I said, squeezing her wrist tighter in my hand. "It was in her clutch. She still had it on her, attached to her belt. So if this is here . . ." I gripped it between my fingers. "Then she put it here." I looked at Lola again. "She put it here for us to find. They must have taken them back to the island. This is simply her way of telling us that."

She groaned. "But how? When?"

I shrugged. "Maybe Blondella told her guards that if anything should happen to her that they take our husbands back to the island. Maybe the traitors need them as bargaining chips. Who knows? All we know is that they're missing and headed back there."

"Presumably," she made note.

I let go of her wrist. "We'll go outside and do a quick sweep." I forced a comforting smile. "Three hundred years of being with someone, Lola, day in and day out, with no sleep, no breaks, let me tell you, I know Dara, know her almost as well as I know myself. And, trust me, this little souvenir was left here on purpose." Heck, I'd almost convinced myself. As if I had a choice, right?

"Fine, Creature," she said, her face resigned, defeated looking. "You've got me this far. I trust you."

In fact, I wasn't exactly sure where I'd gotten her, or any of us for that matter, but I was glad she still had faith. As Huey Lewis used to sing, *that's the power of love*. Then again, Huey was dead now, so what did he know?

We exited the way we came in, avoiding the smooshed queen as we did so. Thankfully, if I could still use the word and not get struck by lightning, our chariot awaited us. That is to say, the guards either didn't notice our golf cart or were to busy escaping to do it any harm. We then drove around and around, the cart's speaker on, my voice projected outward, searching for our husbands.

An hour or so into our mission, Lola put her hand over mine. "Stop," she said. I stopped and turned her way. "If they had turned zombie and were released, they couldn't have gotten far, correct?"

"Correct."

"So they were taken to the island then."

I nodded my head ever so slightly. "It seems so, Lola. The only other scenario I can think of is that they took them from the disco and released them farther away from here, but, apart from being sinister, which, don't get me wrong, Blondella was, I don't see the point in that. She had allies, maybe just a couple or more, but, for whatever reason, she had them. And they're clearly back on Liberty Island."

She sighed. "I hate the thought of leaving here in case they're just around a corner somewhere."

"But, if they're headed back to the island, we're giving them too great of a head start. As it is, they're probably already there, the salt running dangerously low or completely out already."

"Rock and a hard place?" she groaned.

And though I usually quite enjoyed hard places, not this time. "We have to go, Lola. Now. Back to the island and, fingers crossed, find them there."

It was now her turn to nod. "Go," she said, now staring straight ahead, her hand again in her lap, a warm breeze blowing the hair behind her.

So go I did, heading back to the marina once again.

"Um, in case you didn't already realize it, I don't know how to drive a boat, Creature."

"Neither do I," I admitted. "But how hard can it be?" A nervous chuckle worked its way free from between my cracked lips. "Look how well I can drive a golf cart, though."

"I hazard to guess that the two are quite different."

Not surprisingly, she wasn't far off the mark on that one. In fact, she was, pardon the expression, *dead on.*

***

We made it back to the marina a short while later. It was then we encountered a problem far greater than the fact that we didn't know how to drive a boat, namely that it had been more than three hundred years since any of them had even been started and, unlike the golf cart, there were no solar-powered vessels to be found, if they even existed in the first place. In other words, we were screwed, and not the good kind of screwed either.

"The ferry that the Libetians use," I told her, "has been in continual usage all this time. Such in not the case for any other vessel around here." I looked and looked and then added, "And whatever Blondella used during her attack isn't around here either."

Lola nodded her head and walked to the end of the pier, staring out at the rather tranquil bay in front of us, the sun glimmering off the water. I shuddered, despite the beauty of it. Water, after all, was the enemy of the undead, or, more to the point, to the radiation that kept us up and running. On the ferry, we were high above it, safe, but standing so close to it now, a mere couple of feet above, well, it gave me the creeps, truth be told. Because once you see a zombie go up and/or down in a puff of smoke, melting like so much rotted flesh, you tend to stay clear of water, let alone a whole body of it, whenever possible.

I say all this now, admitting my well-based aquaphobia, because Lola wasn't suddenly pointing out so much as down.

My eyes landed on her arm, then hand, then to the water below. "No to the fucking way, Lola."

She turned and looked at me. "It's the only *fucking* way, Creature."

I cringed as I gazed upon the tarped kayak down below. It was one of those long and narrow numbers, the kind used in competitive rowing or perhaps to travel down the Nile with, transporting Cleopatra. And, queen though I may be, I was a land-locked one and smartly so.

"Not to rain on your little floating parade, Lola, but there are only two of us, and . . ." I began to count. "Ten oars."

She was still turned my way, but pointing beyond where I was standing. "Take your pick."

I also turned, hundreds of zombies milling around behind me, all of them clueless as to what she had in mind—lucky them, not so lucky me. "Please tell me you're joking."

"Not without the promise of a raucous applause or a standing ovation," she retorted, taking our standard tip reply and one-upping it.

I groaned louder than the zombies behind me. "You're not making this easy on me."

"I'll do your hair and makeup along the way."

My groan turned ecstatic moan. "I'll gather the troops. You go find me a pretty frock and some makeup." I pointed to the stores behind us. "Something nautical, please."

"Awhore there, Captain!" she replied, saluting.

"Ahoy," I corrected her.

She shrugged and was off. "You say potato . . ."

"Let's call the whole thing off," I grumbled to myself, finishing the song's refrain.

In any case, with clearly no choice in the matter, I went right as she careened left, heading in to a dense pocket of undead.

"Pick the biggest one!" she hollered back my way.

I nodded my head, turned it back toward the milling throng and shouted. "Halt!" They halted. And, fine, I'll admit it, that part of my zombiehood I enjoyed. It wasn't a cold, frothy margarita, but the subservience was exhilarating just the same.

Through the lifeless horde I walked, searching for the strongest and, fine, best-looking men I could find. Shallow? Yes. But the waters beyond were deep enough for me, so a little superficiality was clearly in order.

And so with eight of them now following me, we converged with Lola, bags in her hands, a smile of sorts on her face. We then meandered our way down the metal plank, arriving at our vessel a short while later.

I stared at it and gulped, as usual if only in my head. "Think she's seaworthy?"

Lola nodded. "She looks to be made of some sort of polymer, clearly not wood, not after all these years. We just have to take the tarp off of her and hop in."

I couldn't help but laugh. "Hop?"

She scratched her head. "Okay, so *hop* might not have been the best choice of words. But with ten of us here, we can all help."

I lifted my hand up to stop her cold, so to speak. "They can do it. We can watch. Or, better yet, I can get de-boyed and then get re-girled while they de-tarp and help each other and then us onto that . .

. that . . . *thing*."

She nodded. "Deal."

Great, so we had a deal. Except, our hands came up with all low-numbered cards, not a pair or a full house or even a lovely queen to be had. In other words, while I slipped into a rather fetching pair of navy slacks and a white satin blouse with gold brocades along the shoulders, a sensible pair of flats on my feet and a short, well-styled if not frightfully dusty wig on my head, the zombies, upon my command, removed the tarp and hopped in. That is to say, after an hour or so, the tarp was floating in the bay, the six of them scattered around it, the current taking them to unknown shores.

"Well, that was fun," I said, staring down at the lucky remaining pair. "And see what can happen when we attempt to hop?" I pointed to the body-barges that were floating a few hundred yards away now. It would take a while for the water to seep in. I was glad I didn't have to witness it.

She sighed and stood arms akimbo. "Got it. Now go round up six more."

"You're serious?" Again I pointed to the floating corpses.

While she, in turn, pointed to the safe duo, both of them groaning as they stood like statues within the kayak. "We'll simply learn from our mistakes."

I turned and headed back to the throng, mumbling and grumbling all the while. "Yeah, because zombies are such terrific students."

CHAPTER 16
ROW, ROW, ROW YOUR BOAT

Somehow we "recruited" more rowers—two more times, one mishap following the next—and somehow we all made it aboard, seated, with oars in hand. Then we had to teach eight dead guys had to paddle—without splashing and without capsizing us—and we were off. Simple as that!

I then turned to Lola and she turned to me, makeup at the ready. "You know," I said, "if this thing tips over we're all dead."

"Er."

I nodded as she began to apply. "Dead*er*, right."

"Think of it as an adventure, Creature," she said as she began to lay down ample foundation.

"Let's see," I said, between pursed lips. "I flew across the country, landed on a tiny strip of runway beneath the Statue of Liberty, broke into a stadium, rescued a Tony Award-winning actress, killed my once close friend in a disco, with a disco ball no less, with radiation I shot out of my friggin' eyeballs, and you want me to seek out even *more* adventures?"

"Two-time," she said, starting in on my eye shadow.

"Two-time what?"

"Two-time Tony Award-winning actress."

I stifled a grin. "*That's* what you got out of my tirade?"

She shrugged and swiped the brush across my fluttering lid. "I stopped listening after that."

"You know," I said, "I think you might have been a drag queen in a past life. You certainly talk like one."

She grimaced, her hand frozen above my eye. "My past life ended three hundred years ago, Creature. Right about now, I'm concentrating on salvaging my next one."

I reached out and patted her knee. "I'm sorry, Lola," I apologized. "I'll . . . I'll stop complaining."

She nodded and continued with her ritual. "Really?"

I stopped patting and tilted my head up to the warming sun. "Probably not. But you were being maudlin, so I opted for contrite. To be frank, neither fit us all that well."

She chuckled and probably accidentally on purpose smudged my makeup. In any case, I shut up and she continued, the makeover calming me, temporarily helping me forget that we were whisking our way across lethal water at that very moment, with quite a distance to go. Then again, with our undead rowing team, at least we didn't have to worry about anyone getting a cramp.

Once we made out of the East River we could see the torch far off in the distance, the sun glinting off of it. "Well," said Lola, her work on me complete, a dusty mirror held up for close inspection, "there's the statue, but how are we going to get to her without being seen?"

I turned my head this way and that. Lola was no slouch in the makeup department, thank goodness. I then looked from her to the massive steely drag queen far across the bay. "We'll take a left, down to Governor's Island, then it's a straight shot across the Hudson River. Virtually everyone lives either on Ellis Island or the stretch of pontoons that connects it to Liberty Island. If we come around the back, to the south end of the statue, it's next to near impossible for them to spot us, especially so low to the water."

"Next to near, but not impossible," she replied.

I shrugged. "So what? Even if they spot us, we play dumb."

"Er."

I grinned. "Yes, dumb*er*. Anyway, we're not the enemy, at least to most of them. After all, they came and got me out of Utah to help rescue them from Blondella. Which, need I remind you, we've already done."

She squinted her eyes as she gazed across the choppy water. "No, they don't know about Blondella. They only know they were being attacked. In fact, when you think about it, you killed their goddess."

Again I tried to gulp. "Okay, so, if they spot us, we just stick with the dumb routine, no mention of Blondella, no mention of the plot to kill them all, no mention of the traitors in their midst. Only we'll know that we're there to save our husbands. As to Blondella, they're already saved from her, so I've done my part for them. Then, once we rescue the hubbies, I just have to save my friends back in Utah . . . somehow." I frowned. "Sounds harder once you say it out loud."

She shook her head. "Nope, it sounded hard even before you said it."

After that, I simply stopped talking. Pointing out the obvious was only making us both nervous. That is to say nervous*er*. Because crossing the Hudson against the current was no easy going. And if I hadn't already been bluish gray, I'm sure I would have been so green that even Kermit would've been less than thrilled with me, perhaps even made up a new Muppety song: *It's Not Easy Being Dead.*

***

It had to have been at least an hour before the tarted-up statue was looming high overhead. As suspected, no one seemed to have spotted us, not with us coming in from around their backside, as it were. Or, if they had, there were certainly no alarms going off. There was just us and the kayak and, praise be to Allah or Buddha or Confucius or any other god of your choosing, a place to pull up to and a relatively short stairwell to climb.

I turned to the zombies as Lola and I again stood on solid ground. "Go back the exact way we came. Climb out of the kayak when you arrive at the marina. Good luck."

I saluted them. They groaned and began to paddle once again. "Bon voyage," Lola said as we turned away.

"Falling on dead ears," I told her.

"Don't you mean deaf?" She thought about it and shrugged. "In any case, it never hurts to be friendly."

I thought of how I had left the comfort of my factory in Utah, all in the name of being, to a certain degree, *friendly*, but neglected to rub it in. I mean, why kick a zombie when she's down? "So now what?" I asked, instead.

She stopped and turned my way. "We act dumb, just as planned."

"And avoid the priestess, Topaz, and VaVa, the one that clearly worships Blondella. They were the two that looked suspicious when they thought they'd seen the disco-ball-crushed queen. They're the traitors."

177

"And probably the ones who are holding our husbands then," Lola interjected. "So is it better to avoid them or buddy up to them?"

"Keep your friends close and your enemies closer?"

She nodded and touched fingertip to nose, missing it by just an inch. "Damn," she said.

"Yeah, that's a hard one."

And so we moved, keeping to the periphery, lurking in the shadows. Because, even though we weren't the enemy, we were still zombies, and it was easy to believe that the islanders we encountered would strike first and ask questions later. And, truth be told, I'd been struck enough as of late—enough to last, well, a deathtime.

"Any ideas where they might have been taken?" asked Lola as we huddled beneath an ancient oak.

I nodded. "Ellis Island." I pointed into the distance. "The museum there, it's one of the few buildings not used for housing." I then pointed much closer. "Or here, just below Lady Liberty. It's where the priestess, Topaz, lives. There are rooms inside, an easy place to hide someone or ones."

Lola looked from one point to the other. "It would take us much longer to get across to Ellis Island, with a higher risk of being spotted. I vote we search here first."

My nodding continued. "I second that, though we'll need to wait until it's dark then because there are still humans around, too many eyes to easily spot a tottering zombie or two with, especially inside."

Lola frowned. "Which means more time for our husbands to revert, if they haven't already."

"I'm afraid so," I told her.

"And if they revert, if they're released out here after that happens?"

My frown hung even lower than hers. After all, I'd seen what humans did to zombies when they encountered them. "Look, if they're really being used for bargaining chips, if they're here to prevent us from attacking, then they won't be released, cognizant or not."

"Sorry, but no then," she said after a lengthy pause, surprising me to the quick. "No, I can't risk my husband turning zombie with a chance of staying that way forever, with a chance of never seeing me again or me him."

"But what choice do we have?"

And with that the tiniest of smiles appeared on her glorious face. "What if the bad guys were ordered to release our husbands?"

"Ordered?" I said. "By whom? Topaz would be the highest in command, I assume, and she's the enemy."

"But there's a higher power than even the priestess?"

"There is?" I asked, lost as usual. "Who?"

Her smile grew and grew. "Who do the people worship, Creature? Who have they already seen, according to what you told me? Who did they see, in fact, back at the marina?"

"Blondella?" I coughed out. "But she's dead, and truly dead this time, not her usual form of dead."

"No one knows that but us."

I held her hand in mine and gave it a squeeze. "It'll never work, Lola. They saw me from a distance last time. Up close, they'll know I'm a zombie, they'll know I'm not her. I'm too, too . . ."

"Decrepit?"

"Well, you don't have say it like that."

It was now her turn to squeeze my hand. "But one of us is not, Creature. Not decrepit, that is. And one of us is quite the good actress. Tony-winning in fact."

At last, a smile broke free from my face. "Two-time!"

With her next attempt at touching fingertip to nose, she actually hit the mark. "Silence!" she then shouted, sounding like Blondella to a tee. And with my blonde wig atop her head, she'd be looking like her in no time flat. And not the zombie version either. No ma'am, no how.

Plus, I had a secret weapon to ensure our success.

***

We found one of the island's many golf carts in a parking area to the side of the statue. Lola covered me with a blanket that had been sitting in the back seat. With my wig on and a fresh coat of makeup, she looked human. Me, I looked like a lump, but a talking one just the same, telling my friend where to head to.

Twenty minutes later, give or take, we'd traversed the pontoons instead of searching around Libby, no one the wiser that zombies were in their midst. As for searching the statue, we'd have to wait until it was dark outside, and so we pulled up to the side of the museum instead. A side door was open, the two of us slipping in unseen. As with our last two times in there, the place was empty.

"Whoa," said Lola, taking it all in, the mural especially.

I couldn't help but smile. "My friends were some fierce bitches."

"Blondella included." She pointed up to the mural, the sun from an upper window illuminating the panel like the holy shrine that is was.

"Death, for you, for me, was quick and painless, Lola," I explained. "For her, it was long and agonizing. It warped her, made her into what you witnessed. Though, to be fair, even in life she was one taco short of a combination plate. Perhaps that's what made her so unique in the first place."

"And the people here, they worship this uniqueness now, worship your friends?" she asked, still admiring the scenery.

I shrugged. "They worship a legend. I suppose all throughout history the same could be said. In any case, the society they've formed, it has seemed to work for three hundred years, so why rock a boat that's clearly in choppy waters to begin with?"

"Good point." She turned and looked at me. "But why are we here?"

I grabbed her hand and walked her over to the cases, to their clothes. "The cherry on the sundae." I pointed to the last case.

"Those . . . those were *hers*?"

"Nope."

She looked at me, confused. "Nope? What do you mean *nope*?"

"I mean nope," I replied. "Blondella clearly wasn't killed in the zombie attack that the mural depicts. She's not buried out back. And these weren't her clothes. They're too small—*for her,* that is."

In an instant, she understood what I was getting at. "This pantsuit, it's my size."

"Well, more your size than hers, that's for sure."

"And with this wig and just the right makeup . . ."

"You'll be the spitting image of the Blondella in the mural, the only version of her they have," said I. "Though, of course, zombies don't spit, but still."

She rattled the back of the case, her smile going horizontal in an instant. "It's locked."

I shrugged. "Sure, to anyone without a key."

"You have a key, Creature?"

"Nope."

She groaned. "Please, not that again."

"I mean *nope*, don't need one," I replied. I stood before the case, atoms burbling and bubbling and super-colliding, the heat inside enough to melt, if only temporarily, even the coldness of death. I jumped as the beam exploded from my eyes, concentrated, thin, the metal lock turning from silver to molten red before promptly falling to the ground in a soft *clink*. "There you go," I then said, the beam just as quickly flicked off.

"That does come in handy," Lola said with an appreciative whistle that sounded more like a dying engine.

"Yes, that one never gets any easier. Don't try snapping either. It just makes things worse." And with that, I grabbed the clothes from the case and led us to a nearby bathroom.

Once inside, Lola began to get undressed. "Turn around, please," she barked, modestly.

"Um, in case you've forgotten, I've already seen you naked." I pointed to my X-ray vision eyes.

"Do you *want* to see me naked again, Creature?"

I blushed, which, like snapping and whistling, didn't go over too well. "Oh, um, no thanks." I turned around while she finished the job.

"Okay," she proclaimed a short while later. Well, actually, it was a bit of a longish time later, seeing as a zombie changing in and out of clothes was only slightly less awkward than a zombie whistling or snapping or blushing.

In any case, I turned as Lola handed me the makeup kit. And makeup, zombie or not, was something I could still handle quite well, what with several centuries of practice, I mean. So, not twenty minutes later, there she stood, shorter than the real deal, slimmer, sure, but looking exactly like the queen in the mural just the same. "Amazing what a pound of makeup can do."

Her face went instantly stony. "Halt! Silence! Kill them!" she then shouted, her voice echoing around the tiled room.

I grinned. "You look like her, sound like her and are easily just as bitchy."

"Thanks . . . I think."

We headed out of the bathroom, hanging her old clothes up where her new duds had previously been. From a distance, no one would be the wiser. I then prayed that no one would get up close in the near future.

While we were there, I had a look around. That is to say, a wide beam again popped out of my eyeballs, my X-ray vision slicing through the walls as easily as a Ginsu through a tin can. Round and round I went until the entire building had been scanned.

"Well?" she asked.

"Sorry," I replied, rather glumly. "They're not here, at least not in the museum. Though the island, apart from the hundreds of homes, is littered with other buildings. They could, in fact, be hidden anywhere."

"But, more than likely, somewhere with the priestess," she tacked on.

I nodded. "Again, that makes the most sense."

"And if she's holding them, wouldn't it also make sense that they're being guarded, perhaps with ample weapons?"

And still I nodded. "Yep, that would also make sense," I reluctantly agreed. "Are you going somewhere with all this?"

She smiled, wickedly, looking so much like Blondella that I very nearly cringed. "Going, yes, as in you and me are going to her, the mountain going to Mohammed, as it were."

"I'm Jewish, though. Or half. Non-practicing. Though come Chanukah, if you're so inclined to bestow eight day's worth of presents upon me, I won't object."

She sighed. I was having that effect on her. Go figure. "Okay then, Mount Sinai going to Moses, as it were, then. That better?"

I shrugged. "Suit yourself. But that eight-gift idea still stands."

She shrugged, chuckled and wisely changed the subject. And the location. Meaning, we were out of there in no time flat and back inside the golf cart, the blanket now draped over the top, blocking us from anyone's line of vision. I drove with nothing but my X-ray vision to lead the way. Was the covered cart an odd sight? Sure. But, then again, this was a town of nothing but drag queens, so odd was par for the course. Odd, in fact, was a hole in one. In fact, from the looks of things, anyone that spotted us merely clapped as if we were putting on a show.

"Applause," I gleefully purred. "Ah, how I missed it."

Lola patted my hand. "Welcome to the club then. Three hundred years of nothing but groaning does make a person miss the sound of two hands clapping. Even if these people haven't a clue what in the hell they're clapping for."

I shot her a smirk as we continued onward. We were close now. So close that I could feel it.

Little did I know that we weren't alone in that regard.

***

We reached the Statue of Liberty and pulled the cart right on up to the steps. I got out and ran to help Lola, whom I shielded with the blanket. Me they were allowed to see, had in fact seen before; her they could not, at least not yet.

Up we climbed, slowly, which was the only way we could, really. When we reached the top of the first tier, I stopped and turned around, the covered Lola doing the same. By then, several of the Libetians had witnessed our ascent. After all, a zombie and a blanket-swathed person weren't something easily missed, especially not atop their sacred shrine.

"Gather the others!" I bellowed, my voice echoing outwards. And when Saint Creature bellows, people listen.

After that, we stood there and waited. Thankfully, we didn't have to wait long. Word, it seemed, travelled fast that I had returned and with a surprise no less.

"What's happening?" asked Lola from beneath the blanket.

"The islanders are amassing in, um, masses," I replied. In fact, we could hear them soon enough, hundreds upon hundreds of voices reaching, within minutes, our long-dead ears, the sound like a rock concert, the excitement contagious. Even I was trembling with it, and I knew what was to come. "Are you ready?" I asked, talking above the din so that she could hear me.

"As I'll ever be," she yelled back.

I grinned. "Time for that third Tony?"

The blanket bobbed and shook. "From your lips to God's ears."

"Yeah, I hope he's listening. We could use any help we can get right about now." And then I lifted my hands up into the air, wide, before shouting at the top of my lungs, "Silence!"

The hush started from the first row of islanders and quickly spread to the back, the crowd so large now that I could only see where it started and not even close to where it ended. They were packed in beneath the gilded statue, extending far onto the platoons.

I had been brought there to save them, I told myself. I'd done just that, miracle of miracles. Now it was their turn to return the favor.

"Friends," I said. "I bring you good news." I patted the standing, still-covered *present*. "And so much more than that."

"Show us!" the crowd chanted, the sound making my very bones tremble, my knees quake.

Again I held up my hands. "I will, but first the news." I paused for effect, every eye on me now, every mouth hushed. The crowd, the great beast, pushed even closer, not wanting to miss a word of what I had to say. I smiled. Ah, stardom. "Firstly, you are all safe now. There will be no more zombie attacks, not now, not ever!"

The collective roar was very nearly deafening, the crowd undulating as their hands went up high in waves and thunderous applause. "The blanket!" I heard, the words swirling like a serpent through the crowd before striking me. "The blanket, the blanket, the blanket!"

Again I lifted my hands, the crowd almost instantly growing silent, watching, waiting. "Friends!" I shouted. "I bring you . . . your savior!" And with this, I yanked the blanket up and over and down. "I give you . . . Blondella Bombshell!"

It was not a sound I'd ever heard before, a multitude of mouths instantly sucking in their breaths, an incalculable number of simultaneous gasps as the person in the mural came to life for them before their very eyes.

Lola stood there, regally, taking it all in. She then flung her arms up—no easy feat, mind you—and shouted so that even the back row could hear. "Your goddess has returned!"

We were nearly knocked over with the adulation that rocketed from the crowd. It was Blondella, it had to be, especially if I, their saint, had said so. And with that in mind, they fell to their knees, shouted in praise, beat their chests and cried in revelry.

I turned to Lola as she turned to me. "Well, that went well."

She nodded. "Ready for the rest of it?"

I lifted my index finger in the air. "Give it a minute. Let them get it out of their systems. After all, it's not everyday that a goddess makes an unannounced appearance."

"Good point," she allowed, turning back their way. "Besides, since I'm never going to get to play Madison Square Garden, this will have to do."

Minutes into this, with the crowd still at a fevered pitch, we started hearing the calls, coming in from all sides. "Why have you returned?" And, "Where have you been all this time?" And, of course, seeing as who and what they were, "Who are you wearing?"

Again Lola lifted her arms up high and again the crowd grew silent. "My people," she shouted. "I have come to reveal the traitors in your midst! They are the cause of the recent zombie attacks!"

The gasps returned, louder this time. After all, this was a small community, not to mention a mostly idyllic one, and what Lola was saying went well beyond shocking.

"Who are they?" shouted the crowd? "Bring them to us!" we heard. "Kill the traitors!" it was even hollered. Plus, of course, "Who are you wearing?" Because once a drag queen, always a drag queen.

"Silence!" Lola wailed. The crowd again hushed. "These traitors have captured two of my subjects, two zombies, yes, but two who are friends, two who wish you no harm. Find these two zombies and you will find the turncoats!"

"Where should we look?" we heard next, the crowd one *thing* now, anger and shock blanketing all the faces at once.

And now it was my turn. I flung around and pointed to the statue itself. "Inside you will find your traitor!" I shouted. "Find the priestess and you will find our zombie friends!"

My latest outburst, suffice it to say, brought the biggest gasp yet. This, after all, was their spiritual leader, their connection to the goddesses, to all that they were and held so dearly. And yet, when Lola shouted, "Find the zombies at once!" they did not hesitate. Instead, they stormed up the stairs, trampling past us as they raced inside the statue in search of Dara and Ricky. Those who remained outside merely prostrated themselves and prayed at our feet.

"I can see how someone could get used to this," I whispered into Lola's ear.

She turned and replied, "But we're tricking them, Creature. I'm not the goddess and you're no saint."

A knot formed in my long-dead belly. She was right of course and yet not right as well. But things here were not so black and white; this was a gray area, to be certain—and this coming from someone who knew gray all too well, who stared gray in the face each and every day for centuries. "They are traitors, Lola," I replied. "They were helping

Blondella to bring about their own people's destruction, to snuff out, by all accounts, the last vestiges of mankind." I stared at the moaning masses beneath us. "Or at least dragkind."

She held my hand in hers. "I know you're right, but . . ."

"You're an actress, Lola," I told her, gripping her hand in mine. "This is just another role for you, albeit one with grave consequences if the play closes too soon."

She shut her eyes and nodded. When she opened them again, the smile had returned to her face. "And the play, as they say, must go on."

"Thatta girl."

She released my hand. "Thatta *goddess* you mean."

And then, at last, the crowd reemerged from the statue, Topaz pushed to the front, fear plastered across her face. With her was VaVa. So, yes, two birds, one stone. Except, two was all there were, two and no more.

"Where are they!" barked Lola, her eyes practically aflame.

Those directly behind the prisoners cowered, the one closest to us replying, "They were alone, Goddess. There are no others within."

To which another added, "We searched everywhere, Goddess. They are not inside."

Lola closed the gap between them, her face up close to the priestess'. "Where are they?"

Topaz blinked. It was clear she thought she was gazing at Blondella and then clear again that she knew she wasn't. "I am not a traitor, *Goddess*," she replied.

"And that's not what I asked you."

Topaz gazed on, still in fear, but with a smidge of curiosity thrown in; I could see it in her eyes. "I do not know of whom you speak, but I surmise that it amounts to the same thing: I am no traitor and I do not have the answer to your question."

It was my turn to move in, while the crowd retreated a few feet in reverse, equally as afraid of the zombie and the goddess as the prisoners were. "I saw you at the marina, Topaz."

"Funny," she replied, "I did not see you, Creature."

We were now eye to eye, hers staring down into mine. "But you did see Blondella. You did recognize her." I turned to VaVa. "You both recognized her, neither all that shocked to see her, not like the others were. I know what I saw. Do you deny it?"

The queens stared at each other and then back to us. "We are not traitors, Creature," said VaVa.

"We do not know who you seek or where they are hidden," added Topaz. "But perhaps we know who does." The briefest of smiles broke free from her face, wiped away completely with what she saw next.

Though, to be fair, there wasn't a smile to be found once that happened—except perhaps on the true Blondella's disco-ball-crushed face.

CHAPTER 17
ENERGY BOOST

I looked past her and spotted the smallish boat docked in the same spot that we had docked. She must've been close behind the entire time. Which meant that we should've been looking aft as well as forward.

She approached us slowly. Given her present state, it was a wonder she could do even that. She was also well guarded, a crush of undead underlings all around her, every human within a hundred feet moving in reverse at the sight of them, not to mention the smell.

"Not good," I muttered.

"Nope," agreed Lola.

"Nope," agreed Topaz.

"Not even close," added VaVa.

The humans below watched her progress, confused, as well they should have been, at what they were witnessing. I had, after all, just promised them that there would be no more zombie attacks, and yet here the zombies were. I had just offered them their goddess, and yet another had arrived that bore the same resemblance, albeit squashed and gray and withered though it was. And so they stood their ground and we stood ours and the goddess in question got carried up the stairs, half-crushed face twisted in an angry snarl all the while as she stared at me and me at her.

"Damn, girl," I said, once she was set down, "you look like crap." I flinched when she moved in even closer. "Plus, I, uh, thought you were, you know, *dead.*"

The faintest of grins inched its way up her ghastly face. "I was. Have been for centuries, *old friend.* Gonna take a lot more than a disco ball to finish the deed, though." She then turned to the crowd and brayed as she pointed our way, "Here are your traitors!"

Lola pushed between us and addressed the crowd. "No!" she shouted. "This one is the traitor. This one intends on your destruction!"

"Liar!" shouted the first Blondella.

"Bitch!" shouted the second, the faces in the crowd moving from one to the other and back again, like a good—or perhaps bad, as in *very bad*—tennis volley.

The first Blondella, the unfortunately real one, paused, grinned and then responded by lifting her hand up into the air. In it she held a pistol, the same pearl-inlayed one she held in the mural, the one every islander recognized all too well. She fired it, the sound exploding all around us. "Yeah, I am a bitch. Too bad for you."

And amen to that.

***

Surprisingly, considering that just moments before we were welcomed as heroes, we suddenly found ourselves locked inside a room in a house just below the statue, guarded by a team of well-armed humans. Seems the pistol was the clincher when it came to deciding who the real Blondella was, especially once Lola's wig got ripped away and the makeup smudged off to reveal the zombie beneath, the imposter easily identified. Plus, it'd been several hundred years, so of course Blondella looked like she did. Stood to reason, right? Well, that's what we figured they figured, once she was free and were summarily imprisoned.

"I'm *so* not enjoying my afterlife, Creature," bemoaned Lola as the door slammed in our faces. "Where are all the angels and the pearly gates, not to mention the unlimited chocolate?"

I shrugged. I think she had our story confused with Willy Wonka's. Still, I replied, "The way things are looking, we might find out soon enough."

"And then the husbands will be left here all alone," she added, despondently, face half hers, half our enemy's. "We can't let that happen."

"We need help then."

She looked up. "Gee, ya think?"

I shook my head. "I mean, Topaz and VaVa, they said they weren't the traitors, they implied that they knew who was. They seemed just as shocked and disturbed at Blondella's reappearance as we did. Given that, can't we assume that they're still on our side?"

She didn't look convinced. "Even after we sent the entire island after them, turned their friends against them, accused them of what we accused them of?"

I turned away from her and faced the door. "Doesn't matter. If they recognized Blondella at the marina, if they know what she is and what she means to do to them, to all of them, then they're still on our side, even after what we did, because we're their only hope."

She chuckled. "Says the man—"

"Drag queen."

Again she chuckled. "Says the *drag queen* imprisoned inside a guarded room."

I focused my X-ray vision outward, scanning it this way and that. The crowd was still outside, Blondella speaking to them, promising Lord only knew what. Though a false sense of security was what it must've been. Topaz was now standing by her side, the priestess by her goddess.

I switched the waves around, X-ray turning to radio. I focused the beam, aiming it straight for Topaz, hoping, praying that only she could hear what I had to say. "We need you," I said inside my head, inside hers.

"Creature?" she replied.

"Who else?"

"But how, where—"

"Never mind that," said I, cutting her off. "You're not the traitor?"

She had little to lose now, no reason to lie. "I am the priestess," she replied. "My people are who I serve."

"Not the goddess?"

She laughed. "Hard to worship *that*."

"But someone still does."

She sighed, if only in her head. "Three hundred years have come and gone since your time became ours. One priestess rises when another falls, the teachings passed down."

In an instant, I knew what she was getting at. "You've always known about Blondella then?"

Her sigh repeated. "Yes, even while I've venerated her and taught others to do the same. It's my way, the way of the priestess. To say otherwise would be to contradict all that we've stood for, all that we've built."

"And VaVa?"

"VaVa runs the ferries. She'd seen Blondella. She came to me for guidance," Topaz explained, her voice echoing in my head. "She's on our side."

"But there is a traitor, at least one," I replied. "There is someone or ones communicating with Blondella from the island."

The final sigh was the loudest, the longest. "When the zombies last attacked, just before we came for your assistance, I assumed that Blondella had help to pull off the raid. It stood to reason. She would need to know where to attack, when, would even need help landing her vessel and debarking, even as she needed help today."

"And do you know who helped her both then and now?"

She paused, silence filling my head. "I . . . I think so. I had my suspicions before, and when I saw said help approaching the statue just before Blondella, they were confirmed."

"But how was she able to help?" I asked. "We destroyed their communication device. This traitor had no way of knowing that we were headed here, that Blondella was also headed here?"

"No?" she replied. "And yet you and I are indeed communicating. Besides, who's to say that what you destroyed was their sole means. The city is full of discarded equipment, as was the island."

I turned and looked at Lola. "Fuck."

She grimaced. "What now?"

"Blondella," I told her. "She must have had other ways of reaching the traitor."

She nodded her head. "Makes sense. Bitch, it appears, is nothing if not resourceful."

I focused my mind back into Topaz's. "Not to alarm you, Priestess, but your goddess has an arsenal of explosives, which she probably already planted, at least a portion of, around the island, probably with the help of the traitor. This, it seems, was the real reason she attacked just before you came and got me, apart from getting me to come in the first place."

"Not to alarm me, though."

I shrugged, at least inside my head. "Um, okay, to alarm you then.

And, I'm guessing, the rest of the arsenal is aboard the boat she arrived on today, perhaps being planted even as we, uh, speak."

"Fuck," said the priestess.

"Yeah," said I. "Been there, done that."

Again there was a pause in our communication. When she returned, she told me, "Blondella is done with her speech. The islanders now believe she's returned to lead them."

"Yeah. Lead them to their doom, that is."

"Yes," she replied. "Though I'll stay close to her now, keep an eye on her. She doesn't know what I know of her. As to her plan, the explosives, these zombies you seek, I will do my best to make sure they are all taken care of."

"And us?" I couldn't help but ask.

"You're prisoners," she responded.

"Duh."

Her voice in my head grew softer, as if she was moving away. "One problem at a time, Creature . . ."

And then she was gone, the voice silenced, the connection broken.

Again I turned to Lola. "Good news or bad news first?" I said.

"Good news, please."

I moved away from the door and closer to her. "Topaz and VaVa are on our side. They're going to help."

"And the bad news?" she asked, looking at me reluctantly.

"If they rescue us now, they'll throw suspicion their way."

"Ah," she ahed. "Bad news indeed. Because I'm the star. And stars don't patiently sit in the wings all that well."

"Tell me about it," I replied, "Still, if you want, I could radiate our way through the door and then battle the guards outside. We may end up with a few holes in our bodies, perhaps faces, but we'll be no worse the wear, or at least no deader."

She lifted her index finger in the air, contemplated my remark, and then said, "Okay, I suppose I could wait in the wings a little while longer, though not patiently, of course."

"Of course."

***

So wait we did. Until we no longer needed to. That is to say, until

192

the play came to us.

In she walked, or at least hobbled, badly. "My, my," she said, closing the door behind her. "You all do seem to make a habit of getting caught."

"And escaping," I couldn't help but remind her.

"Except now you have me, my zombie guards, which replaced the human ones, and an entire island of humans against you," she, in turn, couldn't help but remind me. "Check and mate."

I grinned, despite the dire circumstances, if only to piss her off. "Not check, not yet, not while there are still two queens on the board."

"Temporarily," she intoned. The atoms inside of me started to bump and grind, but then just as quickly and surprisingly got tamped down. "Tut, tut, Creature," she added. "Fool me once, shame on you; fool me twice—"

"And smash you with a disco ball?"

She cringed, but them seemed to regain her composure, if only too piss me off. So, yes, the queens on the board were indeed evenly matched. "In any case, Creature, thanks to you, I now know of my other powers, and mine seem to cancel yours out. So no funny stuff, please. Which, if memory serves, was never much your forté anyway."

She had me there; I felt it, internally speaking. My snapping and crackling were fine, but my popping went poop whenever I tried. "So why are you here then, Blondella? For old time's sake? To, *blech*, kiss and make up?"

She shrugged. "Nope. Just a nice little gloat." She grinned, or at least tried to. It didn't come off that well, all things considered—all things being a half-smooshed face, that is. "*Gloat*," she then barked, just before she left us alone again, the door closing behind her.

Lola's tensed shoulders eased down a tad. "She doesn't make it easy to like her, does she?"

"Not when she was alive—"

"And certainly not in death." Lola interrupted, grinning, and it was one of those delicious cat-eating-the-canary type of grins, even though there were no more cats, no more canaries, and we certainly couldn't eat. "But she has given me an idea."

"Really? An idea or a headache? Because both come from the same source."

Her smile remained. "She has your powers now."

I frowned. "And?"

"*And* she can tamp your powers down with hers."

I held my hand up for her to stop. "Speaking of headaches, Lola, just get to the good part, please."

She nodded her head. "Got it," she agreed. "In any case, if she can tamp your powers down with hers, then perhaps you can bump my powers up with yours. Maybe all it takes for me to use mine is a little three hundred year boost of yours."

"But you don't have any powers," I reminded her. "You tried and failed in that regard. You told me so yourself."

Her head was still in the nod position. "Just because I failed doesn't mean I don't have the ability, Creature. Maybe all I need is some extra go-go juice."

"Uh huh," I said. "So you think I should shoot my rays inside of you in the odd chance that I'll push your energy levels over the threshold and not fry you like an onion ring in doing so?"

She cringed. "You do have a way with words, Creature."

"It's a gift," I replied, with a self-satisfied smile.

"Is it returnable?"

My smile vanished. "Sorry." I closed the gap between us. "You sure you want me to try it out, though? Because I really could do some major harm. Remember how a certain steel cable snapped and dropped a disco ball on a certain nasty someone."

She looked around, at the guarded door holding us, at the walls on all sides of us, at the floor and ceiling, and then said, "What choice do we have? Plus, if I do have powers, then it'll be more ammunition for us when we need it. Two against one."

"But that's one hell of a big if."

She reached her hand out and placed it over mine, her smile fairly lighting the dim room up. "We've come this far, Creature, back from the dead even, so why not go just a little bit further?"

I paused. "Well, if you're sure . . ."

She gave my hand a squeeze. "Just do it, Creature. Now. Before I change my mind."

I backed a few inches away and once again set my atoms on a collision course with one another. In no time flat, I was bubbling over, except, this time, rather than slicing through her, I lowered the intensity just a bit and simply bombarded her with a healthy(?) dose of radiation.

"Well?" I asked, unsure if she was standing there like that, stone-faced, unmoving, because she was in pain (doubtful) or dying (even more doubtful) or not feeling anything at all (possible).

"Wait," she replied. "Keep going. Just a little bit more."

And so I beamed away, theoretically filling her reserves. That is, until the theory was now fact.

"Well?" I asked again.

She grinned. "You have a Tasmanian devil tattoo on your upper thigh."

I covered my crotch, little good it did me. "Hey!"

She chuckled. "See, not so nice when the shoe is on the other foot, is it?"

"Turn it off," I told her, my beam now shut down.

"Off," she said. "And nice tat. Pretty big, too."

"Yeah, I'm not all bitch; there's a little butch thrown in for good measure."

She shrugged, clearly not believing me. "In any case, when you're helping me, I have the same powers that you have." She gazed at the wall. Nothing happened. I gave her another boost, and, lo and behold, a tiny hole began to sizzle its way through. "See!"

"Neat!" Truth be told, neat it was, yet another Superqueen power we had, adding to our growing roster. Plus, we really were two against one now.

"It is neat, isn't it?!"

"Why are we shouting?!"

She stopped drilling, as it were, into the wall. "Sorry. It's just, I've never had super powers before, apart from learning an entire script, then delivering it . . . with a British accent."

"Show off."

She grinned and laughed. "Plus, I was playing it blind and in a wheelchair."

"Electric?"

She nodded. "Yeah."

"Call me when you had to use your hands then." I snorted. "*Electric*. Please, Mary."

"So now what?" she asked, wisely changing the subject. Because I could go on like that forever. Seriously. Forever.

"Now we sit tight," I replied. I didn't enjoy saying it any more than she enjoyed hearing it, but we had no choice.

That is to say, until we did.

***

The war didn't start with a bang. Mainly because it began, it seemed to us, with an earth-shaking *BOOM!* The house, our prison, shook a moment later.

"What happened?" Lola asked.

I released my X-ray beam, sending it toward the pontoons. "Huh."

"Huh what?"

"Nothing," I replied. "No fires, no smoke." And so my beams went in the other direction. "Huh," I repeated.

"Again with the huh?"

I nodded. "Lots of fire, lots of smoke," I replied. "Coming from where her boat must be. Maybe some of her explosives went off unplanned?" And then another *BOOM!* boomed, a second one barely a split-second behind that one.

I waved my hands in front of my face as the smoke quickly filled the room. "Hurry," I then heard, the speaker still unseen. "This way."

I grabbed Lola's hand, hard as it was to find it as the room turned smoky black. We followed the voice as it led us through the freshly made hole in the wall. In seconds, we were standing behind the house, the black turning to gray as we realized what had happened.

"You used that second blast to mask the third one, the one that freed us?" I asked, staring up at VaVa, a face to the voice. She was covering her mouth as she nodded my way.

She coughed and replied, "Somehow another boat slammed into the one down by the dock."

"Somehow?"

She shrugged. "It happens. There were lots of boats set adrift when the solar flare occurred. Some still come sailing by every now and then, freed by a storm or simply time." Though, of course, that's not what happened, just meant to look like it had.

"That explains the blast aboard her ship, if she asks, but how do you explain this one?" I pointed behind us as we gave some distance to the wreckage.

She gazed at my point. "We don't. Topaz will lead Blondella to what's left of her boat. All we've done is created a temporary diversion for you. Plus, she'll now have to explain why she had explosives on her in the first place, and that, I suppose, will take a good bit of time."

"And what if her guards warn her of our escape before she makes it to her boat?"

She smiled. "How will a bunch of zombies open the now-locked door they're trapped behind?" Seems a certain drag queen or two had been busy during our brief incarceration.

Lola asked a question for a question. "And why free us now, so soon I mean? I thought Topaz was going to handle things, find out what she could and then put a plan into action."

VaVa's smile remained. "She did, she did, and you are."

"Lost me," I commented, not for the first time or the last.

"She handled things and is continuing to handle things, which is why she's still with Blondella." The smile briefly faltered as she said the vile zombie's name. "As to the finding out what she could, the two zombies you seek have indeed been found. As to the plan, well, the ball is in your court, or so I believe the expression goes."

I sucked in my breath, or at least tried my best to. Came out a nasty wheeze. Points for trying, though. "You found the zombies?"

Lola's hand was still in my own. She squeezed it extra tight. "Where are they? Are they okay? When can we see them?"

VaVa was moving again, helping us across the rubble and to a waiting golf cart. It was slow going, but at least it was going. "All we know is where they are," she told us. "Topaz, thank goodness, had an idea where to look."

"But you haven't seen them?" I asked, confused yet again.

Her smiled returned. "Seen, no?" she replied. "Smelled, well, to be honest, your kind isn't exactly hard to, um, *spot* in that regard."

"Tell me about it," I said, glad for the first time ever for the stench of death and decay.

"Better yet," said Lola. "Show us."

CHAPTER 18
BEAT THE BITCH

Along with the golf cart, VaVa had new wigs and sunglasses waiting for us. It wasn't ideal, but it'd do in a pinch. Plus, the wigs were on the expensive side, one a flaming red, the other an incandescent blue. In other words, I wasn't complaining. Though when Blondella passed us on the narrow road, I was holding my breath just the same, or at least making a valiant effort to do so.

"That was close," said Lola as the two carts whizzed by one another.

I turned to my newfound friend. "She must have other things on her mind, like trying to think of a viable explanation as to why her vessel had explosives on it."

VaVa quickly looked my way. "Why did she have explosives?"

It pained me to tell her the truth. "She means to destroy the island, or at least as much of it as she can. Best bet, she already hid much of her cache when she recently attacked you. Now she's back to finish the job under the pretense of leading you to a brighter tomorrow."

"But why?" VaVa asked. "We worship her. Isn't that enough?"

I shrugged. "She's demented, I suppose. That and you all are a reminder of what she no longer is and can never be again."

Again VaVa glanced my way. "Is that a guess or . . ."

I looked off into the distance. "It's hard to be with you, yes. It's like standing outside in the cold and looking in through smudged windows, seeing a home you once lived in, the key to get inside forever misplaced."

"And yet you live, pardon the wording, with humans. That's how we found you."

I turned back her way. She was frowning. "Strictly out of necessity."

"Oh," she ohed.

"Sad," said Lola.

"You get used to it," I lied.

Thankfully, my melancholy was short-lived, which made one of us, because soon enough we were pulling up behind the Ellis Island museum.

"They can't be here," Lola made note. "We already checked."

"Where did you check?" asked VaVa as she clicked off the ignition.

"Inside," I replied. "I even scanned around the nearby buildings."

"Scanned?" the drag queen asked.

"Long story," I remarked. "In any case, they weren't here."

VaVa extricated herself from the cart and then helped us do the same. "Inside, no," she replied. "Around, no."

"And, again, lost me." She motioned with her brightly-manicured index finger for us to follow her, which we did, arriving around the backside of the museum before standing in front of the eternal flame. It was then that I smelled the familiar smell, one I'd long ago grown accustomed to. "But where is the aroma coming from?" I looked all around, but saw nothing, just the flame as is it sparked and flickered. "Wait," I said. "Not inside or around, but—"

"Down!" shouted Lola. "The flame is fed below ground!"

"Of course!" I shouted in return. "Ginger told us that the fuel source is kept safely below ground." And the smile I'd been smiling got wiped clear away. "Ginger, the keeper of the eternal flame?"

Lola tilted her head to the side. "She was jealous of a flame? She wanted to be eternal, too? So she made a deal with the devil?"

VaVa put her hand on Lola's shoulder. "I don't think that's it."

"Then what?" I asked.

She pointed to the graves behind us. "Your friends, they meant a lot to you?"

I nodded. "In retrospect, the world." Even Blondella meant that to me, at least the way she once had been.

VaVa nodded. "Same for all of us, Ginger included. And her sole job on the island is to tend to the flame, to commemorate your friends there, just as it was for her mother and her mother before that."

"So what you're saying is . . ."

She nodded. "It's only a guess, but that job of hers means everything to her. It's special. Meant for one person and one person only."

Lola also nodded her head. "And if she was eternal, she'd have that job forever."

"Or close to it," I said. "And only one person can promise immortality around these parts."

"Blondella," groaned Lola. "Of course." She turned to VaVa. "Does Ginger ever go into the city?"

VaVa nodded once again. "To get the fuel, yes. Perhaps every six months or so. We think it's safer if it's kept in the stadium rather than here." She pointed all around us. "Because if we ever had a fire, a bad one—"

"Got it," I said. "And a bad one is coming, brought by the worst bitch imaginable."

"And one who clearly divided and conquered at some point in the recent past," added Lola with a frown. "And how can a person say no to someone they worship?"

"Poor Ginger," I said.

"Poor everyone," said VaVa, "if Blondella succeeds."

Topaz being the priestess, I assumed, also meant that she was like the priests of my day. Meaning, people came to her, confessed their sins, asked for guidance. Perhaps that's why she suspected Ginger. It made sense, as much as anything did in this place. In any case, it wasn't Ginger or Topaz I was thinking of at that very moment.

"Can we go rescue our husbands now?" I asked.

"Is that who's down there?" asked VaVa. "Dara? And this zombie's husband?"

"My *friend's*, yes."

Funny, as much as I hated being around humans, it always surprised me when it became clear that the humans felt the same way about us. The way VaVa said *zombie* brought that to light yet again. Still, I couldn't be upset with her; she was looking through the same smudged window as I was, simply from the other side of things.

"Topaz assumes they're down there," she said, "because of the smell coming from the flame. That makes sense. However—"

Lola lifted her hand up. "It's locked, right?"

VaVa nodded. "And only Ginger has the key."

"Wanna make a bet?" said Lola, eyeing the ground all around us. "Here!" she soon shouted. "There's a door in the cement!" She looked at me, eyes wide, filled with hope all of a sudden.

"Care to do the honors?" I asked with a flourish of my withered hand.

"Please," she replied.

And so I bubbled up as she bubbled up, giving her the boost she needed. Seconds later, the metal door was glowing red around the keyhole, the smell of burning metal filling my sinus cavity.

"What's going on?" asked VaVa, jaw hanging low as she watched.

Slowly I bent down and pulled on the handle. Luckily, it gave. "Again, long story. Now please help us down these stairs."

***

It took a while for two zombies and a drag queen in seven-inch stiletto heels to climb through a narrow door in the ground, down an equally narrow stairwell and into a hallway with a ceiling that was barely five feet high, but, considering what was possibly at the end of the line, we made it in record time. That is to say, it took us five minutes to move about ten feet.

"Lester," moaned Lola.

I wasn't sure if the moan was because of the way he looked, which wasn't nearly as preserved as she was, not by a long shot, or because it was obvious by his blank stare that we were too late. In any case, her moan got joined by one of my own. "Dara," I said, the word falling on mostly deaf ears, or at least clearly uninterested ones.

And still she moved to him, drawn by a love that quite literally spanned the ages. I watched, letting her have her moment. As for the two zombies, they simply groaned and stared into the oblivion.

She lifted her hand up, slowly, unsteadily, and rubbed the back of her fingers against his weather-beaten cheek. "Lester," she repeated. "I'm here for you, baby." And still he groaned. She turned and whimpered. "Help him, please."

"We need salt," I told her, then turned to VaVa. "Is there any nearby? It has to be iodized. Like radiation sickness pills, it tamps down the energy inside of them, allows their inner human to come out at play."

VaVa frowned. "We'd have to go get it, and you can't come with me, and *they* certainly can't. The islanders will kill . . . um, do some heavy damage to you if they spot you, especially now."

I also frowned. "Which will take time, and time is something we have little to spare." I turned to Lola. "If we leave them here, they'll be safe, and we can come back for them once it's all over."

"No!" she barked, her voice bouncing off the walls and cutting me to the quick. "I'm not leaving him. Not now. Not after all we've been through to find him."

"But—"

She gripped her hands into fists. "Creature, no. I'm sorry, but I can't leave him." And then she unclenched. "Besides, I have another idea."

"But nothing can cure them," I told her. "Nothing but salt."

She shook her head. "Before."

"Before what?" asked VaVa.

Lola looked from her to her husband and then to me. "Before we discovered that we were Superqueens."

VaVa smiled. "Ooh, Superqueens. Now that I like the sound of."

"Figures," said I. "And what makes you think our powers will work on them?" I asked her.

"They will," she replied, now staring deeply into her husband's eyes. "They have to."

And so, like Blondella had done to me, I willed my radiation to tamp down his. I pushed with all my might, energy pouring from me and into him. It was like using a controlled fire to contain a wild one. "Help me, Lola," I grunted.

She nodded and appeared to concentrate. "Pushing," she said, and a moment later added, "I can feel it now, Creature. Can feel your radiation advancing. Can feel his receding." She glanced my way. "Push harder!"

My entire body was tensing now as I poured and poured my energy into him, until it looked like he was fairly glowing.

And then, suddenly . . .

"Lola," he said, the word just barely a whisper, but piercing the silence just the same.

"Ricky," I sighed.

"Lester," she managed to squeak out. "You came back to me."

The slightest of grins worked its way up his face. "You would have killed me if I hadn't."

She laughed, which was so much easier to do than cry. "Horse is way out of the barn on that one, hon."

"Hell," said VaVa, "the barn burnt to the ground ages ago."

I grinned and turned to Dara. "Now your turn, my love."

Lola walked behind me and put her hand on my shoulder. "Ready."

"Set."

"Go already," said VaVa. "There's still a power-hungry rabid zombie bitch to take care of."

I shrugged. "You forgot disco-ball smooshed, but, okay, good enough." And so yet again I bubbled up and over, and Lola bubbled up and over, and me and her bubbled together, pouring our very essence into Dara, working as a united front.

"Fuck," my lover groaned, soon enough. Then she blinked, once, twice. "Oops, didn't know there was a lady present. Didn't know anyone was present, present company included, namely me." She smiled and reached her hand out to mine. "What took you so long? And since when can you do whatever it is you just did."

VaVa sighed. "Long story. Can we go now, though, please? Before Blondella blows the island sky high and us along with it."

"Wait," barked Lester cum Ricky. "I just need to do something first."

We all turned to him as he turned to Lola.

He grinned. She grinned. And, since it was fairly contagious by then, we all grinned. "How was your show?" he asked, his hand on her hips, their faces mere millimeters apart.

She chuckled. "Longest standing ovation in show biz history, my love."

Their lips at long last met, eyelids fluttering as they melted into another, Dara's hand in mine, her head resting on my shoulder. "So that's Lola Fontaine, huh?" he said as the kiss went on and on. "She's even prettier in, um, person."

"*The* Lola Fontaine," I amended. "And, yes. Does everyone know who she is but me?"

"She's won a Tony, sweetie."

And with that, the kiss was broken. "Two," she uttered. "Two Tonys."

Again VaVa sighed. "What's a Tony?" And then she held her hand up. "Never mind. Let's just go, please."

I turned to Dara and then to Ricky. "Blondella is on the island. The islanders are behind her and against us. She has explosives hidden and plans to blow this place to kingdom come."

Lola raised a finger. "And we smashed her with a disco ball."

But before we could elucidate further, VaVa was already headed out. "Yada, yada, long story, right. Now we're all caught up. Move!"

I shrugged. Lola shrugged. The four of us followed. "Someone forgot her anti-bitch medication this morning," Dara whispered in my ear.

"Oh, I took it," grumbled VaVa, apparently hearing what had been said. "You should see me when I don't."

"Or, better yet," whispered Lola, "*not.*"

And then we were outside again. VaVa looked at us and wisely thought to ask, "So then, how long before these two revert back without some handy-dandy salt inside of them."

I froze. "Good question." I turned to Dara. "Well?"

She turned to Ricky. "Well?"

And he turned to VaVa. "Best guess?"

Poor girl. She clearly wasn't pleased with any of this or any of us. "Humor me."

He shrugged. "Feels exceedingly temporary, a brief reprieve, the darkness creeping in even as we speak."

I tensed. "How long then?"

"An hour at most," came the weary reply.

VaVa again looked my way. "But you can do whatever it is you did again, if they need it, right?"

And still I tensed. "Except, my own salt is quickly running out, quicker now that I've unleashed all my radiation. It's the radiation, after all, that makes us zombies. And with me letting it run amok, it's bringing the change on even quicker. I can feel it."

Lola nodded. "Me too."

And VaVa's sigh went ten on the Richter. "So, just to be clear, there's a chance that I'll be surrounded by four hell-bent zombies in less than an hour."

I nodded. "Five, if you include Blondella." To which I added. "So, um, maybe we should get the salt first. Is your house nearby?"

Her frown sagged further on her face. "I'm guessing you need quite a lot of it, right? For all four of you, I mean."

"At least an entire canister. Why, is that a problem?" I replied.

"We live on a small island, Creature," she informed. "Everything is doled out evenly so that everyone has the same amounts, and even then we're only able, as a community, to store in our homes what's needed for at most six months at a time."

I knew what she was getting at. "So you're saying that you don't have a canister of salt, that no one does?"

"I don't even use salt," she informed. "Leads to water retention. And my dresses are tight enough as it is."

She had a point. "So where do you all keep your reserves then?"

Her gulp was telltale. "Remember the stadium we visited?"

If I could've echoed her gulp, I would have. "The one where everything was smashed to bits."

She touched fingertip to nose. It landed dead on. Damn the living. "That's the one."

"And if we start going door to door now?" added Lola.

"Then we're dead," said Dara. "Or, um, dead*er*. Because no way are they going to greet us with open arms, let alone give us their salt."

"And if we're killed or captured again," said I, "then there's no one left to battle Blondella." I tossed up my hands. They went about two and a half inches high. "Suggestions?"

"Beat the bitch now," said Lola. "Beat her now and get the salt in us later, even after we possibly turn."

I looked at VaVa, who was now eyeing me uncertainly. Either that or one of her enormous eyelashes was wonky. "Can you do that?" I asked. "If we turn, can you get the salt into us later?"

"Get the salt into you?" she asked, those uncertain eyes now wide. "You mean hold four zombies down and dump salt into their mouths?"

I forced a smile. "Well, you did promise me that you'd return us to Utah. Good luck with that if we're rampaging zombies."

"Yeah," said Dara. "Good luck with that."

VaVa sighed, yet again. "Fine, let's just, as you said, beat the bitch."

"Beat the bitch!" shouted Lola.

"Beat the bitch!" shouted Ricky.

"And if we turn," said I, "watch that you don't scrape your hands against my incisors. Ten to one, you won't be taking a dirt nap for a long time to come then."

"A long, *long* time," tossed in Dara.

VaVa squinted her eyes shut. "Oh goody." Then she opened them again. "Now please, let's just go already!"

***

Of course, now we had a new problem to contend with, apart from the fact that we had less than an hour to kill Blondella and apart from the risk of all of us turning and killing VaVa and apart from the island possibly blowing up at any moment. *KAPOW!* See, the problem was that four zombies and one drag queen in one small golf cart was next to near impossible to miss. Actually, we'll just go with impossible, seeing as everyone we passed immediately spotted us, fabulous wigs or no fabulous wigs.

"Stop them!" we soon heard.

"Traitors!" came next.

"Kill the zombies!" Not surprisingly, that seemed to be a popular one.

And, lastly, "Who are you wearing?"

VaVa's sigh returned. "We'll have to stop teaching that in school," she groaned. "Provided there are still schools to teach in." She looked in her rearview mirror as we all in turn looked behind us. "And provided that the islanders don't capture us first." Which was a distinct possibility, considering that a few dozen were now giving chase. And, yes, it is easy to outrace a golf cart. Normally. Then again, when all few dozen were running in three-inch heels or better, well, not so easily as it turned out. Thank goodness.

In other words, we made it to the end of the island, back to Lady Liberty, with about a four-minute lead, give or take.

Up to the pier we drove, Blondella's boat still on fire, belching black smoke into the air, Blondella herself fuming nearby. As to explaining why she had the explosives in the first place, it seemed, judging by the fact that she was still free, she'd convinced the islanders of her innocence. Given that she was their goddess, it probably didn't take too much convincing. Which was indeed ironic because Blondella was many things, but innocent, nuh uh, not so much. Not three hundred years ago and certainly not now.

In any case, she quickly spotted us as we were spotting her. "Seize them!" she bellowed, bony finger aimed our way.

"I think she missed us," I moaned, extricating myself from the cart.

"Maybe she was lonely," said Dara, now standing by my side.

"Or loony," I amended with.

Lola and Ricky appeared on my other side, until we four were staring down at her and her advancing minions, the islanders from the pier behind them, and the islanders that had been following us a mere hundred yards or so away. In other words, trapped would've been putting it mildly.

"Now what do we do?" asked Dara, tugging my sleeve.

I looked all around, angry humans and menacing zombies on all sides. And still I managed a grin. "Do?" I said, atoms colliding inside of me, mashing and smashing together. "Why, the grand finale, of course."

Lola rubbed her hands together. Or at least tried to. "Show time!"

Dara's smile was brighter than the sun overhead. "Finally!"

While Ricky simply scratched his head. "As long as I, um, *live*, I'll never understand you . . ." He had to pause to find the right word. "*Women*."

I turned and patted his hand. "No need to understand, Ricky. Just follow our lead."

He nodded his head. "Ah, now that I can do."

And so side by side we stood, knowing something that Blondella clearly didn't know, namely that we could combine our strengths. And she might have been strong, could command legions of undead if she so chose, but she'd never, ever have what we had, namely the power of love, of friendship. "Goodbye, old girl," I said, the message going from my head to hers, the look on her face switching from anger to confusion to, finally, pain. Oh sure, generally we couldn't feel that, what with us being dead and all, but when four zombies are zapping you at once with all the energy they have, pain is sort of a forgone conclusion.

She tried to fight it, to tamp it down as she'd done before, but now the odds were far in our favor. "NO!" she howled, her ghastly complexion going from gray to a blistering orange, glowing like the flame held aloft by the statue high overhead.

"Yes," I grunted as I pushed and pushed, willing all my strength at her. "Hell to the yes, in fact. And have a great time while you're down there, sweetie."

She stopped in her tracks. Actually, at the sight of her, illuminated with radiation now that she was, everyone stopped, every human, every zombie, every living and undead being all around. In fact, we all stopped and stared as the goddess quickly and utterly and completely (not to mention final-fucking-ly) became one with the cosmos.

In other words, as the ship exploded one last time, its contents flying high up into the air, so did Blondella.

"Well," I said as I powered down, "she always did like to end the show with a bang."

And then I felt it, felt it closing in on me. It'd been hundreds and hundreds of years, but still I knew the feeling, remembered it like it was only yesterday. Death was coming, seeking me out yet again as it had when the sun went all crazy on our asses.

I turned to Dara as she turned to me. "I love you," I managed to say just as I slipped into the oblivion, just as the blackness became all encompassing.

And the last words I heard were, "I love you, too, Creature. See you on the other side."

CHAPTER 19
HOME

I blinked my eyes open, a vision of loveliness filling my field of vision, a halo of white at the periphery. "God?" I croaked out.

She laughed. "No, Creature. Just Topaz. But thanks for saying so."

I pushed myself up on my elbows, or at least tried and failed to. It was then that I noticed that the ground beneath me was strangely vibrating. "But I was dead."

"Technically . . ."

I nodded. "All the way dead, I mean. My salt, it ran out." I panicked. "Dara! Where is she?" My head moved right, left. And then I realized where we were. "But how?"

Topaz was grinning. "We made a promise to you, Creature. We're just keeping our end of the bargain."

I looked over at the small, round window, clouds passing by in great white patches. My eyes then landed on my friends, all tied to their seats, all still very much lifeless.

"Welcome back, Creature." It was Aflo Sheen, holding me down. And when a several hundred pound drag queen is holding, down is where you stay. "We thought we'd do you first."

I nodded. "Thanks. For, um, *doing me*. And, again, how?"

I heard the shout from the front of the plain next. "Bait!" hollered VaVa, our pilotress.

"Bait?" I asked, looking at Aflo. "And you can get off me now. I promise not to bite." Seriously. Promise. *Ugh.*

Aflo grinned and helped push me up until my torso was now at the vertical. Then she pointed at the bait, Ginger frowning from the seat in back. "After she told us where the rest of the explosives were hidden, she was good enough to lead you all to the plane."

Topaz chuckled. "Well, forced to, but why mince words? Anyway, you all followed, flesh-hungry zombies that you were, and, well, here you all now are."

"And Blondella?" I thought to ask, just to make sure. Because even in death, bitch had nine lives.

"Gone," replied Topaz.

"Way gone!" shouted VaVa.

Aflo nodded. "Her remains, what's left of them, will finally be buried next to your friends, Creature. Just where they belong."

"Better late than never." I pointed to the salt canister in her hand. "And that?"

"Seems *the goddess* had a few crates of it on the boat she arrived on," she replied. "When it exploded, the contents went flying." She aimed her pudgy finger to the front of the cabin, a large stack of charred but otherwise whole canisters sitting at the ready.

I laughed. "We only need one or two, you know."

Topaz shrugged at my remark. "Better safe than sorry."

"Good idea," I allowed. "There's been too much sorry and not nearly enough safe as of late." I was now staring at Dara, a pit in my stomach at the lifeless sight of her, her eyes open, gazing into the nothingness, her body tightly bound to the seat. "Open your mouth, sweetie," I told her. "All of you, open wide."

And though I might not have been a goddess, at least not on paper, they obeyed just the same, one mouth after the next unclenching, hanging limp. Topaz and Aflo then helped me up before handing me a full canister. "All yours, sweetie," said Topaz. "After all, *you* don't have to watch for those nasty incisors."

I nodded. "Again, good idea." I turned to the tethered zombies. "Heads back everyone." And to their best ability, heads back is just what they did. I then hobbled over, salt poured down Dara's, then Lola's, then Ricky's throats. "Now come back to me," I told them, rather pleadingly. "And please hurry."

I heard the first cough a minute later, a second one quick to follow, a third, clouds of salt wafting through the cabin a moment after that, sparkling in the sunlight.

Dara's eyes blinked, a smile inching northward on her face. "This the other side, hon?"

I shrugged. "If by 'other side' you mean Utah-bound, then yes, other side it is."

Her smile quivered. "Utah? You mean no more drag queens? No more gilded statues? No more fabulous frocks and flowing wigs and towering stilettos?"

I paused before answering.

As to that, I'd already given it some thought, back when I was being held prisoner. I mean, a lot could be said for what the Libetians had created, oddly grounded in myth though it all might've been— that is to say, grounded in a bunch of drag queens who, in life, had far bigger livers than hearts. In any case, the islanders were just as trapped as we had been, surrounded on all sides by millions of zombies, and yet they'd managed to make metallic green shine as gold, to turn a veritable hell into a beautiful Eden. And so I gazed upon my love and stroked her cheek. "The stilettos, well, probably not such a swell idea, all things considered, but the rest . . ." I grinned, my mind already picturing it all. And what a pretty picture it was indeed. "Yeah, I think we can work on that."

***

They left us as they'd picked us up: quickly and with fabulous aplomb, gowns blowing in the wind and kisses thrown as the plane door closed behind them. After all, they had explosives to get rid of, prisoners to incarcerate, libations to drink. Lucky humans. While we had marauding zombies to wait for, a potential war to fight once they arrived. Still, for the time being, New San Francisco was safe from harm.

After that, I gave our friends a quick tour. "So this is Utah," said Lola, her hand in her husband's. It'd stayed there since I'd reawakened them. "Any stages, costumes, fanfare?"

I grinned. "Nope, nope, and . . ." I pointed at the thousands of zombies on the other side of the fence, all of them loudly groaning. "That count as fanfare?"

She cringed. "We'll have to do something about that."

I smiled at her and then at Ricky and then at Dara, whose hand was in mine, also where it had remained since our flight back home. I'd taken so much for granted over the centuries, missed so many opportunities, but, more importantly, had come to realize that what currently was didn't necessarily have to be. That is to say, it might've been Utah and might have been a salt factory, but that didn't mean it couldn't, in time, be so much more.

And time, of course, we had plenty to spare. Strangely, or maybe not, all things considered, that thought didn't bother me nearly as much as it used to.

"Yes," I replied to her, smiling widely. "Yes, we will do something about that. Might take a little paint and some wood and nails, a bit of elbow grease, maybe even a tube of Poligrip or two, but why should those Libetians have all the fun?"

Dara squeezed my hand in hers and laughed.

"What's so funny?" asked Ricky.

"Let me guess," said I. "You used to know a drag queen by that name? Polly Grip?"

She shook her head. "Actually, no," she replied, pointing with her free hand at one of our minions. "At least not yet."

***

So, like I've said, I can feel it—the radiation, I mean—feel it snap, crackle and pop inside of me. All these years later, decades now, centuries even. Only, now, with my friends by my side, with a promise of a brighter, music-driven, gown-wearing, factory-painted future in front of me, in front of *us*, I don't really mind it so much.

In fact, Superqueen that I now am, I kind of like it.

Heck, maybe even love it.

And, yes, a big, mighty amen to that.

The End?
Nope, nowhere in sight, sweeties.

If you enjoyed *Creature Comfort*, please check out my other novels:
Sparkle: The Queerest Book You'll Ever Love
Divas Las Vegas
Hot Lava
Southern Fried
Queerwolf
Vamp
Queens of the Apocalypse
And my erotica collection, *Good & Hot*

I am also the editor of the following anthologies:
Lust in Time: Erotic Romance Through the Ages
Men of the Manor: Erotic Encounters between Upstairs Lords and Downstairs Lads
Best Gay Erotica 2015
Warlords and Warriors: Gay Erotic Romance and Adventure

And feel free to visit my website for more on me, my work and my life: www.therobrosen.com

Or drop me an email at: robrosen@therobrosen.com

Much Love,

Rob

www.ingramcontent.com/pod-product-compliance
Lightning Source LLC
Chambersburg PA
CBHW070821120626
46556CB00002B/604